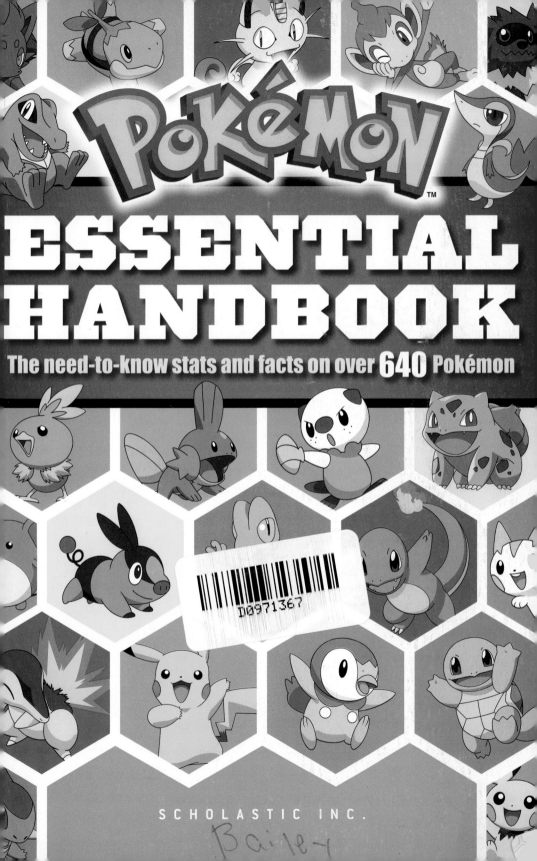

Pokémon

ESSENTIAL HANDBOOK

The need-to-know stats and facts on over **640** Pokémon

SCHOLASTIC INC.

ISBN 978-0-545-42771-5

© 2012 Pokémon. © 1995-2012 Nintendo/Creatures Inc./GAME FREAK inc. TM and ®
and character names are trademarks of Nintendo. All rights reserved.
Published by Scholastic Inc.
SCHOLASTIC and associated logos are trademarks and/or registered trademarks of Scholastic Inc.

Special thanks to Cris Silvestri

12 13 14 15 16 17/0

12 11 10 9 8 7 6 5 4 3 2 1

40

Designed by Henry Ng and Two Red Shoes Design
Printed in the U.S.A.
First printing, August 2012

WELCOME TO THE WORLD OF POKÉMON!

Pokémon Trainers know that the key to success with Pokémon is staying informed. Certain things, like a Pokémon's type, species, weight, and more can make the difference in raising, battling, and evolving Pokémon.

In this book, you'll get all the details you need about over 640 Pokémon. You'll find out how each Pokémon evolves, which moves are most common to them, and even which region they hail from. And it's all in alphabetical order for easy reference.

Get ready, Trainers: With this handy guide, you'll be able to master almost any Pokémon challenge!

HOW TO READ THE ESSENTIAL HANDBOOK

NAME: A Pokémon's name—the first step in knowing your Pokémon.

SPECIES: All Pokémon belong to a specific species. These are interesting classes that highlight what makes some Pokémon so unique. Did you know Tepig was a Fire Pig Species Pokémon?

PRONOUNCED: How can you train a Pokémon if you can't say its name correctly? Learn how to pronounce each name with this handy entry.

POSSIBLE MOVES: There are a ton of moves that Pokémon could be taught, but there are only a few that might be naturally instilled into your Pokémon. This is that list.

TYPE: Some Pokémon have one type, some are dual types—but every Pokémon has a type, and there are 17 in all. Types allow you to anticipate what a Pokémon's strengths and weaknesses will be in battle.

HEIGHT: Who's the tallest? The shortest?

WEIGHT: Who's the heaviest? The lightest?

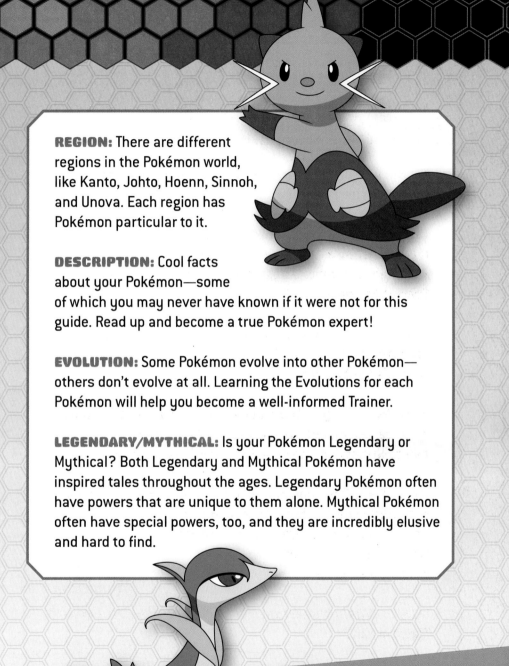

REGION: There are different regions in the Pokémon world, like Kanto, Johto, Hoenn, Sinnoh, and Unova. Each region has Pokémon particular to it.

DESCRIPTION: Cool facts about your Pokémon—some of which you may never have known if it were not for this guide. Read up and become a true Pokémon expert!

EVOLUTION: Some Pokémon evolve into other Pokémon—others don't evolve at all. Learning the Evolutions for each Pokémon will help you become a well-informed Trainer.

LEGENDARY/MYTHICAL: Is your Pokémon Legendary or Mythical? Both Legendary and Mythical Pokémon have inspired tales throughout the ages. Legendary Pokémon often have powers that are unique to them alone. Mythical Pokémon often have special powers, too, and they are incredibly elusive and hard to find.

ARE YOU READY?

YOUR POKÉMON JOURNEY BEGINS WHEN YOU TURN THE PAGE!

ABOMASNOW
FROST TREE POKÉMON

Known as the Ice Monster, Abomasnow can create blizzards across wide areas in the mountains.

Pronounced: uh-BOM-a-snow
Possible Moves: Ice Punch, Powder Snow, Leer, Razor Leaf, Icy Wind, GrassWhistle, Swagger, Mist, Ice Shard, Ingrain, Wood Hammer, Blizzard, Sheer Cold
Type: Grass-Ice
Height: 7' 03"   **Weight:** 298.7 lbs.
Region: Sinnoh

SNOVER

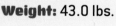

ABOMASNOW

ABRA
PSI POKÉMON

This Pokémon has the ability to teleport itself at any time.

Pronounced: AH-bra
Possible Moves: Teleport
Type: Psychic
Height: 2' 11"   **Weight:** 43.0 lbs.
Region: Kanto

ABRA

KADABRA

ALAKAZAM

ABSOL
DISASTER POKÉMON

When you see Absol, it means that disaster is imminent—so don't stay put! Absol only appears to those it wants to warn.

Pronounced: AB-sol
Possible Moves: Scratch, Feint, Leer, Taunt, Quick Attack, Razor Wind, Pursuit, Swords Dance, Bite, Double Team, Slash, Future Sight, Sucker Punch, Detect, Night Slash, Me First, Psycho Cut, Perish Song
Type: Dark
Height: 3' 11"   **Weight:** 103.6lbs.
Region: Hoenn

DOES NOT EVOLVE

ACCELGOR
SHELL OUT POKÉMON

Having shed its heavy shell, Accelgor is light and moves like a ninja when it fights. But it weakens if its body dries out, so it wraps itself in layers of thin membrane to prevent dehydration.

Pronounced: ak-SELL-gohr
Possible Moves: Leech Life, Acid Spray, Double Team, Quick Attack, Struggle Bug, Mega Drain, Swift, Me First, Agility, Giga Drain, U-turn, Bug Buzz, Recover, Power Swap, Final Gambit
Type: Bug
Height: 2' 07"   **Weight:** 55.8 lbs.
Region: Unova

SHELMET

ACCELGOR

AERODACTYL

FOSSIL POKÉMON

Aerodactyl's teeth are as sharp as blades, and it has flown the skies since ancient times.

Pronounced: AIR-row-DACK-tull
Possible Moves: Ice Fang, Fire Fang, Thunder Fang, Wing Attack, Supersonic, Bite, Scary Face, Roar, Agility, AncientPower, Crunch, Take Down, Sky Drop, Iron Head, Hyper Beam, Rock Slide, Giga Impact
Type: Rock-Flying
Height: 5' 11"   **Weight:** 130.1 lbs.
Region: Kanto

DOES NOT EVOLVE

AGGRON

IRON ARMOR POKÉMON

Aggron digs tunnels by using its steel horns to burrow through bedrock. It digs the tunnels while seeking iron for food.

Pronounced: AGG-ron
Possible Moves: Tackle, Harden, Mud-Slap, Headbutt, Metal Claw, Iron Defense, Roar, Take Down, Iron Head, Protect, Metal Sound, Iron Tail, Autotomize, Heavy Slam, Double-Edge, Metal Burst
Type: Steel-Rock
Height: 6' 11"   **Weight:** 793.7 lbs.   **Region:** Hoenn

ARON

LAIRON

AGGRON

AIPOM
LONG TAIL POKÉMON

Aipom uses its tail to grab things that are out of its reach, since its tail is more effective than its hands.

Pronounced: AY-pom
Possible Moves: Scratch, Tail Whip, Sand-Attack, Astonish, Baton Pass, Tickle, Fury Swipes, Swift, Screech, Agility, Double Hit, Fling, Nasty Plot, Last Resort
Type: Normal
Height: 2' 07"
Weight: 25.4 lbs.
Region: Johto

AIPOM

AMBIPOM

ALAKAZAM
PSI POKÉMON

With an IQ of over 5,000, Alakazam is a force to be reckoned with. It can recall everything it has ever done—including moves in battle.

Pronounced: AH-la-kuh-ZAM
Possible Moves: Teleport, Kinesis, Confusion, Disable, Miracle Eye, Ally Switch, Psybeam, Reflect, Telekinesis, Recover, Psycho Cut, Calm Mind, Psychic, Future Sight, Trick
Type: Psychic   **Height:** 4' 11"   **Weight:** 105.8 lbs.   **Region:** Kanto

ABRA   KADABRA   ALAKAZAM

ALOMOMOLA
CARING POKÉMON

Alomomola floats through the open sea surrounded by a special membrane that heals wounds. When it meets an injured Pokémon, it embraces it and takes it to shore.

Pronounced: uh-LOH-muh-MOH-luh
Possible Moves: Pound, Water Sport, Aqua Ring, Aqua Jet, DoubleSlap, Heal Pulse, Protect, Water Pulse, Wake-Up Slap, Soak, Wish, Brine, Safeguard, Helping Hand, Wide Guard, Healing Wish, Hydro Pump
Type: Water
Height: 3' 11"
Weight: 69.7 lbs.
Region: Unova

DOES NOT EVOLVE

ALTARIA
HUMMING POKÉMON

Altaria looks like a fluffy cloud, and likes to hum in a soprano voice.

Pronounced: all-TAR-ee-uh
Possible Moves: Pluck, Peck, Growl, Astonish, Sing, Fury Attack, Safeguard, Mist, Take Down, Natural Gift, DragonBreath, Dragon Dance, Cotton Guard, Refresh, Dragon Pulse, Perish Song, Sky Attack
Type: Dragon-Flying
Height: 3' 07"
Weight: 45.4 lbs.
Region: Hoenn

SWABLU

ALTARIA

AMBIPOM
LONG TAIL POKÉMON

Sometimes, two tails are better than one! Ambipom has been known to form big groups by linking its tails with other Ambipom.

Pronounced: AM-bih-pom
Possible Moves: Scratch, Tail Whip, Sand-Attack, Astonish, Baton Pass, Tickle, Fury Swipes, Swift, Screech, Agility, Double Hit, Fling, Nasty Plot, Last Resort
Type: Normal
Height: 3' 11"
Weight: 44.8 lbs.
Region: Sinnoh

AIPOM

AMBIPOM

AMOONGUSS
MUSHROOM POKÉMON

To lure prey, Amoonguss dances and waves its Poké Ball-like arm caps in a swaying motion. Not many Pokémon are fooled.

Pronounced: uh-MOON-gus
Possible Moves: Absorb, Growth, Astonish, Bide, Mega Drain, Ingrain, Faint Attack, Sweet Scent, Giga Drain, Toxic, Synthesis, Clear Smog, SolarBeam, Rage Powder, Spore
Type: Grass-Poison
Height: 2' 00"
Weight: 23.1 lbs.
Region: Unova

FOONGUS

AMOONGUSS

AMPHAROS
LIGHT POKÉMON

The tail on Ampharos shines so bright, people once used it to send signals.

Pronounced: AMF-fah-ros

Possible Moves: Fire Punch, Tackle, Growl, ThunderShock, Thunder Wave, Cotton Spore, Charge, ThunderPunch, Electro Ball, Cotton Guard, Discharge, Signal Beam, Light Screen, Power Gem, Thunder

Type: Electric

Height: 4' 07"

Weight: 135.6 lbs.

Region: Johto

MAREEP

FLAAFFY

AMPHAROS

ANORITH
OLD SHRIMP POKÉMON

Anorith uses its massive claws to hunt its prey. It lives in the sea and was reanimated from a fossil, just like Lileep.

Pronounced: AN-no-rith

Possible Moves: Scratch, Harden, Mud Sport, Water Gun, Metal Claw, Protect, AncientPower, Fury Cutter, Slash, Rock Blast, Crush Claw, X-Scissor

Type: Rock-Bug

Height: 2' 04"   **Weight:** 27.6 lbs.

Region: Hoenn

ANORITH

ARMALDO

ARBOK
COBRA POKÉMON

Arbok uses the pattern on its belly to intimidate foes, and then constricts them while they are frozen with fear.

Pronounced: ARE-bock

Possible Moves: Ice Fang, Thunder Fang, Fire Fang, Wrap, Leer, Poison Sting, Bite, Glare, Screech, Acid, Crunch, Stockpile, Swallow, Spit Up, Acid Spray, Mud Bomb, Gastro Acid, Haze, Coil, Gunk Shot

Type: Poison

Height: 11' 06"

Weight: 143.3 lbs.

Region: Kanto

EKANS

ARBOK

ARCANINE
LEGENDARY POKÉMON

Arcanine is a very proud and regal Pokémon, which makes it a favorite among humans.

Pronounced: ARE-ka-nine

Possible Moves: Thunder Fang, Bite, Roar, Fire Fang, Odor Sleuth, ExtremeSpeed

Type: Fire

Height: 6' 03"

Weight: 341.7 lbs.

Region: Kanto

GROWLITHE

ARCANINE

ARCEUS
ALPHA POKÉMON

Arceus emerged from an egg in a place where there was nothing. It is believed to have shaped the world.

Pronounced: AR-key-us
Possible Moves: Seismic Toss, Cosmic Power, Natural Gift, Punishment, Gravity, Earth Power, Hyper Voice, ExtremeSpeed, Refresh, Future Sight, Recover, Hyper Beam, Perish Song, Judgment
Type: Normal
Height: 10' 06"
Weight: 705.5 lbs.
Region: Sinnoh

DOES NOT EVOLVE

MYTHICAL POKÉMON

ARCHEN
FIRST BIRD POKÉMON

This Pokémon, which was revived from a fossil, is thought to be the ancestor of all avian Pokémon. Archen cannot fly, however—it hops from branch to branch.

Pronounced: AR-ken

Possible Moves: Quick Attack, Leer, Wing Attack, Rock Throw, Double Team, Scary Face, Pluck, AncientPower, Agility, Quick Guard, Acrobatics, DragonBreath, Crunch, Endeavor, U-turn, Rock Slide, Dragon Claw, Thrash

Type: Rock-Flying

Height: 1' 08"   **Weight:** 20.9 lbs.

Region: Unova

ARCHEN → ARCHEOPS

ARCHEOPS
FIRST BIRD POKÉMON

A better runner than a flier, Archeops uses a running start to take to the air. It is smart enough to cooperate with other Archeops to hunt prey, which it chases by running as fast as a car.

Pronounced: AR-kee-ops

Possible Moves: Quick Attack, Leer, Wing Attack, Rock Throw, Double Team, Scary Face, Pluck, AncientPower, Agility, Quick Guard, Acrobatics, DragonBreath, Crunch, Endeavor, U-turn, Rock Slide, Dragon Claw, Thrash

Type: Rock-Flying

Height: 4' 07"

Weight: 70.5 lbs.

Region: Unova

ARCHEN → ARCHEOPS

ARIADOS
LONG LEG POKÉMON

Ariados can attach a silken thread to a foe, then follow the thread to its lair and attack it and any acquaintances that happen to be hanging around!

Pronounced: AIR-ree-uh-dose
Possible Moves: Bug Bite, Poison Sting, String Shot, Scary Face, Constrict, Leech Life, Night Shade, Shadow Sneak, Fury Swipes, Sucker Punch, Spider Web, Agility, Pin Missile, Psychic, Poison Jab, Cross Poison
Type: Bug-Poison
Height: 3' 07"
Weight: 73.9 lbs.
Region: Johto

SPINARAK → ARIADOS

ARMALDO
PLATE POKÉMON

Armaldo evolved into its sturdy armor after going ashore to track down foes and food sources.

Pronounced: ar-MAL-do
Possible Moves: Scratch, Harden, Mud Sport, Water Gun, Metal Claw, Protect, AncientPower, Fury Cutter, Slash, Rock Blast, Crush Claw, X-Scissor
Type: Rock-Bug
Height: 4' 11"   **Weight:** 150.4 lbs.
Region: Hoenn

ANORITH → ARMALDO

ARON
IRON ARMOR POKÉMON

Hunger may drive Aron to eat railroad tracks and cars. It lives deep in mountains.

Pronounced: AIR-ron
Possible Moves: Tackle, Harden, Mud-Slap, Headbutt, Metal Claw, Iron Defense, Roar, Take Down, Iron Head, Protect, Metal Sound, Iron Tail, Autotomize, Heavy Slam, Double-Edge, Metal Burst
Type: Steel-Rock
Height: 1' 04"
Weight: 132.3 lbs.
Region: Hoenn

 ARON

 LAIRON

 AGGRON

ARTICUNO
FREEZE POKÉMON

By freezing moisture in the air, Articuno can create blizzards.

LEGENDARY POKÉMON

Pronounced: ART-tick-COO-no
Possible Moves: Gust, Powder Snow, Mist, Ice Shard, Mind Reader, AncientPower, Agility, Ice Beam, Reflect, Roost, Tailwind, Blizzard, Sheer Cold, Hail
Type: Ice-Flying
Height: 5' 07"
Weight: 122.1 lbs.
Region: Kanto

DOES NOT EVOLVE

AUDINO
HEARING POKÉMON

Audino can sense a person's feelings by touching that person with its feelers and listening to the heartbeat. Audino's amazing hearing also helps it sense its environment through faint sounds.

Pronounced: AW-dih-noh
Possible Moves: Pound, Growl, Helping Hand, Refresh, DoubleSlap, Attract, Secret Power, Entrainment, Take Down, Heal Pulse, After You, Simple Beam, Double-Edge, Last Resort
Type: Normal
Height: 3' 07"   **Weight:** 68.3 lbs.
Region: Unova

DOES
NOT
EVOLVE

AXEW
TUSK POKÉMON

Axew uses its tusks to crush berries for food and cut gashes in trees to mark its territory. Its fangs are strong and sharp because they grow constantly. If one breaks, a replacement grows quickly.

Pronounced: AKS-yoo
Possible Moves: Scratch, Leer, Assurance, Dragon Rage, Dual Chop, Scary Face, Slash, False Swipe, Dragon Claw, Dragon Dance, Taunt, Dragon Pulse, Swords Dance, Guillotine, Outrage, Giga Impact
Type: Dragon
Height: 2' 00"
Weight: 39.7 lbs.
Region: Unova

AXEW   FRAXURE   HAXORUS

AZELF
WILLPOWER POKÉMON

Also known as The Being of Willpower, this Pokémon keeps the world in balance. It is said that Uxie, Mesprit, and Azelf all came from the same egg.

Pronounced: AZ-elf
Possible Moves: Rest, Confusion, Imprison, Detect, Swift, Uproar, Future Sight, Nasty Plot, Extrasensory, Last Resort, Natural Gift, Explosion
Type: Psychic
Height: 1' 00"
Weight: 0.7 lbs.
Region: Sinnoh

DOES
NOT
EVOLVE

LEGENDARY
POKÉMON

AZUMARILL
AQUA RABBIT POKÉMON

Azumarill has natural camouflage—the patterns on its body can fool even those standing right next to it.

Pronounced: ah-ZU-mare-rill
Possible Moves: Tackle, Defense Curl, Tail Whip, Water Gun, Rollout, BubbleBeam, Aqua Ring, Double-Edge, Rain Dance, Aqua Tail, Hydro Pump
Type: Water
Height: 2' 07"
Weight: 62.8 lbs.
Region: Johto

AZURILL → MARILL → AZUMARILL

AZURILL
POLKA DOT POKÉMON

Azurill is a water-dwelling Pokémon that loves to bounce on its springy tail, which is filled with nutrients.

Pronounced: uh-ZOO-rill
Possible Moves: Splash, Charm, Tail Whip, Bubble, Slam, Water Gun
Type: Normal   **Height:** 0' 08"   **Weight:** 4.4 lbs.
Region: Hoenn

AZURILL → MARILL → AZUMARILL

BAGON
ROCK HEAD POKÉMON

Bagon leaps off cliffs every day in the hopes that one day it will be able to fly.

Pronounced: BAY-gon
Possible Moves: Rage, Bite, Leer, Headbutt, Focus Energy, Ember, DragonBreath, Zen Headbutt, Scary Face, Crunch, Dragon Claw, Double-Edge
Type: Dragon
Height: 2' 00"
Weight: 92.8 lbs.
Region: Hoenn

BAGON   SHELGON   SALAMENCE

BALTOY
CLAY DOLL POKÉMON

Considered a very rare Pokémon, Baltoy was discovered in ancient ruins.

Pronounced: BAL-toy
Possible Moves: Confusion, Harden, Rapid Spin, Mud-Slap, Psybeam, Rock Tomb, Selfdestruct, AncientPower, Power Trick, Sandstorm, Cosmic Power, Extrasensory, Guard Split, Power Split, Earth Power, Heal Block, Explosion
Type: Ground-Psychic
Height: 1' 08"
Weight: 47.4 lbs.
Region: Hoenn

BALTOY   CLAYDOL

BANETTE
MARIONETTE POKÉMON

Banette became a Pokémon after being abandoned by its owner. It spends most of its time seeking out that owner.

Pronounced: bane-NETT
Possible Moves: Knock Off, Screech, Night Shade, Curse, Spite, Shadow Sneak, Will-O-Wisp, Faint Attack, Hex, Shadow Ball, Sucker Punch, Embargo, Snatch, Grudge, Trick
Type: Ghost
Height: 3' 07"
Weight: 27.6 lbs.
Region: Hoenn

SHUPPET

BANETTE

BARBOACH
WHISKERS POKÉMON

Barboach is able to use its sensitive whiskers to detect prey. It covers its body in slimy fluid so it's harder for predators to grasp.

Pronounced: bar-BOACH
Possible Moves: Mud-Slap, Mud Sport, Water Sport, Water Gun, Mud Bomb, Amnesia, Water Pulse, Magnitude, Rest, Snore, Aqua Tail, Earthquake, Future Sight, Fissure
Type: Water-Ground
Height: 1' 04"   **Weight:** 4.2 lbs.
Region: Hoenn

BARBOACH

WHISCASH

BASCULIN
HOSTILE POKÉMON

Red-Striped Form

Blue-Striped Form

Basculin is a hostile Pokémon. The two forms of this Pokémon don't get along and fight each other on sight. Sometimes, however, members of one group will mingle with another.

Pronounced: BASS-kyoo-lin
Possible Moves: Tackle, Water Gun, Uproar, Headbutt, Bite, Aqua Jet, Chip Away, Take Down, Crunch, Aqua Tail, Soak, Double-Edge, Scary Face, Flail, Final Gambit, Thrash
Type: Water
Height: 3' 03"   **Weight:** 39.7 lbs.
Region: Unova

DOES NOT EVOLVE

BASTIODON
SHIELD POKÉMON

Bastiodon protects its young by forming a wall with other Bastiodon. It is a calm Pokémon that feeds on berries and grass.

Pronounced: BAS-tee-oh-donn
Possible Moves: Tackle, Protect, Taunt, Metal Sound, Take Down, Iron Defense, Swagger, AncientPower, Block, Endure, Metal Burst, Iron Head, Heavy Slam
Type: Rock-Steel
Height: 4' 03"
Weight: 329.6 lbs.
Region: Sinnoh

SHIELDON → BASTIODON

BAYLEEF
LEAF POKÉMON

Need a pick-me-up? Hang out around Bayleef! The spicy aroma from the ring of leaves around its neck can improve people's moods.

Pronounced: BAY-leaf
Possible Moves: Tackle, Growl, Razor Leaf, PoisonPowder, Synthesis, Reflect, Magical Leaf, Natural Gift, Sweet Scent, Light Screen, Body Slam, Safeguard, Aromatherapy, SolarBeam
Type: Grass
Height: 3' 11"
Weight: 34.8 lbs.
Region: Johto

CHIKORITA → BAYLEEF → MEGANIUM

BEARTIC
FREEZING POKÉMON

Beartic freezes its breath to create fangs and claws of ice to fight with. Cold northern areas are its habitat.

Pronounced: BAIR-tick
Possible Moves: Superpower, Powder Snow, Growl, Bide, Icy Wind, Fury Swipes, Brine, Endure, Swagger, Slash, Flail, Icicle Crash, Rest, Blizzard, Hail, Thrash, Sheer Cold
Type: Ice
Height: 8' 06"   **Weight:** 573.2 lbs.
Region: Unova

CUBCHOO → BEARTIC

BEAUTIFLY
BUTTERFLY POKÉMON

Beautifly uses its long, narrow mouth to drain fluid from prey.

Pronounced: BUE-tee-fly

Possible Moves: Absorb, Gust, Stun Spore, Morning Sun, Mega Drain, Whirlwind, Attract, Silver Wind, Giga Drain, Bug Buzz, Quiver Dance

Type: Bug-Flying

Height: 3' 03"

Weight: 62.6 lbs.

Region: Hoenn

WURMPLE → SILCOON → BEAUTIFLY

BEEDRILL
POISON BEE POKÉMON

Beedrill loves to stick and move—flying around at high speeds and stinging enemies, then flying away.

Pronounced: BEE-dril

Possible Moves: Fury Attack, Focus Energy, Twineedle, Rage, Pursuit, Toxic Spikes, Pin Missile, Agility, Assurance, Poison Jab, Endeavor

Type: Bug-Poison   **Height:** 3' 03"   **Weight:** 65.0 lbs.

Region: Kanto

WEEDLE → KAKUNA → BEEDRILL

BEHEEYEM
CEREBRAL POKÉMON

Beheeyem's psychic power can manipulate a target's memory and even control its brain. It seems to communicate by flashing its three fingers, which are different colors.

Pronounced: BEE-hee-ehm
Possible Moves: Confusion, Growl, Heal Block, Miracle Eye, Psybeam, Headbutt, Hidden Power, Imprison, Simple Beam, Zen Headbutt, Psych Up, Psychic, Calm Mind, Recover, Guard Split, Power Split, Synchronoise, Wonder Room
Type: Psychic   **Height:** 3' 03"
Weight: 76.1 lbs.   **Region:** Unova

ELGYEM BEHEEYEM

BELDUM
IRON BALL POKÉMON

While in a group, Beldum can move in perfect unison and talk to one another by using magnetic pulses.

Pronounced: BELL-dum
Possible Moves: Take Down
Type: Steel-Psychic
Height: 2' 00"   **Weight:** 209.9 lbs.
Region: Hoenn

BELDUM

METANG

METAGROSS

BELLOSSOM
FLOWER POKÉMON

Bellossom will dance in the open sunlight after the rainy season ends.

Pronounced: bell-LAHS-um
Possible Moves: Leaf Blade, Mega Drain, Sweet Scent, Stun Spore, Sunny Day, Magical Leaf, Leaf Storm
Type: Grass
Height: 1' 04"
Weight: 12.8 lbs.
Region: Johto

ODDISH ➤ GLOOM ➤ BELLOSSOM

BELLSPROUT
FLOWER POKÉMON

Bellsprout uses its vines to capture prey. It likes to live in hot environments.

Pronounced: BELL-sprout
Possible Moves: Vine Whip, Growth, Wrap, Sleep Powder, PoisonPowder, Stun Spore, Acid, Knock Off, Sweet Scent, Gastro Acid, Razor Leaf, Slam, Wring Out
Type: Grass-Poison   **Height:** 2' 04"   **Weight:** 8.8 lbs.
Region: Kanto

BELLSPROUT ➤ WEEPINBELL ➤ VICTREEBEL

BIBAREL
BEAVER POKÉMON

Bibarel can swim fast in water, but moves slowly on land. Bibarel is known as a hard-working Pokémon.

Pronounced: BEE-bear-ull
Possible Moves: Tackle, Growl, Defense Curl, Rollout, Water Gun, Headbutt, Hyper Fang, Yawn, Amnesia, Take Down, Super Fang, Superpower, Curse
Type: Normal-Water
Height: 3' 03"
Weight: 69.4 lbs.
Region: Sinnoh

BIDOOF

BIBAREL

BIDOOF
PLUMP MOUSE POKÉMON

Bidoof is known to chew on rocks and logs to dull the edge of its sharp teeth. But be careful—this Pokémon is more agile than it appears.

Pronounced: BEE-doof
Possible Moves: Tackle, Growl, Defense Curl, Rollout, Headbutt, Hyper Fang, Yawn, Amnesia, Take Down, Super Fang, Superpower, Curse
Type: Normal
Height: 1' 08"   **Weight:** 44.1 lbs.
Region: Sinnoh

BIDOOF

BIBAREL

BISHARP
SWORD BLADE POKÉMON

Bisharp hunts prey with a large group of Pawniard and battles to become their leader. It is expelled from the group if it loses.

Pronounced: BIH-sharp

Possible Moves: Metal Burst, Scratch, Leer, Fury Cutter, Torment, Faint Attack, Scary Face, Metal Claw, Slash, Assurance, Metal Sound, Embargo, Iron Defense, Night Slash, Iron Head, Swords Dance, Guillotine

Type: Dark-Steel   **Height:** 5' 03"

Weight: 154.3 lbs.   **Region:** Unova

PAWNIARD

BISHARP

BLASTOISE
SHELLFISH POKÉMON

Beware of the jets from this Pokémon's shell—they can punch through thick steel.

Pronounced: BLAS-toyce

Possible Moves: Flash Cannon, Tackle, Tail Whip, Bubble, Withdraw, Water Gun, Bite, Rapid Spin, Protect, Water Pulse, Aqua Tail, Skull Bash, Iron Defense, Rain Dance, Hydro Pump

Type: Water   **Height:** 5' 03"   **Weight:** 188.5 lbs.

Region: Kanto

SQUIRTLE

WARTORTLE

BLASTOISE

BLAZIKEN
BLAZE POKÉMON

Blaziken's wrists spout flames that cover its knuckles. It uses its fiery punches to singe its opponents.

Pronounced: BLAZE-uh-ken
Possible Moves: Fire Punch, Hi Jump Kick, Scratch, Growl, Focus Energy, Ember, Double Kick, Peck, Sand-Attack, Bulk Up, Quick Attack, Blaze Kick, Slash, Brave Bird, Sky Uppercut, Flare Blitz
Type: Fire-Fighting
Height: 6' 03"
Weight: 114.6 lbs.
Region: Hoenn

TORCHIC

COMBUSKEN

BLAZIKEN

BLISSEY
HAPPINESS POKÉMON

This Pokémon can sense feelings of sadness, and also nurses sick Pokémon back to health.

Pronounced: BLISS-sey
Possible Moves: Defense Curl, Pound, Growl, Tail Whip, Refresh, DoubleSlap, Softboiled, Bestow, Minimize, Take Down, Sing, Fling, Heal Pulse, Egg Bomb, Light Screen, Healing Wish, Double-Edge
Type: Normal
Height: 4' 11"
Weight: 103.2 lbs.
Region: Johto

HAPPINY → CHANSEY → BLISSEY

BLITZLE
ELECTRIFIED POKÉMON

When the sky is covered in thunderclouds, Blitzle appears. It communicates with other Blitzle by flashing its mane, which can catch and store lightning. Its mane shines when it discharges that electricity.

Pronounced: BLIT-zul
Possible Moves: Quick Attack, Tail Whip, Charge, Shock Wave, Thunder Wave, Flame Charge, Pursuit, Spark, Stomp, Discharge, Agility, Wild Charge, Thrash
Type: Electric
Height: 2' 07"
Weight: 65.7 lbs.
Region: Unova

BLITZLE → ZEBSTRIKA

BOLDORE
ORE POKÉMON

Boldore searches caves for underground water. When it can't contain excess energy, orange crystals form on its body, and these crystals glow when its power overflows.

Pronounced: BOHL-dohr
Possible Moves: Tackle, Harden, Sand-Attack, Headbutt, Rock Blast, Mud-Slap, Iron Defense, Smack Down, Power Gem, Rock Slide, Stealth Rock, Sandstorm, Stone Edge, Explosion
Type: Rock
Height: 2' 11"
Weight: 224.9 lbs.
Region: Unova

ROGGENROLA → BOLDORE → GIGALITH

BONSLY
BONSAI POKÉMON

Don't worry, Bonsly isn't sad! This Pokémon adjusts its fluid levels by eliminating the excess water from its body through tears.

Pronounced: BON-sly
Possible Moves: Fake Tears, Copycat, Flail, Low Kick, Rock Throw, Mimic, Block, Faint Attack, Rock Tomb, Rock Slide, Slam, Sucker Punch, Double-Edge
Type: Rock
Height: 1' 08"
Weight: 33.1 lbs.
Region: Sinnoh

BONSLY → SUDOWOODO

BOUFFALANT
BASH BUFFALO POKÉMON

Bouffalant recklessly charges and headbutts anything. Though it attacks with enough force to derail a train, its fluffy fur absorbs the damage of even the most violent headbutt.

Pronounced: BOO-fuh-lahnt
Possible Moves: Pursuit, Leer, Rage, Fury Attack, Horn Attack, Scary Face, Revenge, Head Charge, Focus Energy, Megahorn, Reversal, Thrash, Swords Dance, Giga Impact
Type: Normal
Height: 5' 03"   **Weight:** 208.6 lbs.
Region: Unova

DOES NOT EVOLVE

BRAVIARY
VALIANT POKÉMON

This brave warrior battles for its friends with no thought for its own safety. The more scars a Braviary has, the more its peers respect it. It can fly while carrying a car.

Pronounced: BRAY-vee-air-ee
Possible Moves: Peck, Leer, Fury Attack, Wing Attack, Hone Claws, Scary Face, Aerial Ace, Slash, Defog, Tailwind, Air Slash, Crush Claw, Sky Drop, Superpower, Whirlwind, Brave Bird, Thrash
Type: Normal-Flying
Height: 4' 11"
Weight: 90.4 lbs.
Region: Unova

RUFFLET

BRAVIARY

BRELOOM
MUSHROOM POKÉMON

Though Breloom appears to have short arms, they will stretch when Breloom throws punches at its foes.

Pronounced: BRELL-loom
Possible Moves: Absorb, Tackle, Stun Spore, Leech Seed, Mega Drain, Headbutt, Mach Punch, Counter, Force Palm, Sky Uppercut, Mind Reader, Seed Bomb, DynamicPunch
Type: Grass-Fighting
Height: 3' 11"
Weight: 86.4 lbs.
Region: Hoenn

SHROOMISH

BRELOOM

BRONZONG
BRONZE BELL POKÉMON

This Pokémon was known in ancient times as the bringer of plentiful harvests, because it produced rain clouds.

Pronounced: brawn-ZONG
Possible Moves: Sunny Day, Rain Dance, Tackle, Confusion, Hypnosis, Imprison, Confuse Ray, Extrasensory, Iron Defense, Safeguard, Block, Gyro Ball, Future Sight, Faint Attack, Payback, Heal Block, Heavy Slam
Type: Steel-Psychic
Height: 4' 03"   **Weight:** 412.3 lbs.
Region: Sinnoh

BRONZOR

BRONZONG

BRONZOR
BRONZE POKÉMON

Bronzor is shaped like an ancient artifact. No one really knows what it is made of.

Pronounced: BRAWN-zor
Possible Moves: Tackle, Confusion, Hypnosis, Imprison, Confuse Ray, Extrasensory, Iron Defense, Safeguard, Gyro Ball, Future Sight, Faint Attack, Payback, Heal Block, Heavy Slam
Type: Steel-Psychic
Height: 1' 08"   **Weight:** 133.4 lbs.
Region: Sinnoh

BRONZOR > BRONZONG

BUDEW
BUD POKÉMON

The pollen that is released from Budew's bud can cause runny noses and sneezing.

Pronounced: Buh-DOO
Possible Moves: Absorb, Growth, Water Sport, Stun Spore, Mega Drain, Worry Seed
Type: Grass-Poison
Height: 0' 08"   **Weight:** 2.6 lbs.
Region: Sinnoh

BUDEW > ROSELIA > ROSERADE

BUIZEL
SEA WEASEL POKÉMON

The sac around Buizel's neck acts like an innertube, which allows it to float with its head above water. It moves by spinning its tail like a propeller.

Pronounced: BWEE-zull
Possible Moves: SonicBoom, Growl, Water Sport, Quick Attack, Water Gun, Pursuit, Swift, Aqua Jet, Agility, Whirlpool, Razor Wind, Aqua Tail
Type: Water
Height: 2' 04"
Weight: 65.0 lbs.
Region: Sinnoh

BUIZEL

FLOATZEL

BULBASAUR
SEED POKÉMON

Shortly after it hatches, this Pokémon can obtain nourishment from the seed on its back.

Pronounced: BUL-buh-sore
Possible Moves: Tackle, Growl, Leech Seed, Vine Whip, PoisonPowder, Sleep Powder, Take Down, Razor Leaf, Sweet Scent, Growth, Double-Edge, Worry Seed, Synthesis, Seed Bomb
Type: Grass-Poison
Height: 2' 04"
Weight: 15.2 lbs.
Region: Kanto

BULBASAUR ➔ **IVYSAUR** ➔ **VENUSAUR**

BUNEARY
RABBIT POKÉMON

Buneary can unwrap its sharp ears to fight foes. On chilly nights, it will curl up and sleep with its head buried in its fur.

Pronounced: buh-NEER-ree
Possible Moves: Splash, Pound, Defense Curl, Foresight, Endure, Frustration, Quick Attack, Jump Kick, Baton Pass, Agility, Dizzy Punch, After You, Charm, Entrainment, Bounce, Healing Wish
Type: Normal
Height: 1' 04"
Weight: 12.1 lbs.
Region: Sinnoh

BUNEARY ➔ **LOPUNNY**

BURMY GRASS CLOAK
BAGWORM POKÉMON

Burmy can camouflage itself by burying itself in leaves and twigs. If it's uncovered in battle, it can quickly cover itself back up.

Pronounced: BURR-mee
Possible Moves: Protect, Tackle, Bug Bite, Hidden Power
Type: Bug
Height: 0' 08"
Weight: 7.5 lbs.
Region: Sinnoh

BURMY
(GRASS CLOAK)

♀

WORMADAM
(GRASS CLOAK)

♂

MOTHIM

BURMY SANDY CLOAK
BAGWORM POKÉMON

Did you know that each Burmy covers up with the objects around it? This Burmy uses rocks and sand for protection.

Pronounced: BURR-mee
Possible Moves: Protect, Tackle, Bug Bite, Hidden Power
Type: Bug
Height: 0' 08"
Weight: 7.5 lbs.
Region: Sinnoh

BURMY
(SANDY CLOAK)

♀

WORMADAM
(SANDY CLOAK)

♂

MOTHIM

BURMY TRASH CLOAK
BAGWORM POKÉMON

If you're looking for Burmy with a Trash Cloak, try poking around inside a few buildings. You might get lucky!

Pronounced: BURR-mee
Possible Moves: Protect, Tackle, Bug Bite, Hidden Power
Type: Bug
Height: 0' 08"
Weight: 7.5 lbs.
Region: Sinnoh

BURMY
(TRASH CLOAK)

♀

♂

WORMADAM
(TRASH CLOAK)

MOTHIM

BUTTERFREE
BUTTERFLY POKÉMON

Butterfree can smell honey from great distances, and will often find its way to meadows with even minute traces of honey or pollen.

Pronounced: BUT-er-free
Possible Moves: Confusion, PoisonPowder, Stun Spore, Sleep Powder, Gust, Supersonic, Whirlwind, Psybeam, Silver Wind, Tailwind, Rage Powder, Safeguard, Captivate, Bug Buzz, Quiver Dance
Type: Bug-Flying   **Height:** 3' 07"   **Weight:** 70.5 lbs.
Region: Kanto

CATERPIE   **METAPOD**   **BUTTERFREE**

CACNEA
CACTUS POKÉMON

Because of its balloon shape, Cacnea can survive up to thirty days in the desert by living off the water stored in its body.

Pronounced: CACK-nee-uh
Possible Moves: Poison Sting, Leer, Absorb, Growth, Leech Seed, Sand-Attack, Pin Missile, Ingrain, Faint Attack, Spikes, Sucker Punch, Payback, Needle Arm, Cotton Spore, Sandstorm, Destiny Bond
Type: Grass
Height: 1' 04"
Weight: 113.1 lbs.
Region: Hoenn

CACNEA

CACTURNE

CACTURNE
SCARECROW POKÉMON

Cacturne is a nocturnal Pokémon. It waits patiently for prey that are tired from traipsing around the desert all day.

Pronounced: CACK-turn
Possible Moves: Revenge, Poison Sting, Leer, Absorb, Growth, Leech Seed, Sand-Attack, Pin Missile, Ingrain, Faint Attack, Spikes, Sucker Punch, Payback, Needle Arm, Cotton Spore, Sandstorm, Destiny Bond
Type: Grass-Dark
Height: 4' 03"   **Weight:** 170.6 lbs.
Region: Hoenn

CACNEA

CACTURNE

CAMERUPT
ERUPTION POKÉMON

If too much magma builds up in Camerupt's body, the volcanoes on its back will shudder, then erupt violently.

Pronounced: CAM-err-rupt

Possible Moves: Growl, Tackle, Ember, Magnitude, Focus Energy, Flame Burst, Take Down, Amnesia, Lava Plume, Rock Slide, Earth Power, Earthquake, Eruption, Fissure

Type: Fire-Ground

Height: 6' 03"

Weight: 485.0 lbs.

Region: Hoenn

NUMEL

CAMERUPT

CARNIVINE
BUG CATCHER POKÉMON

Carnivine attracts its prey by emitting a sweet-smelling scent. Once its prey is caught, it takes Carnivine a whole day to digest it.

Pronounced: CAR-nuh-vine

Possible Moves: Bind, Growth, Bite, Vine Whip, Sweet Scent, Ingrain, Faint Attack, Leaf Tornado, Stockpile, Spit Up, Swallow, Crunch, Wring Out, Power Whip

Type: Grass

Height: 4' 07"

Weight: 59.5 lbs.

Region: Sinnoh

DOES NOT EVOLVE

CARRACOSTA
PROTOTURTLE POKÉMON

Carracosta can live in the water or on land. It can puncture a tanker's hull with one slap, and its jaws can chew up rocks and steel beams along with its prey.

Pronounced: kar-ruh-KOSS-tuh

Possible Moves: Bide, Withdraw, Water Gun, Rollout, Bite, Protect, Aqua Jet, AncientPower, Crunch, Wide Guard, Brine, Smack Down, Curse, Shell Smash, Aqua Tail, Rock Slide, Rain Dance, Hydro Pump

Type: Water-Rock

Height: 3' 11"   **Weight:** 178.6 lbs.

Region: Unova

TIRTOUGA

CARRACOSTA

CARVANHA
SAVAGE POKÉMON

Carvanha's sharp fangs have been known to destroy boat hulls, and they swarm any foe that invades their territory.

Pronounced: car-VAH-na

Possible Moves: Leer, Bite, Rage, Focus Energy, Scary Face, Ice Fang, Screech, Swagger, Assurance, Crunch, Aqua Jet, Agility, Take Down

Type: Water-Dark

Height: 2' 07"

Weight: 45.9 lbs.

Region: Hoenn

CARVANHA

SHARPEDO

CASCOON
COCOON POKÉMON

Cascoon never forgets the face of an enemy, but then again, it rarely sees them, since this Pokémon spends all of its time in a hardened cocoon.

Pronounced: CAS-koon
Possible Moves: Harden
Type: Bug
Height: 2' 04"
Weight: 25.4 lbs.
Region: Hoenn

WURMPLE　　CASCOON　　DUSTOX

CASTFORM
WEATHER POKÉMON

Castform has the ability to change its appearance to match changes of weather.

Pronounced: CAST-form
Possible Moves: Tackle, Water Gun, Ember, Powder Snow, Headbutt, Rain Dance, Sunny Day, Hail, Weather Ball, Hydro Pump, Fire Blast, Blizzard
Type: Normal
Height: 1' 00"
Weight: 1.8 lbs.
Region: Hoenn

DOES NOT EVOLVE

Regular Form

Sunny Form

Rainy Form

Snowy Form

CATERPIE
WORM POKÉMON

How does Caterpie grow? By repeatedly shedding its skin. How does it survive? By releasing a horrible stench from its antennae.

Pronounced: CAT-er-pee
Possible Moves: Tackle, String Shot, Bug Bite
Type: Bug
Height: 1' 00"
Weight: 6.4 lbs.
Region: Kanto

CATERPIE

METAPOD

BUTTERFREE

CELEBI
TIME TRAVEL POKÉMON

Celebi can travel through time, but is rumored to appear only in peaceful times.

Pronounced: SEL-ih-bee
Possible Moves: Leech Seed, Confusion, Recover, Heal Bell, Safeguard, Magical Leaf, AncientPower, Baton Pass, Natural Gift, Heal Block, Future Sight, Healing Wish, Leaf Storm, Perish Song
Type: Psychic-Grass
Height: 2' 00"
Weight: 11.0 lbs.
Region: Johto

DOES
NOT
EVOLVE

MYTHICAL
POKÉMON

CHANDELURE
LURING POKÉMON

Chandelure's flames will consume a spirit, which Chandelure absorbs as fuel. It waves the flames on its arms to hypnotize foes.

Pronounced: shan-duh-LOOR
Possible Moves: Smog, Confuse Ray, Flame Burst, Hex
Type: Ghost-Fire
Height: 3' 03"
Weight: 75.6 lbs.
Region: Unova

LITWICK   LAMPENT   CHANDELURE

CHANSEY
EGG POKÉMON

Chansey is a very compassionate Pokémon, delivering happiness and sharing its egg with injured people and Pokémon.

Pronounced: CHAN-see
Possible Moves: Defense Curl, Pound, Growl, Tail Whip, Refresh, DoubleSlap, Softboiled, Bestow, Minimize, Take Down, Sing, Fling, Heal Pulse, Egg Bomb, Light Screen, Healing Wish, Double-Edge
Type: Normal
Height: 3' 07"
Weight: 76.3 lbs.
Region: Kanto

HAPPINY   CHANSEY   BLISSEY

CHARIZARD
FLAME POKÉMON

You don't want to mess with Charizard after it has experienced a tense battle—the fire emanating from it burns hotter when it is stressed.

Pronounced: CHAR-i-zard
Possible Moves: Dragon Claw, Shadow Claw, Air Slash, Scratch, Growl, Ember, SmokeScreen, Dragon Rage, Scary Face, Fire Fang, Flame Burst, Wing Attack, Slash, Flamethrower, Fire Spin, Inferno, Heat Wave, Flare Blitz
Type: Fire-Flying
Height: 5' 07"
Weight: 199.5 lbs.
Region: Kanto

CHARMANDER → CHARMELEON → CHARIZARD

CHARMANDER
LIZARD POKÉMON

If Charmander is healthy, the fire on its tail burns intensely.

Pronounced: CHAR-man-der
Possible Moves: Scratch, Growl, Ember, SmokeScreen, Dragon Rage, Scary Face, Fire Fang, Flame Burst, Slash, Flamethrower, Fire Spin, Inferno
Type: Fire   **Height:** 2' 00"
Weight: 18.7 lbs.
Region: Kanto

CHARMANDER → CHARMELEON → CHARIZARD

CHARMELEON
FLAME POKÉMON

It's easy to spot a Charmeleon's lair in Kanto's rocky mountains. Thanks to this Pokémon's fiery tail, its home shines with the power of intense starlight.

Pronounced: char-MEAL-ee-ehn
Possible Moves: Scratch, Growl, Ember, SmokeScreen, Dragon Rage, Scary Face, Fire Fang, Flame Burst, Slash, Flamethrower, Fire Spin, Inferno
Type: Fire   **Height:** 3' 07"   **Weight:** 41.9 lbs.
Region: Kanto

CHARMANDER   CHARMELEON   CHARIZARD

CHATOT
MUSIC NOTE POKÉMON

Chatot can learn human words. Although it can't speak, Chatot can click its tail feathers to make a rhythmic sound.

Pronounced: CHAH-tot
Possible Moves: Peck, Growl, Mirror Move, Sing, Fury Attack, Chatter, Taunt, Round, Mimic, Echoed Voice, Roost, Uproar, Synchronoise, FeatherDance, Hyper Voice
Type: Normal-Flying
Height: 1' 08"   **Weight:** 4.2 lbs.
Region: Sinnoh

DOES NOT EVOLVE

CHERRIM
BLOSSOM POKÉMON

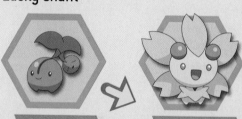

While the sun is out, Cherrim will bloom to full strength, but will return to a bud when sunlight fades.

Pronounced: chuh-RIM
Possible Moves: Morning Sun, Tackle, Growth, Leech Seed, Helping Hand, Magical Leaf, Sunny Day, Petal Dance, Worry Seed, Take Down, SolarBeam, Lucky Chant
Type: Grass
Height: 1' 08"
Weight: 20.5 lbs.
Region: Sinnoh

CHERUBI → CHERRIM

CHERUBI
CHERRY POKÉMON

The small ball attached to Cherubi holds the nutrition that Cherubi needs to evolve. While out in the sun, it will change its color to red.

Pronounced: chuh-ROO-bee
Possible Moves: Morning Sun, Tackle, Growth, Leech Seed, Helping Hand, Magical Leaf, Sunny Day, Worry Seed, Take Down, SolarBeam, Lucky Chant
Type: Grass
Height: 1' 04"
Weight: 7.3 lbs.
Region: Sinnoh

CHERUBI → CHERRIM

CHIKORITA
LEAF POKÉMON

Chikorita loves the sun and uses the leaf on its head to test the weather.

Pronounced: CHICK-oh-REE-ta
Possible Moves: Tackle, Growl, Razor Leaf, PoisonPowder, Synthesis, Reflect, Magical Leaf, Natural Gift, Sweet Scent, Light Screen, Body Slam, Safeguard, Aromatherapy, SolarBeam
Type: Grass
Height: 2' 11"
Weight: 14.1 lbs.
Region: Johto

 CHIKORITA  BAYLEEF  MEGANIUM

CHIMCHAR
CHIMP POKÉMON

Even the rain can't put out Chimchar's fiery tail, which is fueled by the gases in its stomach.

Pronounced: CHIM-char
Possible Moves: Scratch, Leer, Ember, Taunt, Fury Swipes, Flame Wheel, Nasty Plot, Torment, Facade, Fire Spin, Acrobatics, Slack Off, Flamethrower
Type: Fire   **Height:** 1' 08"
Weight: 13.7 lbs.   **Region:** Sinnoh

 CHIMCHAR  MONFERNO  INFERNAPE

CHIMECHO
WIND CHIME POKÉMON

Chimecho can use seven different cries to knock out its prey.

Pronounced: chime-ECK-ko
Possible Moves: Wrap, Growl, Astonish, Confusion, Uproar, Take Down, Yawn, Psywave, Double-Edge, Heal Bell, Safeguard, Extrasensory, Heal Pulse, Synchronoise, Healing Wish
Type: Psychic
Height: 2' 00"   **Weight:** 2.2 lbs.
Region: Hoenn

CHINGLING

CHIMECHO

CHINCHOU
ANGLER POKÉMON

Chinchou's electric attacks are possible thanks to the energy it charges between its two antennae.

Pronounced: CHIN-chow
Possible Moves: Supersonic, Bubble, Thunder Wave, Flail, Confuse Ray, Water Gun, Spark, Take Down, Electro Ball, BubbleBeam, Signal Beam, Discharge, Aqua Ring, Hydro Pump, Charge
Type: Water-Electric
Height: 1' 08"
Weight: 26.5 lbs.
Region: Johto

CHINCHOU

LANTURN

CHINGLING
BELL POKÉMON

Chingling defeats its foes by using a cry that comes from an orb in the back of its throat. When not in battle, it makes a ringing sound as it moves and hops around.

Pronounced: CHING-ling
Possible Moves: Wrap, Growl, Astonish, Confusion, Uproar, Last Resort, Entrainment
Type: Psychic
Height: 0' 08"
Weight: 1.3 lbs.
Region: Sinnoh

CHINGLING

CHIMECHO

CINCCINO
SCARF POKÉMON

Cinccino's white fur has an amazing texture, and its special oil deflects attacks. This fur also repels dust and prevents static electricity.

Pronounced: chin-CHEE-noh
Possible Moves: Bullet Seed, Rock Blast, Helping Hand, Tickle, Sing, Tail Slap
Type: Normal
Height: 1' 08"   **Weight:** 16.5 lbs.
Region: Unova

MINCCINO

CINCCINO

CLAMPERL
BIVALVE POKÉMON

Clamperl will only produce one pearl in its lifetime, which is said to enhance psychic power.

Pronounced: CLAM-perl
Possible Moves: Clamp, Water Gun, Whirlpool, Iron Defense, Shell Smash
Type: Water
Height: 1' 04"
Weight: 115.7 lbs.
Region: Hoenn

CLAMPERL

HUNTAIL

GOREBYSS

CLAYDOL
CLAY DOLL POKÉMON

Claydol was formed when a mysterious ray of light shone down upon an ancient clay figurine.

Pronounced: CLAY-doll
Possible Moves: Teleport, Confusion, Harden, Rapid Spin, Mud-Slap, Psybeam, Rock Tomb, Selfdestruct, AncientPower, Power Trick, Sandstorm, Hyper Beam, Extrasensory, Cosmic Power, Guard Split, Power Split, Earth Power, Heal Block, Explosion
Type: Ground-Psychic
Height: 4' 11"
Weight: 238.1 lbs.
Region: Hoenn

BALTOY

CLAYDOL

CLEFABLE
FAIRY POKÉMON

This Pokémon is very shy. It lives mostly near deserted lakebeds. Clefable can hear you coming, too—its hearing can detect a pin drop from over half a mile away.

Pronounced: cluh-FAY-bull
Possible Moves: Sing, DoubleSlap, Minimize, Metronome
Type: Normal
Height: 4' 03"
Weight: 88.2 lbs.
Region: Kanto

CLEFFA  CLEFAIRY  CLEFABLE

CLEFAIRY
FAIRY POKÉMON

This is one of the most difficult Pokémon to find—it flies mostly at night, collecting moonlight on its wings.

Pronounced: cluh-FAIR-ee
Possible Moves: Pound, Growl, Encore, Sing, DoubleSlap, Defense Curl, Follow Me, Minimize, Wake-Up Slap, Bestow, Cosmic Power, Lucky Chant, Metronome, Gravity, Moonlight, Stored Power, Light Screen, Healing Wish, After You, Meteor Mash
Type: Normal
Height: 2' 00"
Weight: 16.5 lbs.
Region: Kanto

 CLEFFA  CLEFAIRY CLEFABLE

CLEFFA
STAR SHAPE POKÉMON

Cleffa is usually found when shooting stars fill the night skies. It is said to arrive riding on a shooting star.

Pronounced: CLEFF-uh
Possible Moves: Pound, Charm, Encore, Sing, Sweet Kiss, Copycat, Magical Leaf
Type: Normal
Height: 1' 00"
Weight: 6.6 lbs.
Region: Johto

CLEFFA → CLEFAIRY → CLEFABLE

CLOYSTER
BIVALVE POKÉMON

Cloyster fights by shooting spikes from its body and then closing its shell for protection.

Pronounced: CLOY-stir
Possible Moves: Toxic Spikes, Withdraw, Supersonic, Protect, Aurora Beam, Spike Cannon, Spikes, Icicle Crash
Type: Water-Ice
Height: 4' 11"
Weight: 292.1 lbs.
Region: Kanto

SHELLDER → CLOYSTER

COBALION
IRON WILL POKÉMON

Calm and collected, Cobalion has a body and heart of steel—and a glare that demands obedience even from ill-behaved Pokémon. This Legendary Pokémon battled humans to protect other Pokémon.

Pronounced: koh-BAY-lee-un

Possible Moves: Quick Attack, Leer, Double Kick, Metal Claw, Take Down, Helping Hand, Retaliate, Iron Head, Sacred Sword, Swords Dance, Quick Guard, Work Up, Metal Burst, Close Combat

Type: Steel-Fighting

Height: 6' 11"

Weight: 551.2 lbs.

Region: Unova

DOES
NOT
EVOLVE

LEGENDARY
POKÉMON

COFAGRIGUS
COFFIN POKÉMON

Cofagrigus's body is covered in pure gold, and it poses as an ornate coffin to punish grave robbers. It likes to eat gold nuggets, but it's said that it gulps down people who get too close and makes them into mummies.

Pronounced: kof-uh-GREE-guss
Possible Moves: Astonish, Protect, Disable, Haze, Night Shade, Hex, Will-O-Wisp, Ominous Wind, Curse, Power Split, Guard Split, Scary Face, Shadow Ball, Grudge, Mean Look, Destiny Bond
Type: Ghost
Height: 5' 07"   **Weight:** 168.7 lbs.
Region: Unova

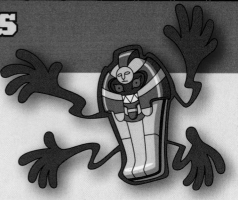

YAMASK

COFAGRIGUS

COMBEE
TINY BEE POKÉMON

Combee collects honey for the rest of the colony and delivers it to Vespiquen.

Pronounced: COHM-bee
Possible Moves: Sweet Scent, Gust, Bug Bite
Type: Bug-Flying
Height: 1' 00"
Weight: 12.1 lbs.
Region: Sinnoh

COMBEE

VESPIQUEN

COMBUSKEN
YOUNG FOWL POKÉMON

Using cries to intimidate its foes, Combusken can kick ten times per second.

Pronounced: com-BUS-ken

Possible Moves: Scratch, Growl, Focus Energy, Ember, Double Kick, Peck, Sand-Attack, Bulk Up, Quick Attack, Slash, Mirror Move, Sky Uppercut, Flare Blitz

Type: Fire-Fighting

Height: 2' 11"

Weight: 43.0 lbs.

Region: Hoenn

TORCHIC

COMBUSKEN

BLAZIKEN

CONKELDURR
MUSCULAR POKÉMON

Conkeldurr uses its concrete pillars like walking canes, but has no trouble swinging them around in battle. It's said that Conkeldurr taught humans how to make concrete over two thousand years ago.

Pronounced: kon-KELL-dur

Possible Moves: Pound, Leer, Focus Energy, Bide, Low Kick, Rock Throw, Wake-Up Slap, Chip Away, Bulk Up, Rock Slide, DynamicPunch, Scary Face, Hammer Arm, Stone Edge, Focus Punch, Superpower

Type: Fighting

Height: 4' 07"

Weight: 191.8 lbs.

Region: Unova

TIMBURR

GURDURR

CONKELDURR

CORPHISH
RUFFIAN POKÉMON

Corphish will use its pincers to grab hold of its prey. Its sturdy nature enables it to adapt to almost any environment.

Pronounced: COR-fish
Possible Moves: Bubble, Harden, ViceGrip, Leer, BubbleBeam, Protect, Knock Off, Taunt, Night Slash, Crabhammer, Swords Dance, Crunch, Guillotine
Type: Water
Height: 2' 00"
Weight: 25.4 lbs.
Region: Hoenn

CORPHISH → CRAWDAUNT

CORSOLA
CORAL POKÉMON

Corsola must live in clean seas (usually in the south) because they can't live in polluted waters.

Pronounced: COR-soh-la
Possible Moves: Tackle, Harden, Bubble, Recover, Refresh, Rock Blast, BubbleBeam, Lucky Chant, AncientPower, Aqua Ring, Spike Cannon, Power Gem, Mirror Coat, Earth Power
Type: Water-Rock
Height: 2' 00"
Weight: 11.0 lbs.
Region: Johto

DOES NOT EVOLVE

COTTONEE
COTTON PUFF POKÉMON

Cottonee travels on the winds, sheltering beneath large trees on rainy days, when its body becomes heavier. If attacked, it shoots cotton from its body, as a decoy to fool the enemy while it escapes.

Pronounced: KAHT-ton-ee
Possible Moves: Absorb, Growth, Leech Seed, Stun Spore, Mega Drain, Cotton Spore, Razor Leaf, PoisonPowder, Giga Drain, Charm, Helping Hand, Energy Ball, Cotton Guard, Sunny Day, Endeavor, SolarBeam
Type: Grass
Height: 1' 00"
Weight: 1.3 lbs.
Region: Unova

COTTONEE → WHIMSICOTT

CRADILY
BARNACLE POKÉMON

Cradily captures its prey by digging up the beaches of warm seas during low tide.

Pronounced: cray-DILLY
Possible Moves: Astonish, Constrict, Acid, Ingrain, Confuse Ray, Amnesia, AncientPower, Gastro Acid, Energy Ball, Stockpile, Spit Up, Swallow, Wring Out
Type: Rock-Grass
Height: 4' 11"
Weight: 133.2 lbs.
Region: Hoenn

LILEEP → CRADILY

CRANIDOS
HEAD BUTT POKÉMON

Cranidos uses its ironclad head to ram into its foes and take them down.

Pronounced: CRANE-ee-dose
Possible Moves: Headbutt, Leer, Focus Energy, Pursuit, Take Down, Scary Face, Assurance, Chip Away, AncientPower, Zen Headbutt, Screech, Head Smash
Type: Rock
Height: 2' 11"
Weight: 69.4 lbs.
Region: Sinnoh

CRANIDOS

RAMPARDOS

CRAWDAUNT
ROGUE POKÉMON

Crawdaunt is highly territorial. It will use its pincers to toss away any intruders that venture near.

Pronounced: CRAW-daunt
Possible Moves: Bubble, Harden, ViceGrip, Leer, BubbleBeam, Protect, Knock Off, Swift, Taunt, Night Slash, Crabhammer, Swords Dance, Crunch, Guillotine
Type: Water-Dark
Height: 3' 07"
Weight: 72.3 lbs.
Region: Hoenn

CORPHISH

CRAWDAUNT

CRESSELIA
LUNAR POKÉMON

The crescent moon shape of Cresselia's wings will sometimes emit shiny particles, making it look like a veil.

Pronounced: cres-SEL-ee-uh
Possible Moves: Confusion, Double Team, Safeguard, Mist, Aurora Beam, Future Sight, Slash, Moonlight, Psycho Cut, Psycho Shift, Lunar Dance, Psychic
Type: Psychic
Height: 4' 11"
Weight: 188.7 lbs.
Region: Sinnoh

DOES NOT EVOLVE

LEGENDARY POKÉMON

CROAGUNK
TOXIC MOUTH POKÉMON

The sacs on Croagunk's cheeks hold a toxic poison. It surprises its foes by jabbing them with its toxic fingers.

Pronounced: CROW-gunk
Possible Moves: Astonish, Mud-Slap, Poison Sting, Taunt, Pursuit, Faint Attack, Revenge, Swagger, Mud Bomb, Sucker Punch, Venoshock, Nasty Plot, Poison Jab, Sludge Bomb, Flatter
Type: Poison-Fighting
Height: 2' 04"   **Weight:** 50.7 lbs.
Region: Sinnoh

CROAGUNK

TOXICROAK

CROBAT
BAT POKÉMON

How does Crobat fly so fast and so quietly? Its lower legs evolved into an extra pair of wings!

Pronounced: CROW-bat
Possible Moves: Cross Poison, Screech, Leech Life, Supersonic, Astonish, Bite, Wing Attack, Confuse Ray, Air Cutter, Mean Look, Acrobatics, Poison Fang, Haze, Air Slash
Type: Poison-Flying   **Height:** 5' 11"
Weight: 165.3 lbs.
Region: Johto

ZUBAT

GOLBAT

CROBAT

CROCONAW
BIG JAW POKÉMON

Croconaw will chomp down and not let go when battling, even if it loses its teeth—which grow back anyway.

Pronounced: CROCK-oh-naw
Possible Moves: Scratch, Leer, Water Gun, Rage, Bite, Scary Face, Ice Fang, Flail, Crunch, Chip Away, Slash, Screech, Thrash, Aqua Tail, Superpower, Hydro Pump
Type: Water
Height: 3' 07"
Weight: 55.1 lbs.
Region: Johto

TOTODILE

CROCONAW

FERALIGATR

CRUSTLE
STONE HOME POKÉMON

With its enormously powerful legs, Crustle can walk for days across arid land while carrying a heavy slab. Its battles for territory are vicious—once a Crustle's boulder is smashed, it loses.

Pronounced: KRUS-tul
Possible Moves: Shell Smash, Rock Blast, Withdraw, Sand-Attack, Faint Attack, Smack Down, Rock Polish, Bug Bite, Stealth Rock, Rock Slide, Slash, X-Scissor, Shell Smash, Flail, Rock Wrecker
Type: Bug-Rock   **Height:** 4' 07"
Weight: 440.9 lbs.   **Region:** Unova

DWEBBLE

CRUSTLE

CRYOGONAL
CRYSTALLIZING POKÉMON

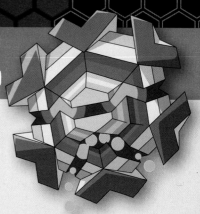

Cryogonal originates inside snow clouds and snags its prey with chains of ice crystals. It turns to steam and vanishes if its body temperature rises, but it turns back into ice once its temperature drops.

Pronounced: kry-AH-guh-nul
Possible Moves: Bind, Ice Shard, Sharpen, Rapid Spin, Icy Wind, Mist, Haze, Aurora Beam, Acid Armor, Ice Beam, Light Screen, Reflect, Slash, Confuse Ray, Recover, SolarBeam, Night Slash, Sheer Cold
Type: Ice   **Height:** 3' 07"
Weight: 326.3 lbs.   **Region:** Unova

DOES NOT EVOLVE

CUBCHOO
CHILL POKÉMON

Cubchoo sniffs its perpetually runny nose—the mucus is needed for its moves. When Cubchoo is unwell, the mucus becomes watery, decreasing the power of Cubchoo's Ice-type moves.

Pronounced: cub-CHOO
Possible Moves: Powder Snow, Growl, Bide, Icy Wind, Fury Swipes, Brine, Endure, Charm, Slash, Flail, Rest, Blizzard, Hail, Thrash, Sheer Cold
Type: Ice
Height: 1' 08"
Weight: 18.7 lbs.
Region: Unova

CUBCHOO → BEARTIC

CUBONE
LONELY POKÉMON

The skull Cubone wears rattles loudly when it cries.

Pronounced: CUE-bone
Possible Moves: Growl, Tail Whip, Bone Club, Headbutt, Leer, Focus Energy, Bonemerang, Rage, False Swipe, Thrash, Fling, Bone Rush, Endeavor, Double-Edge, Retaliate
Type: Ground
Height: 1' 04"
Weight: 14.3 lbs.
Region: Kanto

CUBONE ➔ MAROWAK

CYNDAQUIL
FIRE MOUSE POKÉMON

The flames on Cyndaquil's back will burn more brightly if it is startled.

Pronounced: SIN-da-kwill
Possible Moves: Tackle, Leer, SmokeScreen, Ember, Quick Attack, Flame Wheel, Defense Curl, Flame Charge, Swift, Lava Plume, Flamethrower, Inferno, Rollout, Double-Edge, Eruption
Type: Fire   **Height:** 1' 08"
Weight: 17.4 lbs.
Region: Johto

CYNDAQUIL ➔ QUILAVA ➔ TYPHLOSION

DARKRAI
PITCH-BLACK POKÉMON

Although it is most active on nights with a full moon, legend says that it is on moonless nights that Darkrai lures people to sleep and gives them horrible nightmares.

Pronounced: DARK-rye
Possible Moves: Ominous Wind, Disable, Quick Attack, Hypnosis, Faint Attack, Nightmare, Double Team, Haze, Dark Void, Nasty Plot, Dream Eater, Dark Pulse
Type: Dark
Height: 4' 11"
Weight: 111.3 lbs
Region: Sinnoh

DOES
NOT
EVOLVE

MYTHICAL
POKÉMON

DARMANITAN
BLAZING POKÉMON

If weakened in battle, Darmanitan becomes motionless and resorts to psychic attacks. Powered by an internal fire that burns at 2,500 degrees Fahrenheit, it can wreck a dump truck with just one punch.

Pronounced: dar-MAN-ih-tan
Possible Moves: Tackle, Rollout, Incinerate, Rage, Fire Fang, Headbutt, Swagger, Facade, Fire Punch, Work Up, Thrash, Belly Drum, Flare Blitz, Hammer Arm, Taunt, Superpower, Overheat
Type: Fire
Height: 4' 03"　**Weight:** 204.8 lbs.
Region: Unova

DARUMAKA

DARMANITAN

DARUMAKA
ZEN CHARM POKÉMON

Darumaka's droppings are hot, so people used to stay warm by tucking them inside their clothing. When its internal fire is burning, Darumaka runs around, unable to calm down. Once the fire goes down, it sleeps.

Pronounced: dah-roo-MAH-kuh
Possible Moves: Tackle, Rollout, Incinerate, Rage, Fire Fang, Headbutt, Uproar, Facade, Fire Punch, Work Up, Thrash, Belly Drum, Flare Blitz, Taunt, Superpower, Overheat
Type: Fire　　**Height:** 2' 00"
Weight: 82.7 lbs.　**Region:** Unova

DARUMAKA

DARMANITAN

DEERLING
SEASON POKÉMON

As the seasons change, so does Deerling's fur—people use this as a way to mark the seasons. The color and scent of Deerling's fur matches the mountain grass, where it hides if it senses a threat.

Pronounced: DEER-ling
Possible Moves: Tackle, Camouflage, Growl, Sand-Attack, Double Kick, Leech Seed, Faint Attack, Take Down, Jump Kick, Aromatherapy, Energy Ball, Charm, Nature Power, Double-Edge, SolarBeam
Type: Normal-Grass
Height: 2' 00"
Weight: 43.0 lbs.
Region: Unova

Spring Form

Autumn Form

Winter Form

Summer Form

DEERLING

SAWSBUCK

67

DEINO
IRATE POKÉMON

Approach Deino with care: unable to see, it bites and tackles whatever is around it. This habit often leaves it with injuries all over its body. It is not a picky eater.

Pronounced: DY-noh
Possible Moves: Tackle, Dragon Rage, Focus Energy, Bite, Headbutt, DragonBreath, Roar, Crunch, Slam, Dragon Pulse, Work Up, Dragon Rush, Body Slam, Scary Face, Hyper Voice, Outrage
Type: Dark-Dragon
Height: 2' 07"
Weight: 38.1 lbs.
Region: Unova

DEINO   ZWEILOUS   HYDREIGON

DELCATTY
PRIM POKÉMON

Female Trainers love Delcatty for its beautiful fur—and because it never makes a nest.

Pronounced: dell-CAT-tee
Possible Moves: Fake Out, Attract, Sing, DoubleSlap
Type: Normal
Height: 3' 07"
Weight: 71.9 lbs.
Region: Hoenn

SKITTY

DELCATTY

DELIBIRD
DELIVERY POKÉMON

If people get lost in the mountains, Delibird will share its food, which it carries in its tail.

Pronounced: DELL-ee-bird
Possible Moves: Present
Type: Ice-Flying
Height: 2' 11"
Weight: 35.3 lbs.
Region: Johto

DOES
NOT
EVOLVE

DEOXYS
DNA POKÉMON

Deoxys was formed when a meteor that carried an alien virus crash-landed and underwent a DNA mutation.

Pronounced: dee-OCKS-iss
Possible Moves: Leer, Wrap, Night Shade, Teleport, Knock Off, Pursuit, Psychic, Snatch, Psycho Shift, Zen Headbutt, Cosmic Power, Recover, Psycho Boost, Hyper Beam
Type: Psychic
Height: 5' 07"
Weight: 134.0 lbs.
Region: Hoenn

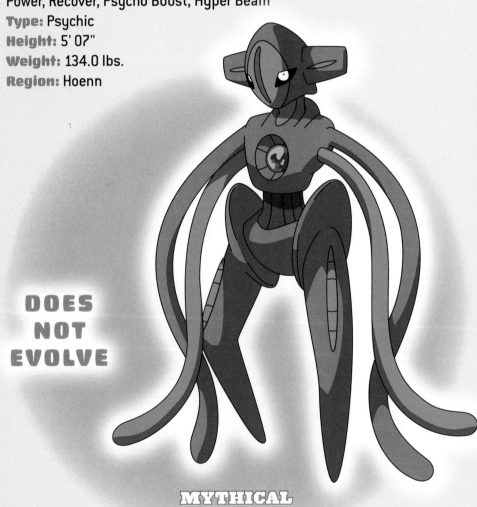

DOES
NOT
EVOLVE

MYTHICAL
POKÉMON

DEWGONG
SEA LION POKÉMON

Because Dewgong's coat is pure white, it can blend into snow to protect it from being seen by predators.

Pronounced: DOO-gong
Possible Moves: Headbutt, Growl, Signal Beam, Icy Wind, Encore, Ice Shard, Rest, Aqua Ring, Aurora Beam, Aqua Jet, Brine, Sheer Cold, Take Down, Dive, Aqua Tail, Ice Beam, Safeguard, Hail
Type: Water-Ice
Height: 5' 07"
Weight: 264.6 lbs.
Region: Kanto

SEEL

DEWGONG

DEWOTT
DISCIPLINE POKÉMON

Dewott learns its flowing double-scalchop techniques through rigorous training. Each Dewott has its own scalchop technique. It always keeps its scalchops in good condition.

Pronounced: DOO-wot
Possible Moves: Tackle, Tail Whip, Water Gun, Water Sport, Focus Energy, Razor Shell, Fury Cutter, Water Pulse, Revenge, Aqua Jet, Encore, Aqua Tail, Retaliate, Swords Dance, Hydro Pump
Type: Water   **Height:** 2' 07"   **Weight:** 54.0 lbs.
Region: Unova

OSHAWOTT

DEWOTT

SAMUROTT

DIALGA
TEMPORAL POKÉMON

This Legendary Pokémon has the ability to distort time. As a matter of fact, it is said that time began when Dialga was born.

Pronounced: dee-AL-guh

Possible Moves: DragonBreath, Scary Face, Metal Claw, Ancient-Power, Slash, Power Gem, Metal Burst, Dragon Claw, Earth Power, Aura Sphere, Iron Tail, Roar of Time, Flash Cannon

Type: Steel-Dragon

Height: 17' 09"

Weight: 1505.8 lbs.

Region: Sinnoh

DOES NOT EVOLVE

LEGENDARY POKÉMON

DIGLETT
MOLE POKÉMON

Diglett avoids the sunlight and lives underground. It is so used to the dark recesses that bright sunlight repels it.

Pronounced: DIG-lit
Possible Moves: Scratch, Sand-Attack, Growl, Astonish, Mud-Slap, Magnitude, Bulldoze, Sucker Punch, Mud Bomb, Earth Power, Dig, Slash, Earthquake, Fissure
Type: Ground
Height: 0' 08"
Weight: 1.8 lbs.
Region: Kanto

DIGLETT

DUGTRIO

DITTO
TRANSFORM POKÉMON

Ditto has the ability to transform into anything it sees by reconstituting and restructuring its cellular composition.

Pronounced: DIT-oh
Possible Moves: Transform
Type: Normal
Height: 1' 00"
Weight: 8.8 lbs.
Region: Kanto

DOES
NOT
EVOLVE

DODRIO
TRIPLE BIRD POKÉMON

Dodrio evolves from Doduo after one of Doduo's heads splits in two. This Pokémon is able to run at almost forty miles per hour!

Pronounced: doe-DREE-oh
Possible Moves: Pluck, Peck, Growl, Quick Attack, Rage, Fury Attack, Pursuit, Uproar, Acupressure, Tri Attack, Agility, Drill Peck, Endeavor, Thrash
Type: Normal-Flying
Height: 5' 11"
Weight: 187.8 lbs.
Region: Kanto

DODUO → DODRIO

DODUO
TWIN BIRD POKÉMON

Using telepathic power, Doduo's two heads can communicate emotions to each other.

Pronounced: doe-DOO-oh
Possible Moves: Peck, Growl, Quick Attack, Rage, Fury Attack, Pursuit, Uproar, Acupressure, Double Hit, Agility, Drill Peck, Endeavor, Thrash
Type: Normal-Flying
Height: 4' 07"
Weight: 86.4 lbs.
Region: Kanto

DODUO → DODRIO

DONPHAN
ARMOR POKÉMON

Donphan attacks by curling up into a ball and rolling into foes, and can bowl over a house with one hit.

Pronounced: DON-fan

Possible Moves: Fire Fang, Thunder Fang, Horn Attack, Growl, Defense Curl, Bulldoze, Rapid Spin, Knock Off, Rollout, Magnitude, Slam, Fury Attack, Assurance, Scary Face, Earthquake, Giga Impact

Type: Ground

Height: 3' 07"   **Weight:** 264.6 lbs.

Region: Johto

PHANPY → DONPHAN

DRAGONAIR
DRAGON POKÉMON

Living in seas and lakes, Dragonair can change weather patterns if its body is affected by auras.

Pronounced: DRAG-uh-NAIR

Possible Moves: Wrap, Leer, Thunder Wave, Twister, Dragon Rage, Slam, Agility, Dragon Tail, Aqua Tail, Dragon Rush, Safeguard, Dragon Dance, Outrage, Hyper Beam

Type: Dragon   **Height:** 31' 01"

Weight: 36.4 lbs.

Region: Kanto

DRATINI → DRAGONAIR → DRAGONITE

DRAGONITE
DRAGON POKÉMON

Dragonite is known for helping guide shipwrecked crews to land.

Pronounced: DRAG-uh-nite

Possible Moves: Fire Punch, ThunderPunch, Roost, Wrap, Leer, Thunder Wave, Twister, Dragon Rage, Slam, Agility, Dragon Tail, Aqua Tail, Dragon Rush, Safeguard, Wing Attack, Dragon Dance, Outrage, Hyper Beam, Hurricane

Type: Dragon-Flying

Height: 7' 03"

Weight: 463.0 lbs.

Region: Kanto

DRATINI ➤ DRAGONAIR ➤ DRAGONITE

DRAPION
OGRE SCORP POKÉMON

Drapion is able to turn its head 180 degrees to see its surroundings. It will use its mighty clawed arms to hold onto its prey.

Pronounced: DRAP-pee-on

Possible Moves: Thunder Fang, Ice Fang, Fire Fang, Bite, Poison Sting, Leer, Knock Off, Pin Missile, Acupressure, Scary Face, Toxic Spikes, Bug Bite, Poison Fang, Hone Claws, Venoshock, Crunch, Cross Poison

Type: Poison-Dark   **Height:** 4' 03"

Weight: 135.6 lbs.   **Region:** Sinnoh

SKORUPI ➤ DRAPION

DRATINI
DRAGON POKÉMON

Dratini is so rare that people are only aware of its existence because of the shed skin it leaves behind.

Pronounced: druh-TEE-nee

Possible Moves: Wrap, Leer, Thunder Wave, Twister, Dragon Rage, Slam, Agility, Dragon Tail, Aqua Tail, Dragon Rush, Safeguard, Dragon Dance, Outrage, Hyper Beam

Type: Dragon

Height: 5' 11"

Weight: 7.3 lbs.

Region: Kanto

DRATINI → DRAGONAIR → DRAGONITE

DRIFBLIM
BLIMP POKÉMON

Since they can't fly, Drifblim will drift into the air at night. No one seems to know where they end up.

Pronounced: DRIFF-blimm

Possible Moves: Constrict, Minimize, Astonish, Gust, Focus Energy, Payback, Hex, Stockpile, Swallow, Spit Up, Ominous Wind, Baton Pass, Shadow Ball, Explosion

Type: Ghost-Flying

Height: 3' 11"

Weight: 33.1 lbs.

Region: Sinnoh

DRIFLOON → DRIFBLIM

DRIFLOON
BALLOON POKÉMON

Drifloon tries to pull children's hands to steal them away, but this lightweight Pokémon doesn't have the power to lift them. Usually, it's Drifloon that ends up getting pulled around!

Pronounced: DRIFF-loon
Possible Moves: Constrict, Minimize, Astonish, Gust, Focus Energy, Payback, Hex, Stockpile, Swallow, Spit Up, Ominous Wind, Baton Pass, Shadow Ball, Explosion
Type: Ghost-Flying
Height: 1' 04"
Weight: 2.6 lbs.
Region: Sinnoh

DRIFLOON → DRIFBLIM

DRILBUR
MOLE POKÉMON

By putting its claws together and spinning at high speed, Drilbur swiftly burrows through the ground. It can dig up to thirty miles per hour, fast enough to race a car driving above ground.

Pronounced: DRIL-bur
Possible Moves: Scratch, Mud Sport, Rapid Spin, Mud-Slap, Fury Swipes, Metal Claw, Dig, Hone Claws, Slash, Rock Slide, Earthquake, Swords Dance, Sandstorm, Drill Run, Fissure
Type: Ground   **Height:** 1' 00"
Weight: 18.7 lbs.   **Region:** Unova

DRILBUR → EXCADRILL

DROWZEE
HYPNOSIS POKÉMON

Drowzee loves fun dreams! It can tell where the dreams are by using its nose to sniff around.

Pronounced: DROW-zee
Possible Moves: Pound, Hypnosis, Disable, Confusion, Headbutt, Poison Gas, Meditate, Psybeam, Psych Up, Synchronoise, Zen Headbutt, Swagger, Psychic, Nasty Plot, Psyshock, Future Sight
Type: Psychic
Height: 3' 03"   **Weight:** 71.4 lbs.
Region: Kanto

DROWZEE

HYPNO

DRUDDIGON
CAVE POKÉMON

The skin on Druddigon's face is harder than rock, and it speeds through narrow caves to catch prey in its sharp claws. Its wings absorb sunlight to warm its body, but it stops moving if its body temperature falls.

Pronounced: DRUD-dih-gun
Possible Moves: Leer, Scratch, Hone Claws, Bite, Scary Face, Dragon Rage, Slash, Crunch, Dragon Claw, Chip Away, Revenge, Night Slash, Dragon Tail, Rock Climb, Superpower, Outrage
Type: Dragon
Height: 5' 03"
Weight: 306.4 lbs.
Region: Unova

DOES
NOT
EVOLVE

DUCKLETT
WATER BIRD POKÉMON

An excellent diver, Ducklett swims around in search of peat moss, its favorite food. If attacked, it splashes water to cover its escape.

Pronounced: DUK-lit
Possible Moves: Water Gun, Water Sport, Defog, Wing Attack, Water Pulse, Aerial Ace, BubbleBeam, FeatherDance, Aqua Ring, Air Slash, Roost, Rain Dance, Tailwind, Brave Bird, Hurricane
Type: Water-Flying
Height: 1' 08"
Weight: 12.1 lbs.
Region: Unova

DUCKLETT

SWANNA

DUGTRIO
MOLE POKÉMON

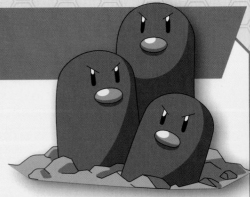

Using its three heads, Dugtrio is able to dig through soil at depths that sometimes reach sixty miles.

Pronounced: dug-TREE-oh
Possible Moves: Night Slash, Tri Attack, Scratch, Sand-Attack, Growl, Astonish, Mud-Slap, Magnitude, Bulldoze, Sucker Punch, Sand Tomb, Mud Bomb, Earth Power, Dig, Slash, Earthquake, Fissure
Type: Ground
Height: 2' 04"   **Weight:** 73.4 lbs.
Region: Kanto

DIGLETT

DUGTRIO

DUNSPARCE
LAND SNAKE POKÉMON

Dunsparce is able to fly for short bursts, but uses its tail to make maze-like nests in the ground.

Pronounced: DUN-sparce
Possible Moves: Rage, Defense Curl, Yawn, Glare, Rollout, Spite, Pursuit, Screech, Roost, Take Down, Coil, AncientPower, Dig, Endeavor, Flail
Type: Normal
Height: 4' 11"
Weight: 30.9 lbs.
Region: Johto

DOES NOT EVOLVE

DUOSION
MITOSIS POKÉMON

Duosion's divided brains sometimes compel it to try two different things at once. When its two brains are thinking the same thing, Duosion shows its greatest power.

Pronounced: doo-OH-zhun
Possible Moves: Psywave, Reflect, Rollout, Snatch, Hidden Power, Light Screen, Charm, Recover, Psyshock, Endeavor, Future Sight, Pain Split, Psychic, Skill Swap, Heal Block, Wonder Room
Type: Psychic   **Height:** 2' 00"   **Weight:** 17.6 lbs.
Region: Unova

SOLOSIS   DUOSION   REUNICLUS

DURANT
IRON ANT POKÉMON

Durant digs nests in the mountains to create mazes of complex, interconnected tunnels. Covered in steel armor to protect itself from Heatmor, it attacks in a group.

Pronounced: dur-ANT
Possible Moves: ViceGrip, Sand-Attack, Fury Cutter, Bite, Agility, Metal Claw, Bug Bite, Crunch, Iron Head, Dig, Entrainment, X-Scissor, Iron Defense, Guillotine, Metal Sound
Type: Bug-Steel
Height: 1' 00"   **Weight:** 72.8 lbs.
Region: Unova

DOES NOT EVOLVE

DUSCLOPS
BECKON POKÉMON

Dusclops's body is hollow, but don't look too closely—it is believed that if you gaze into its body you can be lost in the void.

Pronounced: DUS-klops
Possible Moves: Fire Punch, Ice Punch, ThunderPunch, Gravity, Bind, Leer, Night Shade, Disable, Foresight, Astonish, Confuse Ray, Shadow Sneak, Pursuit, Curse, Will-O-Wisp, Shadow Punch, Hex, Mean Look, Payback, Future Sight
Type: Ghost
Height: 5' 03"
Weight: 67.5 lbs.
Region: Hoenn

DUSKULL   DUSCLOPS   DUSKNOIR

DUSKNOIR
GRIPPER POKÉMON

Dusknoir receives messages from the antennae on its head. Sometimes, it is commanded to take people to the spirit world.

Pronounced: DUSK-nwar
Possible Moves: Fire Punch, Ice Punch, ThunderPunch, Gravity, Bind, Leer, Night Shade, Disable, Foresight, Astonish, Confuse Ray, Shadow Sneak, Pursuit, Curse, Will-O-Wisp, Shadow Punch, Hex, Mean Look, Payback, Future Sight
Type: Ghost
Height: 7' 03"
Weight: 235.0 lbs.
Region: Hoenn

DUSKULL   DUSCLOPS   DUSKNOIR

DUSKULL
REQUIEM POKÉMON

Duskull is a nocturnal Pokémon that spends most of its time seeking out enemies and prey.

Pronounced: DUS-kull
Possible Moves: Leer, Night Shade, Disable, Foresight, Astonish, Confuse Ray, Shadow Sneak, Pursuit, Curse, Will-O-Wisp, Hex, Mean Look, Payback, Future Sight
Type: Ghost   **Height:** 2' 07"   **Weight:** 33.1 lbs.
Region: Hoenn

DUSKULL   DUSCLOPS   DUSKNOIR

DUSTOX
POISON MOTH POKÉMON

This nocturnal Pokémon loves to scavenge leafy goodness from tree-lined boulevards. It is attracted to streetlights.

Pronounced: DUS-tocks
Possible Moves: Confusion, Gust, Protect, Moonlight, Psybeam, Whirlwind, Light Screen, Silver Wind, Toxic, Bug Buzz, Quiver Dance
Type: Bug-Poison
Height: 3' 11"
Weight: 69.7 lbs.
Region: Hoenn

WURMPLE → CASCOON → DUSTOX

DWEBBLE
ROCK INN POKÉMON

The liquid from Dwebble's mouth melts through rock with ease. It makes its home in a suitable rock, but if the rock is broken, it can't relax until it finds a replacement.

Pronounced: DWEHB-bul
Possible Moves: Fury Cutter, Rock Blast, Withdraw, Sand-Attack, Faint Attack, Smack Down, Rock Polish, Bug Bite, Stealth Rock, Rock Slide, Slash, X-Scissor, Shell Smash, Flail, Rock Wrecker
Type: Bug-Rock
Height: 1' 00"   **Weight:** 32.0 lbs.
Region: Unova

DWEBBLE → CRUSTLE

EELEKTRIK
ELEFISH POKÉMON

Eelektrik has a big appetite. Once it sees prey, it attacks, using electricity to paralyze the target. The circular patterns on its body are electricity-generating organs, so Eelektrik can wrap itself around a target and shock it.

Pronounced: ee-LEK-trik

Possible Moves: Headbutt, Thunder Wave, Spark, Charge Beam, Bind, Acid, Discharge, Crunch, Thunderbolt, Acid Spray, Coil, Wild Charge, Gastro Acid, Zap Cannon, Thrash

Type: Electric

Height: 3' 11"

Weight: 48.5 lbs.

Region: Unova

TYNAMO → EELEKTRIK → EELEKTROSS

EELEKTROSS
ELEFISH POKÉMON

By crawling out of the water, Eelektross can attack prey on shore and drag it into the ocean. Once Eelektross draws the target into its sucker mouth, it shocks its prey with electricity from its fangs.

Pronounced: ee-LEK-trahs

Possible Moves: Crush Claw, Headbutt, Acid, Discharge, Crunch

Type: Electric

Height: 6' 11"   **Weight:** 177.5 lbs.

Region: Unova

TYNAMO → EELEKTRIK → EELEKTROSS

EEVEE
EVOLUTION POKÉMON

Eevee is able to take on many different evolutionary forms and adapts to almost any environment.

Pronounced: EE-vee
Possible Moves: Tackle, Tail Whip, Helping Hand, Sand-Attack, Growl, Quick Attack, Bite, Baton Pass, Take Down, Last Resort, Trump Card
Type: Normal
Height: 1' 00"
Weight: 14.3 lbs.
Region: Kanto

VAPOREON

GLACEON

JOLTEON

LEAFEON

EEVEE

FLAREON

UMBREON

ESPEON

EKANS
SNAKE POKÉMON

Ekans is sneaky, gaining the advantage in battle by taking its enemies by surprise.

Pronounced: ECK-ehns
Possible Moves: Wrap, Leer, Poison Sting, Bite, Glare, Screech, Acid, Stockpile, Swallow, Spit Up, Acid Spray, Mud Bomb, Gastro Acid, Haze, Coil, Gunk Shot
Type: Poison
Height: 6' 07"   **Weight:** 15.2 lbs.
Region: Kanto

EKANS

ARBOK

ELECTABUZZ
ELECTRIC POKÉMON

Because it eats so much electricity from power plants, Electabuzz can cause blackouts.

Pronounced: ee-LECK-tuh-buzz
Possible Moves: Quick Attack, Leer, ThunderShock, Low Kick, Swift, Shock Wave, Light Screen, Electro Ball, ThunderPunch, Discharge, Thunderbolt, Screech, Thunder
Type: Electric   **Height:** 3' 07"   **Weight:** 66.1 lbs.
Region: Kanto

ELEKID

ELECTABUZZ

ELECTIVIRE

ELECTIVIRE
THUNDERBOLT POKÉMON

This Pokémon uses the tips of its two tails to let loose with twenty thousand volts of power.

Pronounced: e-LECT-uh-vire
Possible Moves: Fire Punch, Quick Attack, Leer, ThunderShock, Low Kick, Swift, Shock Wave, Light Screen, Electro Ball, ThunderPunch, Discharge, Thunderbolt, Screech, Thunder, Giga Impact
Type: Electric
Height: 5' 11"
Weight: 305.6 lbs.
Region: Sinnoh

ELEKID → ELECTABUZZ → ELECTIVIRE

ELECTRIKE
LIGHTNING POKÉMON

This Pokémon gains reaction speed by stimulating its muscles via electricity stored in its fur.

Pronounced: ee-LEK-trike
Possible Moves: Tackle, Thunder Wave, Leer, Howl, Quick Attack, Spark, Odor Sleuth, Bite, Thunder Fang, Roar, Discharge, Charge, Wild Charge, Thunder
Type: Electric
Height: 2' 00"
Weight: 33.5 lbs.
Region: Hoenn

ELECTRIKE → MANECTRIC

ELECTRODE
BALL POKÉMON

When Electrode is bloated to bursting with electricity, it can drift on the wind.

Pronounced: ee-LECK-trode
Possible Moves: Charge, Tackle, SonicBoom, Spark, Rollout, Screech, Charge Beam, Light Screen, Electro Ball, Selfdestruct, Swift, Magnet Rise, Gyro Ball, Explosion, Mirror Coat
Type: Electric
Height: 3' 11"   **Weight:** 146.8 lbs.
Region: Kanto

VOLTORB

ELECTRODE

ELEKID
ELECTRIC POKÉMON

Elekid spins its arms to create electricity, but it cannot store the electricity it creates.

Pronounced: el-EH-kid
Possible Moves: Quick Attack, Leer, ThunderShock, Low Kick, Swift, Shock Wave, Light Screen, Electro Ball, ThunderPunch, Discharge, Thunderbolt, Screech, Thunder
Type: Electric   **Height:** 2' 00"   **Weight:** 51.8 lbs.
Region: Johto

ELEKID   ELECTABUZZ   ELECTIVIRE

ELGYEM
CEREBRAL POKÉMON

This Pokémon was first seen fifty years ago in the desert. Elgyem uses its psychic power to squeeze an opponent's brain, inflicting unbearable headaches.

Pronounced: ELL-jee-ehm
Possible Moves: Confusion, Growl, Heal Block, Miracle Eye, Psybeam, Headbutt, Hidden Power, Imprison, Simple Beam, Zen Headbutt, Psych Up, Psychic, Calm Mind, Recover, Guard Split, Power Split, Synchronoise, Wonder Room
Type: Psychic   **Height:** 1' 08"
Weight: 19.8 lbs.   **Region:** Unova

ELGYEM

BEHEEYEM

EMBOAR
MEGA FIRE PIG POKÉMON

Emboar is loyal to its friends and adept at quick, powerful fighting moves. It grows a fiery beard, and can use it to set its fists aflame for a blazing punch.

Pronounced: EHM-bohr
Possible Moves: Hammer Arm, Tackle, Tail Whip, Ember, Odor Sleuth, Defense Curl, Flame Charge, Arm Thrust, Smog, Rollout, Take Down, Heat Crash, Assurance, Flamethrower, Head Smash, Roar, Flare Blitz
Type: Fire-Fighting   **Height:** 5' 03"
Weight: 330.7 lbs.
Region: Unova

TEPIG

PIGNITE

EMBOAR

EMOLGA
SKY SQUIRREL POKÉMON

This treetop-dwelling Pokémon generates electricity in its cheeks and stores it in a cape-like membrane. It can glide using the inner surface of the membrane, discharging electricity as it soars.

Pronounced: ee-MAHL-guh
Possible Moves: ThunderShock, Quick Attack, Tail Whip, Charge, Spark, Pursuit, Double Team, Shock Wave, Electro Ball, Acrobatics, Light Screen, Encore, Volt Switch, Agility, Discharge
Type: Electric-Flying   **Height:** 1' 04"
Weight: 11.0 lbs.   **Region:** Unova

DOES NOT EVOLVE

EMPOLEON
EMPEROR POKÉMON

You can tell the leader in a pack of Empoleon by the size of its horns—the leader has the biggest ones, of course! It can swim at speeds that rival jet boats.

Pronounced: em-PO-lee-on
Possible Moves: Tackle, Growl, Bubble, Swords Dance, Peck, Metal Claw, BubbleBeam, Swagger, Fury Attack, Brine, Aqua Jet, Whirlpool, Mist, Drill Peck, Hydro Pump
Type: Water-Steel   **Height:** 5' 07"   **Weight:** 186.3 lbs.
Region: Sinnoh

PIPLUP   PRINPLUP   EMPOLEON

ENTEI
VOLCANO POKÉMON

It is said that when Entei roars, a volcano will erupt somewhere around the globe.

Pronounced: EN-tay
Possible Moves: Bite, Leer, Ember, Roar, Fire Spin, Stomp, Flamethrower, Swagger, Fire Fang, Lava Plume, Extrasensory, Fire Blast, Calm Mind, Eruption
Type: Fire
Height: 6' 11"
Weight: 436.5 lbs.
Region: Johto

DOES NOT EVOLVE

LEGENDARY POKÉMON

ESCAVALIER
CAVALRY POKÉMON

Escavalier wears a Shelmet's shell, and the steel armor protects its entire body. It battles courageously even when it's in trouble, flying around at high speed and attacking with its pointed spears.

Pronounced: ess-KAH-vuh-LEER

Possible Moves: Peck, Leer, Quick Guard, Twineedle, Fury Attack, Headbutt, False Swipe, Bug Buzz, Slash, Iron Head, Iron Defense, X-Scissor, Reversal, Swords Dance, Giga Impact

Type: Bug-Steel   **Height:** 3' 03"
Weight: 72.8 lbs.   **Region:** Unova

KARRABLAST

ESCAVALIER

ESPEON
SUN POKÉMON

When Espeon uses psychic power, the orb on its head will glow. Its fur has the look and feel of velvet.

Pronounced: ESS-pee-on

Possible Moves: Tail Whip, Tackle, Helping Hand, Sand-Attack, Confusion, Quick Attack, Swift, Psybeam, Future Sight, Last Resort, Psych Up, Psychic, Morning Sun, Power Swap

Type: Psychic
Height: 2' 11"
Weight: 58.4 lbs.
Region: Johto

EEVEE

ESPEON

EXCADRILL
SUBTERRENE POKÉMON

Excadrill builds maze-like nests over three hundred feet underground. It creates holes in subway tunnels, but it can also help with tunnel construction.

Pronounced: EKS-kuh-dril
Possible Moves: Scratch, Mud Sport, Rapid Spin, Mud-Slap, Fury Swipes, Metal Claw, Dig, Hone Claws, Slash, Rock Slide, Horn Drill, Earthquake, Swords Dance, Sandstorm, Drill Run, Fissure
Type: Ground-Steel
Height: 2' 04"
Weight: 89.1 lbs.
Region: Unova

DRILBUR

EXCADRILL

EXEGGCUTE
EGG POKÉMON

Exeggcute communicates with the other five in its group by using telepathy. They can gather quickly if separated.

Pronounced: EGGS-egg-cute
Possible Moves: Barrage, Uproar, Hypnosis, Reflect, Leech Seed, Bullet Seed, Stun Spore, PoisonPowder, Sleep Powder, Confusion, Worry Seed, Natural Gift, SolarBeam, Psychic, Bestow
Type: Grass-Psychic
Height: 1' 04"   **Weight:** 5.5 lbs.
Region: Kanto

EXEGGCUTE

EXEGGUTOR

EXEGGUTOR
COCONUT POKÉMON

Also known as The Walking Jungle, it can spawn an Exeggcute if its head becomes too big and falls off.

Pronounced: eggs-EGG-you-tor
Possible Moves: Seed Bomb, Barrage, Hypnosis, Confusion, Stomp, Psyshock, Egg Bomb, Wood Hammer, Leaf Storm
Type: Grass-Psychic
Height: 6' 07"   **Weight:** 264.6 lbs.
Region: Kanto

EXEGGCUTE → EXEGGUTOR

EXPLOUD
LOUD NOISE POKÉMON

This noisy Pokémon emits sound from every port on its body, and when it howls it can be heard from miles away.

Pronounced: ecks-PLOWD
Possible Moves: Ice Fang, Fire Fang, Thunder Fang, Pound, Uproar, Astonish, Howl, Bite, Supersonic, Stomp, Screech, Crunch, Roar, Synchronoise, Rest, Sleep Talk, Hyper Voice, Hyper Beam
Type: Normal   **Height:** 4' 11"   **Weight:** 185.2 lbs.
Region: Hoenn

WHISMUR → LOUDRED → EXPLOUD

FARFETCH'D
WILD DUCK POKÉMON

Farfetch'd can't live without the stalk it constantly holds, which is why it will defend it to the death.

Pronounced: FAR-fetcht
Possible Moves: Poison Jab, Peck, Sand-Attack, Leer, Fury Cutter, Fury Attack, Knock Off, Aerial Ace, Slash, Air Cutter, Swords Dance, Agility, Night Slash, Acrobatics, Feint, False Swipe, Air Slash, Brave Bird
Type: Normal-Flying
Height: 2' 07"
Weight: 33.1 lbs.
Region: Kanto

DOES
NOT
EVOLVE

FEAROW
BEAK POKÉMON

Its powerful wings let it fly all day, but its needle-sharp beak is what you have to watch out for.

Pronounced: FEER-oh
Possible Moves: Pluck, Peck, Growl, Leer, Fury Attack, Pursuit, Aerial Ace, Mirror Move, Agility, Assurance, Roost, Drill Peck, Drill Run
Type: Normal-Flying
Height: 3' 11"
Weight: 83.8 lbs.
Region: Kanto

SPEAROW

FEAROW

FEEBAS
FISH POKÉMON

Feebas can live anywhere because of its ability to eat anything.

Pronounced: FEE-bass
Possible Moves: Splash, Tackle, Flail
Type: Water
Height: 2' 00"
Weight: 16.3 lbs.
Region: Hoenn

FEEBAS

MILOTIC

FERALIGATR
BIG JAW POKÉMON

It's easy to be fooled by Feraligatr's slow gait, but be warned that it becomes lightning fast when battling.

Pronounced: fer-AL-ee-gay-tur
Possible Moves: Scratch, Leer, Water Gun, Rage, Bite, Scary Face, Ice Fang, Flail, Agility, Crunch, Chip Away, Slash, Screech, Thrash, Aqua Tail, Superpower, Hydro Pump
Type: Water   **Height:** 7' 07"   **Weight:** 195.8 lbs.
Region: Johto

TOTODILE

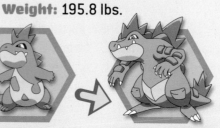

CROCONAW   FERALIGATR

FERROSEED
THORN SEED POKÉMON

By sticking its spikes into a cave wall, Ferroseed absorbs minerals from the rock. When in danger, it shoots a barrage of spikes to cover its escape and rolls away.

Pronounced: fer-AH-seed
Possible Moves: Tackle, Harden, Rollout, Curse, Metal Claw, Pin Missile, Gyro Ball, Iron Defense, Mirror Shot, Ingrain, Selfdestruct, Iron Head, Payback, Flash Cannon, Explosion
Type: Grass-Steel
Height: 2' 00"   **Weight:** 41.4 lbs.
Region: Unova

FERROSEED

FERROTHORN

FERROTHORN
THORN POD POKÉMON

Ferrothorn attaches itself to the ceilings of caves and fires steel spikes at targets below. It fights by swinging its three feelers, whose steel spikes can smash a boulder into rubble.

Pronounced: fer-AH-thorn
Possible Moves: Rock Climb, Tackle, Harden, Rollout, Curse, Metal Claw, Pin Missile, Gyro Ball, Iron Defense, Mirror Shot, Ingrain, Selfdestruct, Power Whip, Iron Head, Payback, Flash Cannon, Explosion
Type: Grass-Steel   **Height:** 3' 03"
Weight: 242.5 lbs.   **Region:** Unova

FERROSEED

FERROTHORN

FINNEON
WING FISH POKÉMON

Nicknamed Beautifly of the Sea, the spots on Finneon's fins will collect sunlight during the day, then shine luminously at night.

Pronounced: FINN-ee-onn
Possible Moves: Pound, Water Gun, Attract, Rain Dance, Gust, Water Pulse, Captivate, Safeguard, Aqua Ring, Whirlpool, U-turn, Bounce, Silver Wind, Soak
Type: Water   **Height:** 1' 04"
Weight: 15.4 lbs.   **Region:** Sinnoh

FINNEON

LUMINEON

FLAAFFY
WOOL POKÉMON

Flaaffy's tail will light up when its coat is completely charged with electricity—and it will shoot electrified hairs from its body!

Pronounced: FLAF-fee
Possible Moves: Tackle, Growl, ThunderShock, Thunder Wave, Cotton Spore, Charge, Electro Ball, Cotton Guard, Discharge, Signal Beam, Light Screen, Power Gem, Thunder
Type: Electric   **Height:** 2' 07"   **Weight:** 29.3 lbs.
Region: Johto

MAREEP   FLAAFFY   AMPHAROS

FLAREON
FLAME POKÉMON

Before a battle, Flareon can raise its body temperature to 1650 degrees Fahrenheit via a flame sac in its body.

Pronounced: FLARE-ae-on
Possible Moves: Tackle, Tail Whip, Helping Hand, Sand-Attack, Ember, Quick Attack, Bite, Fire Spin, Fire Fang, Last Resort, Smog, Scary Face, Fire Blast, Lava Plume
Type: Fire
Height: 2' 11"
Weight: 55.1 lbs.
Region: Kanto

EEVEE

FLAREON

FLOATZEL
SEA WEASEL POKÉMON

Using the flotation tube around its neck, Floatzel can stay afloat easily, and has even assisted in the rescue of drowning people.

Pronounced: FLOAT-zull
Possible Moves: Ice Fang, SonicBoom, Growl, Water Sport, Quick Attack, Water Gun, Pursuit, Swift, Aqua Jet, Crunch, Agility, Whirlpool, Razor Wind, Aqua Tail
Type: Water
Height: 3' 07"   **Weight:** 73.9 lbs.
Region: Sinnoh

BUIZEL

FLOATZEL

FLYGON
MYSTIC POKÉMON

Known as The Desert Spirit, Flygon can create sandstorms with the rapid flapping of its wings.

Pronounced: FLY-gon

Possible Moves: SonicBoom, Sand-Attack, Faint Attack, Sand Tomb, Supersonic, DragonBreath, Screech, Dragon Claw, Sandstorm, Hyper Beam, Dragon Tail

Type:
Ground-Dragon

Height: 6' 07"

Weight: 180.8 lbs.

Region: Hoenn

TRAPINCH

VIBRAVA

FLYGON

FOONGUS
MUSHROOM POKÉMON

For reasons as yet unknown, this Pokémon looks like a Poké Ball. Foongus uses its Poké Ball pattern to lure people close, then releases poison spores—and it does the same to anyone who tries to catch it.

Pronounced: FOON-gus

Possible Moves: Absorb, Growth, Astonish, Bide, Mega Drain, Ingrain, Faint Attack, Sweet Scent, Giga Drain, Toxic, Synthesis, Clear Smog, SolarBeam, Rage Powder, Spore

Type: Grass-Poison

Height: 0' 08"

Weight: 2.2 lbs.

Region: Unova

FOONGUS

AMOONGUSS

FORRETRESS
BAGWORM POKÉMON

The only internal workings of this Pokémon that are visible past its steel shell are its eyes.

Pronounced: FOR-it-TRESS
Possible Moves: Toxic Spikes, Tackle, Protect, Selfdestruct, Bug Bite, Take Down, Rapid Spin, Bide, Natural Gift, Spikes, Mirror Shot, Autotomize, Payback, Explosion, Iron Defense, Gyro Ball, Double-Edge, Magnet Rise, Zap Cannon, Heavy Slam
Type: Bug-Steel
Height: 3' 11"
Weight: 277.3 lbs.
Region: Johto

PINECO ⟩ FORRETRESS

FRAXURE
AXE JAW POKÉMON

Fraxure's tusks can shatter rock, and the fights can get violent when it battles other Fraxure over territory. Since a broken tusk won't regrow, Fraxure carefully sharpens its tusks on river rocks after battling.

Pronounced: FRAK-shur
Possible Moves: Scratch, Leer, Assurance, Dragon Rage, Dual Chop, Scary Face, Slash, False Swipe, Dragon Claw, Dragon Dance, Taunt, Dragon Pulse, Swords Dance, Guillotine, Outrage, Giga Impact
Type: Dragon
Height: 3' 03"
Weight: 79.4 lbs.
Region: Unova

AXEW ⟩ FRAXURE ⟩ HAXORUS

FRILLISH
FLOATING POKÉMON

Frillish lives five miles below the ocean surface, and it drags its prey down to its lair after paralyzing it with poison. It wraps its veil-like arms around a target, then sinks to the ocean floor.

Frillish ♂

Frillish ♀

Pronounced: FRIL-lish
Possible Moves: Bubble, Water Sport, Absorb, Night Shade, BubbleBeam, Recover, Water Pulse, Ominous Wind, Brine, Rain Dance, Hex, Hydro Pump, Wring Out, Water Spout
Type: Water-Ghost   **Height:** 3' 11"
Weight: 72.8 lbs.   **Region:** Unova

FRILLISH

JELLICENT

FROSLASS
SNOW LAND POKÉMON

Froslass may seem to have a solid body, but it is actually hollow. It likes to freeze its foes.

Pronounced: FROS-lass
Possible Moves: Powder Snow, Leer, Double Team, Astonish, Icy Wind, Confuse Ray, Ominous Wind, Wake-Up Slap, Captivate, Ice Shard, Hail, Blizzard, Destiny Bond
Type: Ice-Ghost
Height: 4' 03"
Weight: 58.6 lbs.
Region: Sinnoh

SNORUNT

FROSLASS

FURRET
LONG BODY POKÉMON

Furret uses speed to outmaneuver foes, and lulls its offspring to sleep by curling up around them.

Pronounced: FUR-ret
Possible Moves: Scratch, Foresight, Defense Curl, Quick Attack, Fury Swipes, Helping Hand, Follow Me, Slam, Rest, Sucker Punch, Amnesia, Baton Pass, Me First, Hyper Voice
Type: Normal
Height: 5' 11"
Weight: 71.6 lbs.
Region: Johto

SENTRET

FURRET

GABITE
CAVE POKÉMON

Rumor has it that using the scales from Gabite can heal even the most incurable diseases.

Pronounced: guh-BITE
Possible Moves:
Tackle, Sand-Attack, Dragon Rage, Sandstorm, Take Down, Sand Tomb, Dual Chop, Slash, Dragon Claw, Dig, Dragon Rush
Type: Dragon-Ground
Height: 4' 07"
Weight: 123.5 lbs.
Region: Sinnoh

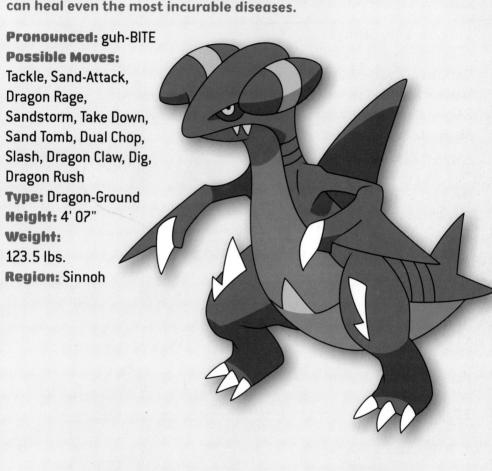

GIBLE > GABITE > GARCHOMP

GALLADE
BLADE POKÉMON

Gallade fights by extending the swords on its elbows. It is very courteous when not battling.

Pronounced: GAL-ade
Possible Moves: Leaf Blade, Night Slash, Leer, Confusion, Double Team, Teleport, Fury Cutter, Slash, Heal Pulse, Swords Dance, Psycho Cut, Helping Hand, Feint, False Swipe, Protect, Close Combat, Stored Power
Type:
Psychic-Fighting
Height: 5' 03"
Weight: 114.6 lbs.
Region: Sinnoh

RALTS

KIRLIA

GALLADE

GALVANTULA
ELESPIDER POKÉMON

It traps prey with its electrically charged web. The web shocks and immobilizes prey so Galvantula can feed at its leisure. If attacked, Galvantula can also spit out charged threads to create an electric barrier.

Pronounced: gal-VAN-choo-luh
Possible Moves: String Shot, Leech Life, Spider Web, Thunder Wave, Screech, Fury Cutter, Electroweb, Bug Bite, Gastro Acid, Slash, Electro Ball, Signal Beam, Agility, Sucker Punch, Discharge, Bug Buzz
Type: Bug-Electric
Height: 2' 07"   **Weight:** 31.5 lbs.
Region: Unova

JOLTIK

GALVANTULA

GARBODOR
TRASH HEAP POKÉMON

Garbodor absorbs garbage into its body. To take down foes, it holds them fast with its left arm and belches putrid, poisonous gas. The fingertips of its right hand shoot poisonous liquid.

Pronounced: gar-BOH-dur
Possible Moves: Pound, Poison Gas, Recycle, Toxic Spikes, Acid Spray, DoubleSlap, Sludge, Stockpile, Swallow, Body Slam, Sludge Bomb, Clear Smog, Toxic, Amnesia, Gunk Shot, Explosion
Type: Poison
Height: 6'03"   **Weight:** 236.6 lbs.
Region: Unova

TRUBBISH

GARBODOR

GARCHOMP
MACH POKÉMON

By spreading its wings and folding up its body, Garchomp can fly as fast as a jet plane.

Pronounced: gar-CHOMP
Possible Moves: Fire Fang, Tackle, Sand-Attack, Dragon Rage, Sandstorm, Take Down, Sand Tomb, Dual Chop, Slash, Dragon Claw, Dig, Crunch, Dragon Rush
Type: Dragon-Ground   **Height:** 6'03"
Weight: 209.4 lbs.   **Region:** Sinnoh

GIBLE

GABITE

GARCHOMP

GARDEVOIR
EMBRACE POKÉMON

Gardevoir is a vigilant and loyal companion that guards its Trainer with its life. It can also see into the future.

Pronounced: GAR-dee-VWAR

Possible Moves: Healing Wish, Growl, Confusion, Double Team, Teleport, Wish, Magical Leaf, Heal Pulse, Calm Mind, Psychic, Imprison, Future Sight, Captivate, Hypnosis, Dream Eater, Stored Power

Type: Psychic
Height: 5' 03"
Weight: 106.7 lbs.
Region: Hoenn

RALTS → KIRLIA → GARDEVOIR

GASTLY
GAS POKÉMON

Gastly is ninety-five percent gas. It can beat a large foe, but the gas is easily blown away by strong winds.

Pronounced: GAST-lee

Possible Moves: Hypnosis, Lick, Spite, Mean Look, Curse, Night Shade, Confuse Ray, Sucker Punch, Payback, Shadow Ball, Dream Eater, Dark Pulse, Destiny Bond, Hex, Nightmare

Type: Ghost-Poison
Height: 4' 03"
Weight: 0.2 lbs.
Region: Kanto

GASTLY → HAUNTER → GENGAR

GASTRODON EAST SEA

SEA SLUG POKÉMON

Gastrodon has different colors depending upon where it's found. If you find your Gastrodon in the east, it will be blue and green. If you find it in the west, it will be pink and brown.

Pronounced: GAS-tro-donn
Possible Moves: Mud-Slap, Mud Sport, Harden, Water Pulse, Mud Bomb, Hidden Power, Rain Dance, Body Slam, Muddy Water, Recover
Type: Water-Ground
Height: 2' 11"
Weight: 65.9 lbs.
Region: Sinnoh

SHELLOS (EAST SEA) → GASTRODON (EAST SEA)

GASTRODON WEST SEA

SEA SLUG POKÉMON

Gastrodon lives in shallow waters. It can grow back any body part that is ripped off.

Pronounced: GAS-tro-donn
Possible Moves: Mud-Slap, Mud Sport, Harden, Water Pulse, Mud Bomb, Hidden Power, Rain Dance, Body Slam, Muddy Water, Recover
Type: Water-Ground
Height: 2' 11"
Weight: 65.9 lbs.
Region: Sinnoh

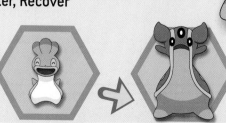

SHELLOS (WEST SEA) → GASTRODON (WEST SEA)

GENGAR
SHADOW POKÉMON

You can tell where Gengar is hiding when the temperature in an area drops by ten degrees Fahrenheit.

Pronounced: GENG-are

Possible Moves: Hypnosis, Lick, Spite, Mean Look, Curse, Night Shade, Confuse Ray, Sucker Punch, Shadow Punch, Payback, Shadow Ball, Dream Eater, Dark Pulse, Destiny Bond, Hex, Nightmare

Type: Ghost-Poison

Height: 4' 11"

Weight: 89.3 lbs.

Region: Kanto

GASTLY ➤ HAUNTER ➤ GENGAR

GEODUDE
ROCK POKÉMON

Geodude watch climbers while masquerading as half-buried rocks. They slam into one another to show how strong they are.

Pronounced: JEE-oh-dood

Possible Moves: Tackle, Defense Curl, Mud Sport, Rock Polish, Rock Throw, Magnitude, Rollout, Rock Blast, Smack Down, Selfdestruct, Bulldoze, Stealth Rock, Earthquake, Explosion, Double-Edge, Stone Edge

Type: Rock-Ground

Height: 1' 04"

Weight: 44.1 lbs.

Region: Kanto

GEODUDE ➤ GRAVELER ➤ GOLEM

GIBLE
LAND SHARK POKÉMON

Nesting in small holes in caves, Gible will pounce on any prey that comes too close.

Pronounced: GIBB-bull
Possible Moves: Tackle, Sand-Attack, Dragon Rage, Sandstorm, Take Down, Sand Tomb, Slash, Dragon Claw, Dig, Dragon Rush
Type: Dragon-Ground   **Height:** 2' 04"
Weight: 45.2 lbs.
Region: Sinnoh

GIBLE   GABITE   GARCHOMP

GIGALITH
COMPRESSED POKÉMON

Gigalith's orange crystals absorb solar energy, which it amplifies and fires from its mouth. This focused energy powers an attack strong enough to blow apart a mountain.

Pronounced: GIH-gah-lith
Possible Moves: Tackle, Harden, Sand-Attack, Headbutt, Rock Blast, Mud-Slap, Iron Defense, Smack Down, Power Gem, Rock Slide, Stealth Rock, Sandstorm, Stone Edge, Explosion
Type: Rock   **Height:** 5' 07"   **Weight:** 573.2 lbs.
Region: Unova

ROGGENROLA   BOLDORE   GIGALITH

GIRAFARIG
LONG NECK POKÉMON

Girafarig's tail can keep away foes that are trying to attack from behind. The tail has a small brain, and never sleeps.

Pronounced: jir-RAF-uh-rig

Possible Moves: Power Swap, Guard Swap, Astonish, Tackle, Growl, Confusion, Odor Sleuth, Stomp, Agility, Psybeam, Baton Pass, Assurance, Double Hit, Psychic, Zen Headbutt, Crunch

Type: Normal-Psychic

Height: 4' 11"

Weight: 91.5 lbs.

Region: Johto

DOES NOT EVOLVE

GIRATINA ALTERED FORME
RENEGADE POKÉMON

Giratina lives in the Reverse World, a strange place with low gravity. Giratina is the only one who can travel between the Reverse World and the normal world.

Pronounced: gear-uh-TEE-na
Possible Moves: DragonBreath, Scary Face, Ominous Wind, AncientPower, Slash, Shadow Sneak, Destiny Bond, Dragon Claw, Earth Power, Aura Sphere, Shadow Claw, Shadow Force, Hex
Type: Ghost-Dragon
Height: 14' 09"
Weight: 1653.5 lbs.
Region: Sinnoh

LEGENDARY POKÉMON

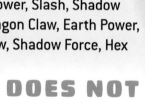

DOES NOT EVOLVE

GIRATINA ORIGIN FORME
RENEGADE POKÉMON

Giratina uses its Origin Forme to fly in the Reverse World. When it enters the normal world, it changes to Altered Forme.

Pronounced: gear-uh-TEE-na
Possible Moves: DragonBreath, Scary Face, Ominous Wind, AncientPower, Slash, Shadow Sneak, Destiny Bond, Dragon Claw, Earth Power, Aura Sphere, Shadow Claw, Shadow Force, Hex
Type: Ghost-Dragon
Height: 14' 09"
Weight: 1653.5 lbs.
Region: Sinnoh

LEGENDARY POKÉMON

DOES NOT EVOLVE

GLACEON

FRESH SNOW POKÉMON

As a defensive measure, Glaceon freezes its fur so that its hairs are razor-sharp needles.

Pronounced: GLACE-ee-on
Possible Moves: Tail Whip, Tackle, Helping Hand, Sand-Attack, Icy Wind, Quick Attack, Bite, Ice Shard, Ice Fang, Last Resort, Mirror Coat, Hail, Blizzard, Barrier
Type: Ice
Height: 2' 07"
Weight: 57.1 lbs.
Region: Sinnoh

EEVEE → GLACEON

GLALIE

FACE POKÉMON

Glalie can freeze the moisture in the air to encase its body in an armor of ice.

Pronounced: GLAY-lee
Possible Moves: Powder Snow, Leer, Double Team, Bite, Icy Wind, Headbutt, Protect, Ice Fang, Crunch, Ice Beam, Hail, Blizzard, Sheer Cold
Type: Ice
Height: 4' 11"
Weight: 565.5 lbs.
Region: Hoenn

SNORUNT → GLALIE

GLAMEOW
CATTY POKÉMON

Even though Glameow can be very fickle, don't underestimate it. It can put a foe into hypnosis with its stare.

Pronounced: GLAM-meow
Possible Moves: Fake Out, Scratch, Growl, Hypnosis, Faint Attack, Fury Swipes, Charm, Assist, Captivate, Slash, Sucker Punch, Attract, Hone Claws
Type: Normal
Height: 1' 08" **Weight:** 8.6 lbs.
Region: Sinnoh

GLAMEOW

PURUGLY

GLIGAR
FLYSCORPION POKÉMON

Gligar will aim for a foe's face while descending from the sky.

Pronounced: GLY-gar
Possible Moves: Poison Sting, Sand-Attack, Harden, Knock Off, Quick Attack, Fury Cutter, Faint Attack, Acrobatics, Screech, Slash, Swords Dance, U-turn, X-Scissor, Guillotine
Type: Ground-Flying
Height: 3' 07"
Weight: 142.9 lbs.
Region: Johto

GLIGAR

GLISCOR

GLISCOR
FANG SCORP POKÉMON

While hanging upside down from branches, Gliscor patiently waits for prey upon which it will swoop at a moment's notice.

Pronounced: GLY-skor
Possible Moves: Thunder Fang, Ice Fang, Fire Fang, Poison Jab, Sand-Attack, Harden, Knock Off, Quick Attack, Fury Cutter, Faint Attack, Acrobatics, Screech, Night Slash, Swords Dance, U-turn, X-Scissor, Guillotine
Type: Ground-Flying
Height: 6' 07"
Weight: 93.7 lbs.
Region: Sinnoh

GLIGAR   GLISCOR

GLOOM
WEED POKÉMON

The drool of honey from Gloom's mouth is so noxious, you can smell it from a mile away.

Pronounced: GLOOM
Possible Moves: Absorb, Sweet Scent, Acid, PoisonPowder, Stun Spore, Sleep Powder, Mega Drain, Lucky Chant, Natural Gift, Moonlight, Giga Drain, Petal Dance
Type: Grass-Poison
Height: 2' 07"
Weight: 19.0 lbs.
Region: Kanto

ODDISH

GLOOM

VILEPLUME   BELLOSSOM

GOLBAT
BAT POKÉMON

Searching for prey at night, Golbat seeks out the blood of both humans and Pokémon.

Pronounced: GOAL-bat
Possible Moves: Screech, Leech Life, Supersonic, Astonish, Bite, Wing Attack, Confuse Ray, Air Cutter, Mean Look, Acrobatics, Poison Fang, Haze, Air Slash
Type: Poison-Flying
Height: 5' 03"
Weight: 121.3 lbs.
Region: Kanto

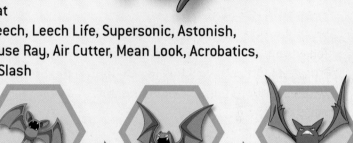

ZUBAT > GOLBAT > CROBAT

GOLDEEN
GOLDFISH POKÉMON

Imbued with the majesty of a queen, Goldeen is a champion swimmer that can reach speeds of five knots. Goldeen relies on the sharp horn on its head for protection.

Pronounced: GOAL-deen
Possible Moves: Peck, Tail Whip, Water Sport, Supersonic, Horn Attack, Water Pulse, Flail, Aqua Ring, Fury Attack, Waterfall, Horn Drill, Agility, Soak, Megahorn
Type: Water
Height: 2' 00"
Weight: 33.1 lbs.
Region: Kanto

GOLDEEN > SEAKING

GOLDUCK
DUCK POKÉMON

Known as the fastest swimmer, this Pokémon lives in lakes. It is faster than any recorded human swimmer.

Pronounced: GOAL-duck
Possible Moves: Aqua Jet, Water Sport, Scratch, Tail Whip, Water Gun, Disable, Confusion, Water Pulse, Fury Swipes, Screech, Soak, Psych Up, Zen Headbutt, Amnesia, Hydro Pump, Wonder Room
Type: Water
Height: 5' 07"
Weight: 168.9 lbs.
Region: Kanto

PSYDUCK

GOLDUCK

GOLEM
MEGATON POKÉMON

Not even big blasts of dynamite can harm this rocky-looking Pokémon, which sheds its skin only once a year.

Pronounced: GOAL-um
Possible Moves: Tackle, Defense Curl, Mud Sport, Rock Polish, Rock Throw, Magnitude, Steamroller, Rock Blast, Smack Down, Selfdestruct, Bulldoze, Stealth Rock, Earthquake, Explosion, Double-Edge, Stone Edge, Heavy Slam
Type: Rock-Ground
Height: 4' 07"
Weight: 661.4 lbs.
Region: Kanto

GEODUDE

GRAVELER

GOLEM

GOLETT
AUTOMATON POKÉMON

It's thought that Golett was created by the science of a mysterious ancient civilization. No one has yet identified the energy that burns inside Golett and enables it to move.

Pronounced: GO-let
Possible Moves: Pound, Astonish, Defense Curl, Mud-Slap, Rollout, Shadow Punch, Iron Defense, Mega Punch, Magnitude, DynamicPunch, Night Shade, Curse, Earthquake, Hammer Arm, Focus Punch
Type: Ground-Ghost
Height: 3' 03"   **Weight:** 202.8 lbs.
Region: Unova

GOLETT

GOLURK

GOLURK
AUTOMATON POKÉMON

Stories say that an ancient people created Golurk to protect people and Pokémon. It flies at mach speeds, but it goes haywire if the seal on its chest is removed.

Pronounced: GO-lurk
Possible Moves: Pound, Astonish, Defense Curl, Mud-Slap, Rollout, Shadow Punch, Iron Defense, Mega Punch, Magnitude, DynamicPunch, Night Shade, Curse, Heavy Slam, Earthquake, Hammer Arm, Focus Punch
Type: Ground-Ghost
Height: 9' 02"
Weight: 727.5 lbs.
Region: Unova

GOLETT

GOLURK

GOREBYSS
SOUTH SEA POKÉMON

Although it is a deep-sea dweller, the body of Gorebyss will turn a brighter shade of pink during the springtime.

Pronounced: GORE-a-biss
Possible Moves: Whirlpool, Confusion, Agility, Water Pulse, Amnesia, Aqua Ring, Captivate, Baton Pass, Dive, Psychic, Aqua Tail, Hydro Pump
Type: Water
Height: 5' 11"
Weight: 49.8 lbs.
Region: Hoenn

CLAMPERL

HUNTAIL   GOREBYSS

GOTHITA
FIXATION POKÉMON

Gothita is always staring at something—it closely observes Trainers and Pokémon, though it seems to see something that others cannot. Its ribbonlike feelers boost its psychic power.

Pronounced: GAH-THEE-tah
Possible Moves: Pound, Confusion, Tickle, Fake Tears, DoubleSlap, Psybeam, Embargo, Faint Attack, Psyshock, Flatter, Future Sight, Heal Block, Psychic, Telekinesis, Charm, Magic Room
Type: Psychic
Height: 1' 04"
Weight: 12.8 lbs.
Region: Unova

GOTHITA   GOTHORITA

GOTHITELLE

GOTHITELLE
ASTRAL BODY POKÉMON

Gothitelle's focused psychic power distorts space, revealing starry skies from thousands of light-years away. It can even predict a Trainer's life span.

Pronounced: GAH-thih-tell
Possible Moves: Pound, Confusion, Tickle, Fake Tears, DoubleSlap, Psybeam, Embargo, Faint Attack, Psyshock, Flatter, Future Sight, Heal Block, Psychic, Telekinesis, Charm, Magic Room
Type: Psychic
Height: 4' 11"
Weight: 97.0 lbs.
Region: Unova

GOTHITA   GOTHORITA   GOTHITELLE

GOTHORITA
MANIPULATE POKÉMON

Starlight is the source of its power, and Gothorita marks star positions by using psychic energy to levitate stones. Gothorita's hypnosis can control people and Pokémon.

Pronounced: GAH-thuh-REE-tah
Possible Moves: Pound, Confusion, Tickle, Fake Tears, DoubleSlap, Psybeam, Embargo, Faint Attack, Psyshock, Flatter, Future Sight, Heal Block, Psychic, Telekinesis, Charm, Magic Room
Type: Psychic   **Height:** 2' 04"
Weight: 39.7 lbs.
Region: Unova

GOTHITA   GOTHORITA   GOTHITELLE

GRANBULL
FAIRY POKÉMON

Using its huge fangs to strike at its foes, Granbull may seem imposing, but most are known to be timid.

Pronounced: GRAN-bull
Possible Moves: Ice Fang, Fire Fang, Thunder Fang, Tackle, Scary Face, Tail Whip, Charm, Bite, Lick, Headbutt, Roar, Rage, Take Down, Payback, Crunch, Outrage
Type: Normal
Height: 4' 07"
Weight: 107.4 lbs.
Region: Johto

SNUBBULL

GRANBULL

GRAVELER
ROCK POKÉMON

Graveler freefall down mountainsides, oblivious to how much of their bodies chip off in the process. They eat a ton of rocks per day!

Pronounced: GRAV-el-er
Possible Moves: Tackle, Defense Curl, Mud Sport, Rock Polish, Rock Throw, Magnitude, Rollout, Rock Blast, Smack Down, Selfdestruct, Bulldoze, Stealth Rock, Earthquake, Explosion, Double-Edge, Stone Edge
Type: Rock-Ground
Height: 3' 03"
Weight: 231.5 lbs.
Region: Kanto

GEODUDE

GRAVELER

GOLEM

GRIMER
SLUDGE POKÉMON

When dirt and filth from a stream were exposed to the moon's X-rays, Grimer was born.

Pronounced: GRIME-er
Possible Moves: Poison Gas, Pound, Harden, Mud-Slap, Disable, Minimize, Sludge, Mud Bomb, Fling, Screech, Sludge Bomb, Acid Armor, Sludge Wave, Gunk Shot, Memento
Type: Poison
Height: 2' 11" **Weight:** 66.1 lbs.
Region: Kanto

GRIMER

MUK

GROTLE
GROVE POKÉMON

Grotle likes to lie out in the sun. The berries that grow on its back can be eaten by other Pokémon.

Pronounced: GRAHT-ull
Possible Moves: Tackle, Withdraw, Absorb, Razor Leaf, Curse, Bite, Mega Drain, Leech Seed, Synthesis, Crunch, Giga Drain, Leaf Storm
Type: Grass
Height: 3' 07" **Weight:** 213.8 lbs. **Region:** Sinnoh

TURTWIG

GROTLE

TORTERRA

123

GROUDON
CONTINENT POKÉMON

After fighting Kyogre ages ago, Groudon now rests underground in a magma cavern.

Pronounced: GRAU-don
Possible Moves: Mud Shot, Scary Face, Lava Plume, Hammer Arm, Rest, Earthquake, AncientPower, Eruption, Bulk Up, Earth Power, Fissure, SolarBeam, Fire Blast
Type: Ground
Height: 11' 06"   **Weight:** 2094.4 lbs.
Region: Hoenn

DOES
NOT
EVOLVE

LEGENDARY
POKÉMON

GROVYLE
WOOD GECKO POKÉMON

Grovyle attacks its foes by jumping from branch to branch in the deep jungles.

Pronounced: GROW-vile
Possible Moves: Pound, Leer, Absorb, Quick Attack, Fury Cutter, Pursuit, Screech, Leaf Blade, Agility, Slam, Detect, False Swipe, Leaf Storm
Type: Grass
Height: 2' 11"
Weight: 47.6 lbs.
Region: Hoenn

TREECKO   GROVYLE   SCEPTILE

GROWLITHE
PUPPY POKÉMON

An extremely obedient Pokémon, Growlithe will wait patiently for orders by its Trainer.

Pronounced: GROWL-ith
Possible Moves: Bite, Roar, Ember, Leer, Odor Sleuth, Helping Hand, Flame Wheel, Reversal, Fire Fang, Flame Burst, Take Down, Flamethrower, Agility, Crunch, Retaliate, Heat Wave, Flare Blitz
Type: Fire
Height: 2' 04"
Weight: 41.9 lbs.
Region: Kanto

GROWLITHE   ARCANINE

GRUMPIG
MANIPULATE POKÉMON

Grumpig gains control over its enemies by dancing and using the black pearls around its neck to increase its psychic power.

Pronounced: GRUM-pig
Possible Moves: Splash, Psywave, Odor Sleuth, Psybeam, Psych Up, Confuse Ray, Magic Coat, Zen Headbutt, Rest, Snore, Psyshock, Payback, Psychic, Power Gem, Bounce
Type: Psychic
Height: 2' 11"　　**Weight:** 157.6 lbs.
Region: Hoenn

SPOINK

GRUMPIG

GULPIN
STOMACH POKÉMON

Gulpin's toxic digestive juices immediately dissolve anything it swallows, and since all of its body is stomach, that's saying a lot.

Pronounced: GULL-pin
Possible Moves: Pound, Yawn, Poison Gas, Sludge, Amnesia, Encore, Toxic, Acid Spray, Stockpile, Spit Up, Swallow, Sludge Bomb, Gastro Acid, Wring Out, Gunk Shot
Type: Poison
Height: 1' 04"　　**Weight:** 22.7 lbs.
Region: Hoenn

GULPIN

SWALOT

GURDURR
MUSCULAR POKÉMON

Gurdurr is so muscular and strong, a team of wrestlers couldn't budge it one bit. It shows off its big muscles to its friends and carries around steel beams to make itself even stronger.

Pronounced: GUR-dur
Possible Moves: Pound, Leer, Focus Energy, Bide, Low Kick, Rock Throw, Wake-Up Slap, Chip Away, Bulk Up, Rock Slide, DynamicPunch, Scary Face, Hammer Arm, Stone Edge, Focus Punch, Superpower
Type: Fighting
Height: 3' 11"
Weight: 88.2 lbs.
Region: Unova

TIMBURR	GURDURR	CONKELDURR

GYARADOS
ATROCIOUS POKÉMON

This Pokémon will not stop its rage until every field and village around it has been destroyed.

Pronounced: GAR-i-dose
Possible Moves: Thrash, Bite, Dragon Rage, Leer, Twister, Ice Fang, Aqua Tail, Rain Dance, Hydro Pump, Dragon Dance, Hyper Beam
Type: Water-Flying
Height: 21' 04"
Weight: 518.1 lbs.
Region: Kanto

MAGIKARP	GYARADOS

HAPPINY
PLAYHOUSE POKÉMON

Happiny loves to carry around white rocks in its pouch to imitate Chansey.

Pronounced: hap-PEE-nee
Possible Moves: Pound, Charm, Copycat, Refresh, Sweet Kiss
Type: Normal
Height: 2' 00" **Weight:** 53.8 lbs.
Region: Sinnoh

HAPPINY CHANSEY BLISSEY

HARIYAMA
ARM THRUST POKÉMON

Hariyama uses its arms—powerful enough to knock over trucks—to thrust, and it loves going up against bigger Pokémon.

Pronounced: HAR-ee-YAH-mah
Possible Moves: Brine, Tackle, Focus Energy, Sand-Attack, Arm Thrust, Vital Throw, Fake Out, Whirlwind, Knock Off, SmellingSalt, Belly Drum, Force Palm, Seismic Toss, Wake-Up Slap, Endure, Close Combat, Reversal, Heavy Slam
Type: Fighting
Height: 7' 07" **Weight:** 559.5 lbs.
Region: Hoenn

MAKUHITA

HARIYAMA

HAUNTER
GAS POKÉMON

Haunter hides in the darkness and inside walls to watch its prey and foes, then licks them to steal their life force.

Pronounced: HAWN-ter
Possible Moves: Hypnosis, Lick, Spite, Mean Look, Curse, Night Shade, Confuse Ray, Sucker Punch, Shadow Punch, Payback, Shadow Ball, Dream Eater, Dark Pulse, Destiny Bond, Hex, Nightmare
Type: Ghost-Poison
Height: 5' 03"
Weight: 0.2 lbs.
Region: Kanto

GASTLY   HAUNTER   GENGAR

HAXORUS
AXE JAW POKÉMON

Haxorus may be kind, but it is relentless when defending territory. Covered in hard armor, it challenges foes with tusks sturdy enough to cut through steel.

Pronounced: HAK-soar-us
Possible Moves: Scratch, Leer, Assurance, Dragon Rage, Dual Chop, Scary Face, Slash, False Swipe, Dragon Claw, Dragon Dance, Taunt, Dragon Pulse, Swords Dance, Guillotine, Outrage, Giga Impact
Type: Dragon   **Height:** 5' 11"
Weight: 232.6 lbs.
Region: Unova

AXEW   FRAXURE   HAXORUS

HEATMOR
ANTEATER POKÉMON

Heatmor has an internal flame and uses a hole in its tail to breathe. Its searing, fiery tongue can pierce the armor of its main prey, Durant.

Pronounced: HEET-mohr
Possible Moves: Incinerate, Lick, Odor Sleuth, Bind, Fire Spin, Fury Swipes, Snatch, Flame Burst, Bug Bite, Slash, Amnesia, Flamethrower, Stockpile, Spit Up, Swallow, Inferno
Type: Fire
Height: 4' 07"   **Weight:** 127.9 lbs.
Region: Unova

DOES NOT EVOLVE

HEATRAN
LAVA DOME POKÉMON

Its cross-shaped feet are perfect for helping it dig into the hard rock walls and cavern ceilings of the volcanic caves where it dwells.

Pronounced: HEE-tran
Possible Moves: AncientPower, Leer, Fire Fang, Metal Sound, Crunch, Scary Face, Lava Plume, Fire Spin, Iron Head, Earth Power, Heat Wave, Stone Edge, Magma Storm
Type: Fire-Steel
Height: 5' 07"   **Weight:** 948.0 lbs.
Region: Sinnoh

LEGENDARY POKÉMON

DOES NOT EVOLVE

HERACROSS
SINGLE HORN POKÉMON

Because of the tremendous strength in its legs and claws, Heracross is strong enough to pick up its foes and throw them great distances.

Pronounced: HAIR-uh-cross
Possible Moves: Night Slash, Tackle, Leer, Horn Attack, Endure, Fury Attack, Aerial Ace, Brick Break, Counter, Take Down, Close Combat, Reversal, Feint, Megahorn
Type: Bug-Fighting
Height: 4' 11"   **Weight:** 119.0 lbs.
Region: Johto

DOES NOT EVOLVE

HERDIER
LOYAL DOG POKÉMON

For ages, Herdier have helped Trainers raise Pokémon, loyally following Trainers' orders. A Herdier's dark fur looks like a cape, but it is extremely hard and helps protect Herdier from damage.

Pronounced: HERD-ee-er
Possible Moves: Leer, Tackle, Odor Sleuth, Bite, Helping Hand, Take Down, Work Up, Crunch, Roar, Retaliate, Reversal, Last Resort, Giga Impact
Type: Normal   **Height:** 2' 11"   **Weight:** 32.4 lbs.
Region: Unova

LILLIPUP   HERDIER   STOUTLAND

HIPPOPOTAS
HIPPO POKÉMON

Hippopotas does not like getting wet. It prefers to cover itself with a layer of sand for protection.

Pronounced: HIP-po-puh-TOSS
Possible Moves: Tackle, Sand-Attack, Bite, Yawn, Take Down, Dig, Sand Tomb, Crunch, Earthquake, Double-Edge, Fissure
Type: Ground
Height: 2' 07"
Weight: 109.1 lbs.
Region: Sinnoh

HIPPOPOTAS

HIPPOWDON

HIPPOWDON
HEAVYWEIGHT POKÉMON

Hippowdon can create powerful twisters by shooting out sand that it has stored in its body, and can crush cars in its powerful jaws.

Pronounced: hip-POW-donn
Possible Moves: Ice Fang, Fire Fang, Thunder Fang, Tackle, Sand-Attack, Bite, Yawn, Take Down, Dig, Sand Tomb, Crunch, Earthquake, Double-Edge, Fissure
Type: Ground
Height: 6' 07"   **Weight:** 661.4 lbs.
Region: Sinnoh

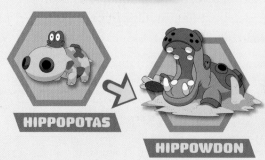

HIPPOPOTAS

HIPPOWDON

HITMONCHAN
PUNCHING POKÉMON

Although Hitmonchan has to rest after three minutes of fighting, its punches can burst through concrete.

Pronounced: HIT-mon-CHAN
Possible Moves: Revenge, Comet Punch, Agility, Pursuit, Mach Punch, Bullet Punch, Feint, Vacuum Wave, Quick Guard, ThunderPunch, Ice Punch, Fire Punch, Sky Uppercut, Mega Punch, Detect, Focus Punch, Counter, Close Combat
Type: Fighting
Height: 4' 07"
Weight: 110.7 lbs.
Region: Kanto

TYROGUE

HITMONLEE

HITMONCHAN

HITMONTOP

HITMONLEE
KICKING POKÉMON

Foes can be surprised by this Pokémon's reach, because its legs can stretch to double their length.

Pronounced: HIT-mon-LEE
Possible Moves: Revenge, Double Kick, Meditate, Rolling Kick, Jump Kick, Brick Break, Focus Energy, Feint, Hi Jump Kick, Mind Reader, Foresight, Wide Guard, Blaze Kick, Endure, Mega Kick, Close Combat, Reversal
Type: Fighting
Height: 4' 11"
Weight: 109.8 lbs.
Region: Kanto

TYROGUE

HITMONLEE

HITMONCHAN

HITMONTOP

HITMONTOP
HANDSTAND POKÉMON

When Hitmontop spins like a whirling top, the power of its attack increases tenfold.

Pronounced: HIT-mon-TOP
Possible Moves: Revenge, Rolling Kick, Focus Energy, Pursuit, Quick Attack, Triple Kick, Rapid Spin, Counter, Feint, Agility, Gyro Ball, Wide Guard, Quick Guard, Detect, Close Combat, Endeavor
Type: Fighting
Height: 4' 07"
Weight: 105.8 lbs.
Region: Johto

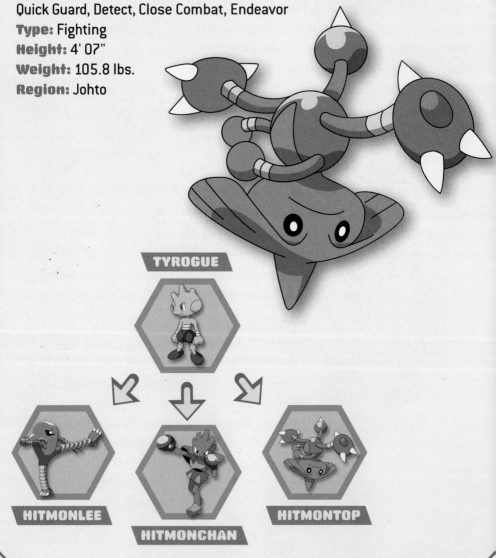

TYROGUE

HITMONLEE

HITMONCHAN

HITMONTOP

HO-OH
RAINBOW POKÉMON

If you see the multicolored Ho-Oh, it is said that you will have eternal happiness.

Pronounced: HOE-OH
Possible Moves: Whirlwind, Weather Ball, Gust, Brave Bird, Extrasensory, Sunny Day, Fire Blast, Sacred Fire, Punishment, AncientPower, Safeguard, Recover, Future Sight, Natural Gift, Calm Mind, Sky Attack
Type: Fire-Flying
Height: 12' 06"
Weight: 438.7 lbs.
Region: Johto

DOES NOT EVOLVE

LEGENDARY POKÉMON

HONCHKROW
BIG BOSS POKÉMON

Honchkrow is a nocturnal Pokémon, and will travel with Murkrow in groups.

Pronounced: HONCH-krow
Possible Moves: Astonish, Pursuit, Haze, Wing Attack, Swagger, Nasty Plot, Foul Play, Night Slash, Quash, Dark Pulse
Type: Dark-Flying
Height: 2' 11"
Weight: 60.2 lbs.
Region: Sinnoh

MURKROW

HONCHKROW

HOOTHOOT
OWL POKÉMON

Even though it has two feet, Hoothoot will only stand on one foot at a time while fighting.

Pronounced: HOOT-HOOT
Possible Moves: Tackle, Growl, Foresight, Hypnosis, Peck, Uproar, Reflect, Confusion, Echoed Voice, Take Down, Air Slash, Zen Headbutt, Synchronoise, Extrasensory, Psycho Shift, Roost, Dream Eater
Type: Normal-Flying   **Height:** 2' 04"
Weight: 46.7 lbs.   **Region:** Johto

HOOTHOOT

NOCTOWL

HOPPIP
COTTONWEED POKÉMON

Hoppip are carried by blowing winds, and when they arrive at a destination, it is said that spring is on the way.

Pronounced: HOP-pip
Possible Moves: Splash, Synthesis, Tail Whip, Tackle, PoisonPowder, Stun Spore, Sleep Powder, Bullet Seed, Leech Seed, Mega Drain, Acrobatics, Rage Powder, Cotton Spore, U-turn, Worry Seed, Giga Drain, Bounce, Memento
Type: Grass-Flying
Height: 1' 04"
Weight: 1.1 lbs.
Region: Johto

HOPPIP → SKIPLOOM → JUMPLUFF

HORSEA
DRAGON POKÉMON

When it senses danger, Horsea will spit out thick ink. It usually rests in the shade of coral reefs.

Pronounced: HORSE-ee
Possible Moves: Bubble, SmokeScreen, Leer, Water Gun, Focus Energy, BubbleBeam, Agility, Twister, Brine, Hydro Pump, Dragon Dance, Dragon Pulse
Type: Water   **Height:** 1' 04"   **Weight:** 17.6 lbs.
Region: Kanto

HORSEA → SEADRA → KINGDRA

HOUNDOOM
DARK POKÉMON

Houndoom's cries and howls are so eerie, people used to think it was the call of the grim reaper.

Pronounced: HOWN-doom
Possible Moves: Thunder Fang, Leer, Ember, Howl, Smog, Roar, Bite, Odor Sleuth, Beat Up, Fire Fang, Faint Attack, Embargo, Foul Play, Flamethrower, Crunch, Nasty Plot, Inferno
Type: Dark-Fire
Height: 4' 07"
Weight: 77.2 lbs.
Region: Johto

HOUNDOUR

HOUNDOOM

HOUNDOUR
DARK POKÉMON

Houndour are pack Pokémon that can eloquently convey their feelings through the different pitch of their cries.

Pronounced: HOWN-dowr
Possible Moves: Leer, Ember, Howl, Smog, Roar, Bite, Odor Sleuth, Beat Up, Fire Fang, Faint Attack, Embargo, Foul Play, Flamethrower, Crunch, Nasty Plot, Inferno
Type: Dark-Fire   **Height:** 2' 00"
Weight: 23.8 lbs.   **Region:** Johto

HOUNDOUR

HOUNDOOM

HUNTAIL
DEEP SEA POKÉMON

Huntail will use its bait-shaped tail to lure its prey from the deepest parts of the seas in which it lives.

Pronounced: HUN-tail
Possible Moves: Whirlpool, Bite, Screech, Water Pulse, Scary Face, Ice Fang, Brine, Baton Pass, Dive, Crunch, Aqua Tail, Hydro Pump
Type: Water
Height: 5' 07"
Weight: 59.5 lbs.
Region: Hoenn

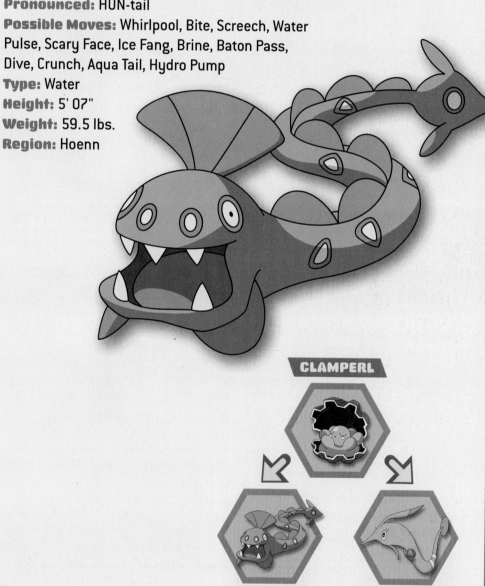

CLAMPERL

HUNTAIL

GOREBYSS

HYDREIGON
BRUTAL POKÉMON

As it flies around on six wings, Hydreigon registers anything that moves as a foe to be attacked. Though all three heads can attack and devour, the heads on its arms have no brains.

Pronounced: hy-DRY-gun
Possible Moves: Tri Attack, Dragon Rage, Focus Energy, Bite, Headbutt, DragonBreath, Roar, Crunch, Slam, Dragon Pulse, Work Up, Dragon Rush, Body Slam, Scary Face, Hyper Voice, Outrage
Type: Dark-Dragon
Height: 5' 11"
Weight: 352.7 lbs.
Region: Unova

DEINO  ZWEILOUS HYDREIGON

HYPNO
HYPNOSIS POKÉMON

Hypno is able to put anyone to sleep at any time using its pendulum.

Pronounced: HIP-no
Possible Moves: Nightmare, Switcheroo, Pound, Hypnosis, Disable, Confusion, Headbutt, Poison Gas, Meditate, Psybeam, Psych Up, Synchronoise, Zen Headbutt, Swagger, Psychic, Nasty Plot, Psyshock, Future Sight
Type: Psychic
Height: 5' 03"   **Weight:** 166.7 lbs.
Region: Kanto

DROWZEE

HYPNO

IGGLYBUFF
BALLOON POKÉMON

It can be very hard to stop Igglybuff from bouncing once it starts.

Pronounced: IG-lee-buff
Possible Moves: Sing, Charm, Defense Curl, Pound, Sweet Kiss, Copycat
Type: Normal
Height: 1' 00"
Weight: 2.2 lbs.
Region: Johto

IGGLYBUFF → JIGGLYPUFF → WIGGLYTUFF

ILLUMISE
FIREFLY POKÉMON

By using its sweet aroma, Illumise can guide Volbeat to draw signs with light in the night sky.

Pronounced: EE-loom-MEE-zay
Possible Moves: Tackle, Sweet Scent, Charm, Moonlight, Quick Attack, Wish, Encore, Flatter, Helping Hand, Zen Headbutt, Bug Buzz, Covet
Type: Bug
Height: 2' 00"
Weight: 39.0 lbs.
Region: Hoenn

DOES NOT EVOLVE

INFERNAPE
FLAME POKÉMON

Infernape's fire never goes out. This Pokémon also uses many different forms of martial arts to defeat its foes.

Pronounced: in-FER-nape

Possible Moves: Scratch, Leer, Ember, Taunt, Mach Punch, Fury Swipes, Flame Wheel, Feint, Punishment, Close Combat, Fire Spin, Acrobatics, Calm Mind, Flare Blitz

Type: Fire-Fighting

Height: 3' 11"

Weight: 121.3 lbs.

Region: Sinnoh

CHIMCHAR > **MONFERNO** > **INFERNAPE**

IVYSAUR
SEED POKÉMON

A sweet aroma is the signal that the bulb on its back will soon be in bloom.

Pronounced: EYE-vee-sore

Possible Moves: Tackle, Growl, Leech Seed, Vine Whip, PoisonPowder, Sleep Powder, Take Down, Razor Leaf, Sweet Scent, Growth, Double-Edge, Worry Seed, Synthesis, SolarBeam

Type: Grass-Poison

Height: 3' 03"

Weight: 28.7 lbs.

Region: Kanto

BULBASAUR **IVYSAUR** **VENUSAUR**

JELLICENT
FLOATING POKÉMON

Jellicent propels itself by expelling seawater from its body. Life energy is its favorite food source. Sometimes entire ships and crew vanish after entering Jellicent territory.

Jellicent ♂

Jellicent ♀

Pronounced: JEL-ih-sent

Possible Moves: Bubble, Water Sport, Absorb, Night Shade, BubbleBeam, Recover, Water Pulse, Ominous Wind, Brine, Rain Dance, Hex, Hydro Pump, Wring Out, Water Spout

Type: Water-Ghost **Height:** 7' 03"

Weight: 297.6 lbs. **Region:** Unova

FRILLISH

JELLICENT

JIGGLYPUFF
BALLOON POKÉMON

By singing a lullaby, Jigglypuff can make everyone drowsy.

Pronounced: JIG-lee-puff

Possible Moves: Sing, Defense Curl, Pound, Disable, Round, Rollout, DoubleSlap, Rest, Body Slam, Gyro Ball, Wake-Up Slap, Mimic, Hyper Voice, Double-Edge

Type: Normal **Height:** 1' 08" **Weight:** 12.1 lbs.

Region: Kanto

IGGLYBUFF   JIGGLYPUFF   WIGGLYTUFF

JIRACHI
WISH POKÉMON

Every thousand years, Jirachi has the ability to grant any wish for one week.

Pronounced: jer-AH-chi
Possible Moves: Wish, Confusion, Rest, Swift, Helping Hand, Psychic, Refresh, Rest, Zen Headbutt, Double-Edge, Gravity, Healing Wish, Future Sight, Cosmic Power, Last Resort, Doom Desire
Type: Steel-Psychic
Height: 1' 00"
Weight: 2.4 lbs.
Region: Hoenn

DOES
NOT
EVOLVE

MYTHICAL
POKÉMON

JOLTEON
LIGHTNING POKÉMON

When it raises the fur on its body, Jolteon looks like it's covered in sharp needles. It can emit 10,000 volts of electricity.

Pronounced: JOLT-ee-on
Possible Moves: Tail Whip, Tackle, Helping Hand, Sand-Attack, ThunderShock, Quick Attack, Double Kick, Pin Missile, Thunder Fang, Last Resort, Thunder Wave, Agility, Thunder, Discharge
Type: Electric
Height: 2' 07"   **Weight:** 54.0 lbs.
Region: Kanto

EEVEE → JOLTEON

JOLTIK
ATTACHING POKÉMON

Joltik clings to large Pokémon and absorbs static electricity, which it stores in an electric pouch. City-dwelling Joltik have figured out how to drain electricity from outlets in houses.

Pronounced: JOHL-tik
Possible Moves: String Shot, Leech Life, Spider Web, Thunder Wave, Screech, Fury Cutter, Electroweb, Bug Bite, Gastro Acid, Slash, Electro Ball, Signal Beam, Agility, Sucker Punch, Discharge, Bug Buzz
Type: Bug-Electric
Height: 0' 04"
Weight: 1.3 lbs.
Region: Unova

JOLTIK →

GALVANTULA

JUMPLUFF
COTTONWEED POKÉMON

Jumpluff scatters cotton spores while traveling by wind current around the world.

Pronounced: JUM-pluff
Possible Moves: Splash, Synthesis, Tail Whip, Tackle, PoisonPowder, Stun Spore, Sleep Powder, Bullet Seed, Leech Seed, Mega Drain, Acrobatics, Rage Powder, Cotton Spore, U-turn, Worry Seed, Giga Drain, Bounce, Memento
Type: Grass-Flying
Height: 2' 07"
Weight: 6.6 lbs.
Region: Johto

HOPPIP   SKIPLOOM   JUMPLUFF

JYNX
HUMAN SHAPE POKÉMON

Although it is impossible to understand Jynx, its cries do sound human.

Pronounced: JINKS
Possible Moves: Pound, Lick, Lovely Kiss, Powder Snow, DoubleSlap, Ice Punch, Heart Stamp, Mean Look, Fake Tears, Wake-Up Slap, Avalanche, Body Slam, Wring Out, Perish Song, Blizzard
Type: Ice-Psychic
Height: 4' 07"   **Weight:** 89.5 lbs.
Region: Kanto

SMOOCHUM

JYNX

KABUTO
SHELLFISH POKÉMON

Protected by a stiff shell, this Pokémon was thought to have existed three hundred million years ago.

Pronounced: kuh-BOO-toe
Possible Moves: Scratch, Harden, Absorb, Leer, Mud Shot, Sand-Attack, Endure, Aqua Jet, Mega Drain, Metal Sound, AncientPower, Wring Out
Type: Rock-Water
Height: 1' 08"
Weight: 25.4 lbs.
Region: Kanto

KABUTO → KABUTOPS

KABUTOPS
SHELLFISH POKÉMON

Because its prey adapted to life on land, this Rock- and Water-type Pokémon evolved so that it can also walk on land.

Pronounced: KA-boo-tops
Possible Moves: Feint, Scratch, Harden, Absorb, Leer, Mud Shot, Sand-Attack, Endure, Aqua Jet, Mega Drain, Slash, Metal Sound, AncientPower, Wring Out, Night Slash
Type: Rock-Water
Height: 4' 03"
Weight: 89.3 lbs.
Region: Kanto

KABUTO → KABUTOPS

KADABRA
PSI POKÉMON

If you see the shadow of this Pokémon, it is said to bring bad luck—and the alpha waves it emits can ruin precision devices.

Pronounced: kah-DA-bruh

Possible Moves: Teleport, Kinesis, Confusion, Disable, Miracle Eye, Ally Switch, Psybeam, Reflect, Telekinesis, Recover, Psycho Cut, Role Play, Psychic, Future Sight, Trick

Type: Psychic

Height: 4' 03"

Weight: 124.6 lbs.

Region: Kanto

ABRA

KADABRA

ALAKAZAM

KAKUNA
COCOON POKÉMON

Kakuna is a master of camouflage, hiding in leaves and tree branches as it waits for Evolution.

Pronounced: ka-KOO-nuh

Possible Moves: Harden

Type: Bug-Poison   **Height:** 2' 00"

Weight: 22.0 lbs.   **Region:** Kanto

WEEDLE

KAKUNA

BEEDRILL

KANGASKHAN
PARENT POKÉMON

Kangaskhan will let its baby come out of its pouch only when it feels safe.

Pronounced: KANG-gus-con
Possible Moves: Comet Punch, Leer, Fake Out, Tail Whip, Bite, Double Hit, Rage, Mega Punch, Chip Away, Dizzy Punch, Crunch, Endure, Outrage, Sucker Punch, Reversal
Type: Normal
Height: 7' 03"   **Weight:** 176.4 lbs.
Region: Kanto

DOES NOT EVOLVE

KARRABLAST
CLAMPING POKÉMON

This mysterious Pokémon targets Shelmet and evolves when it receives electrical stimulation while a Shelmet is present. If Karrablast feels threatened, it spits acid liquid to drive off attackers.

Pronounced: KAIR-ruh-blast
Possible Moves: Peck, Leer, Endure, Fury Cutter, Fury Attack, Headbutt, False Swipe, Bug Buzz, Slash, Take Down, Scary Face, X-Scissor, Flail, Swords Dance, Double-Edge
Type: Bug
Height: 1' 08"
Weight: 13.0 lbs.
Region: Unova

KARRABLAST   ESCAVALIER

KECLEON
COLOR SWAP POKÉMON

The pattern on Kecleon's belly will never change, but it does have the ability to change the color of the rest of its body.

Pronounced: KEH-clee-on
Possible Moves: Thief, Tail Whip, Astonish, Lick, Scratch, Bind, Faint Attack, Fury Swipes, Feint, Psybeam, Shadow Sneak, Slash, Screech, Substitute, Sucker Punch, Shadow Claw, AncientPower, Synchronoise
Type: Normal
Height: 3' 03"   **Weight:** 48.5 lbs.
Region: Hoenn

DOES
NOT
EVOLVE

KINGDRA
DRAGON POKÉMON

Whenever Kingdra moves while on the seafloor, it creates giant whirlpools.

Pronounced: KING-dra
Possible Moves: Yawn, Bubble, SmokeScreen, Leer, Water Gun, Focus Energy, BubbleBeam, Agility, Twister, Brine, Hydro Pump, Dragon Dance, Dragon Pulse
Type: Water-Dragon
Height: 5' 11"   **Weight:** 335.1 lbs.
Region: Johto

HORSEA   SEADRA   KINGDRA

KINGLER
PINCER POKÉMON

Kingler's big pincer is so heavy that it's hard for it to aim—but it is extremely strong.

Pronounced: KING-ler
Possible Moves: Wide Guard, Mud Sport, Bubble, ViceGrip, Leer, Harden, BubbleBeam, Mud Shot, Metal Claw, Stomp, Protect, Guillotine, Slam, Brine, Crabhammer, Flail
Type: Water
Height: 4' 03"
Weight: 132.3 lbs.
Region: Kanto

KRABBY   KINGLER

KIRLIA
EMOTION POKÉMON

When Kirlia is happy it will dance around, and is always "in tune" with its Trainer.

Pronounced: KEERL-lee-ah
Possible Moves: Growl, Confusion, Double Team, Teleport, Lucky Chant, Magical Leaf, Heal Pulse, Calm Mind, Psychic, Imprison, Future Sight, Charm, Hypnosis, Dream Eater, Stored Power
Type: Psychic
Height: 2' 07"
Weight: 44.5 lbs.
Region: Hoenn

RALTS

KIRLIA

GALLADE

GARDEVOIR

KLANG
GEAR POKÉMON

To express its feelings, Klang alters its direction of rotation, rotating faster when it is angry. It can spin its minigears at high speed and fire them at foes, but this can backfire if the gears don't come back.

Pronounced: KLANG
Possible Moves: ViceGrip, Charge, ThunderShock, Gear Grind, Bind, Charge Beam, Autotomize, Mirror Shot, Screech, Discharge, Metal Sound, Shift Gear, Lock-On, Zap Cannon, Hyper Beam
Type: Steel
Height: 2' 00"
Weight: 112.4 lbs.
Region: Unova

KLINK   KLANG   KLINKLANG

KLINK
GEAR POKÉMON

Each Klink is composed of two interlocking minigears that rotate to generate its vital energy. Only the right two minigears can successfully mesh together, and each one simply bounces off any other minigear.

Pronounced: KLEENK
Possible Moves: ViceGrip, Charge, ThunderShock, Gear Grind, Bind, Charge Beam, Autotomize, Mirror Shot, Screech, Metal Sound, Shift Gear, Lock-On, Zap Cannon, Hyper Beam
Type: Steel
Height: 1' 00"
Weight: 46.3 lbs.
Region: Unova

KLINK   KLANG   KLINKLANG

KLINKLANG
GEAR POKÉMON

Klinklang's red core is an energy tank. To generate a quick energy charge, the gear with the core spins at high speed, and Klinklang fires the charged energy from its spikes for an area attack.

Pronounced: KLEENK-klang

Possible Moves: ViceGrip, Charge, ThunderShock, Gear Grind, Bind, Charge Beam, Autotomize, Mirror Shot, Screech, Discharge, Metal Sound, Shift Gear, Lock-On, Zap Cannon, Hyper Beam

Type: Steel

Height: 2' 00"

Weight: 178.6 lbs.

Region: Unova

KLINK   KLANG   KLINKLANG

KOFFING
POISON GAS POKÉMON

The lighter-than-air gases that make up this Pokémon keep it aloft, but they smell terrible and can explode.

Pronounced: CAWF-ing
Possible Moves: Poison Gas, Tackle, Smog, SmokeScreen, Assurance, Clear Smog, Selfdestruct, Sludge, Haze, Gyro Ball, Explosion, Sludge Bomb, Destiny Bond, Memento
Type: Poison
Height: 2' 00"
Weight: 2.2 lbs.
Region: Kanto

KOFFING → WEEZING

KRABBY
RIVER CRAB POKÉMON

Krabby hides in holes it digs on beaches, and its pincers will grow back if they break.

Pronounced: CRA-bee
Possible Moves: Mud Sport, Bubble, ViceGrip, Leer, Harden, BubbleBeam, Mud Shot, Metal Claw, Stomp, Protect, Guillotine, Slam, Brine, Crabhammer, Flail
Type: Water
Height: 1' 04"   **Weight:** 14.3 lbs.
Region: Kanto

KRABBY → KINGLER

KRICKETOT
CRICKET POKÉMON

Kricketot communicate with one another by shaking their heads and knocking their antennae together.

Pronounced: KRICK-eh-tot
Possible Moves: Growl, Bide, Struggle Bug, Bug Bite
Type: Bug
Height: 1' 00"
Weight: 4.9 lbs.
Region: Sinnoh

KRICKETOT

KRICKETUNE

KRICKETUNE
CRICKET POKÉMON

Kricketune shows its emotion by creating melodies. When it cries, it crosses its arms in front of itself.

Pronounced: KRICK-eh-toon
Possible Moves: Growl, Bide, Fury Cutter, Leech Life, Sing, Focus Energy, Slash, X-Scissor, Screech, Taunt, Night Slash, Bug Buzz, Perish Song
Type: Bug
Height: 3' 03"
Weight: 56.2 lbs.
Region: Sinnoh

KRICKETOT

KRICKETUNE

KROKOROK
DESERT CROC POKÉMON

A protective membrane shields Krokorok's eyes from sandstorms. This membrane also senses heat, enabling Krokorok to see in the dark. It lives in small groups.

Pronounced: KRAHK-oh-rahk
Possible Moves: Leer, Rage, Bite, Sand-Attack, Torment, Sand Tomb, Assurance, Mud-Slap, Embargo, Swagger, Crunch, Dig, Scary Face, Foul Play, Sandstorm, Earthquake, Thrash
Type: Ground-Dark
Height: 3' 03"
Weight: 73.6 lbs.
Region: Unova

SANDILE > KROKOROK > KROOKODILE

KROOKODILE
INTIMIDATION POKÉMON

Krookodile never lets prey get away. It has jaws powerful enough to crush a car body and eyes like binoculars, able to see faraway objects.

Pronounced: KROOK-oh-dyle
Possible Moves: Leer, Rage, Bite, Sand-Attack, Torment, Sand Tomb, Assurance, Mud-Slap, Embargo, Swagger, Crunch, Dig, Scary Face, Foul Play, Sandstorm, Earthquake, Outrage
Type: Ground-Dark   **Height:** 4' 11"   **Weight:** 212.3 lbs.
Region: Unova

SANDILE > KROKOROK > KROOKODILE

KYOGRE
SEA BASIN POKÉMON

Kyogre has slumbered in a marine trench for ages, but when it awakes, it could cause downpours that would widen the oceans.

Pronounced: kai-OH-gurr

Possible Moves: Water Pulse, Scary Face, Body Slam, Muddy Water, Aqua Ring, Ice Beam, AncientPower, Water Spout, Calm Mind, Aqua Tail, Sheer Cold, Double-Edge, Hydro Pump

Type: Water

Height: 14' 09" **Weight:** 776.0 lbs.

Region: Hoenn

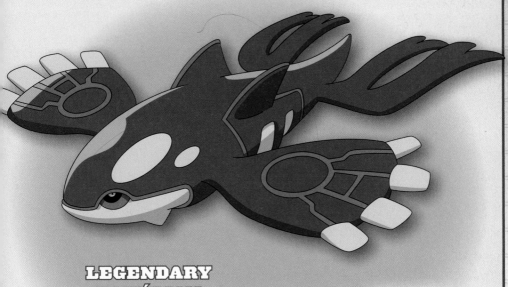

LEGENDARY
POKÉMON

DOES
NOT
EVOLVE

KYUREM
BOUNDARY POKÉMON

Able to create ultracold air, Kyurem can generate a powerful, freezing energy. But when this energy leaked out, its body was frozen.

Pronounced: KYOO-rem
Possible Moves: Icy Wind, Dragon Rage, Imprison, AncientPower, Ice Beam, DragonBreath, Slash, Scary Face, Glaciate, Dragon Pulse, Imprison, Endeavor, Blizzard, Outrage, Hyper Voice
Type: Dragon-Ice
Height: 9' 10"
Weight: 716.5 lbs.
Region: Unova

DOES NOT EVOLVE

LEGENDARY POKÉMON

LAIRON
IRON ARMOR POKÉMON

To bulk up, Lairon digs up and eats iron ore. It also smashes its strong body against others to fight for territory.

Pronounced: LAIR-ron
Possible Moves: Tackle, Harden, Mud-Slap, Headbutt, Metal Claw, Iron Defense, Roar, Take Down, Iron Head, Protect, Metal Sound, Iron Tail, Autotomize, Heavy Slam, Double-Edge, Metal Burst
Type: Steel-Rock
Height: 2' 11"
Weight: 264.6 lbs.
Region: Hoenn

ARON

LAIRON

AGGRON

LAMPENT
LAMP POKÉMON

People fear this ominous Pokémon, which searches through cities for spirits of the fallen. Lampent can even steal the spirit out of a body.

Pronounced: LAM-pent
Possible Moves: Ember, Astonish, Minimize, Smog, Fire Spin, Confuse Ray, Night Shade, Will-O-Wisp, Flame Burst, Imprison, Hex, Memento, Inferno, Curse, Shadow Ball, Pain Split, Overheat
Type: Ghost-Fire   **Height:** 2' 00"   **Weight:** 28.7 lbs.
Region: Unova

LITWICK

LAMPENT

CHANDELURE

LANDORUS
ABUNDANCE POKÉMON

Landorus is hailed as "The Guardian of the Fields" because wherever it goes, a bountiful crop follows. Energy pours from its tail and fertilizes the soil, making crops grow to great size.

Pronounced: LAN-duh-rus

Possible Moves: Block, Mud Shot, Rock Tomb, Imprison, Punishment, Bulldoze, Rock Throw, Extrasensory, Swords Dance, Earth Power, Rock Slide, Earthquake, Sandstorm, Fissure, Stone Edge, Hammer Arm, Outrage

Type: Ground-Flying

Height: 4' 11"

Weight: 149.9 lbs.

Region: Unova

DOES
NOT
EVOLVE

LEGENDARY
POKÉMON

LANTURN
LIGHT POKÉMON

Nicknamed the Deep-Sea Star, Lanturn's light shines so bright that it even lights up the depths of the sea.

Pronounced: LAN-turn

Possible Moves: Bubble, Supersonic, Thunder Wave, Flail, Water Gun, Confuse Ray, Spark, Take Down, Stockpile, Swallow, Spit Up, Electro Ball, BubbleBeam, Signal Beam, Discharge, Aqua Ring, Hydro Pump, Charge

Type: Water-Electric

Height: 3' 11"   **Weight:** 49.6 lbs.

Region: Johto

CHINCHOU

LANTURN

LAPRAS
TRANSPORT POKÉMON

Since it is able to understand humans, Lapras often helps people and Pokémon cross bodies of water.

Pronounced: LAP-russ

Possible Moves: Sing, Growl, Water Gun, Mist, Confuse Ray, Ice Shard, Water Pulse, Body Slam, Rain Dance, Perish Song, Ice Beam, Brine, Safeguard, Hydro Pump, Sheer Cold

Type: Water-Ice

Height: 8' 02"

Weight: 485.0 lbs.

Region: Kanto

DOES NOT EVOLVE

LARVESTA
TORCH POKÉMON

Larvesta dwells at the base of volcanoes and is said to be born from the sun. When it evolves, its entire body is wreathed in flames. Its five horns shoot fire.

Pronounced: lar-VESS-tuh
Possible Moves: Ember, String Shot, Leech Life, Take Down, Flame Charge, Bug Bite, Double-Edge, Flame Wheel, Bug Buzz, Amnesia, Thrash, Flare Blitz
Type: Bug-Fire
Height: 3' 07"
Weight: 63.5 lbs.
Region: Unova

LARVESTA   VOLCARONA

LARVITAR
ROCK SKIN POKÉMON

This Pokémon eats as much soil as it can, then sleeps so it can grow.

Pronounced: LAR-vuh-tar
Possible Moves: Bite, Leer, Sandstorm, Screech, Chip Away, Rock Slide, Scary Face, Thrash, Dark Pulse, Payback, Crunch, Earthquake, Stone Edge, Hyper Beam
Type: Rock-Ground   **Height:** 2' 00"
Weight: 158.7 lbs.
Region: Johto

LARVITAR   PUPITAR   TYRANITAR

LATIAS
EON POKÉMON

Latias can become invisible if it sits in the light the right way, thanks to the light-refracting down that covers its body.

Pronounced: LAT-ee-ahs
Possible Moves: Psywave, Wish, Helping Hand, Safeguard, DragonBreath, Water Sport, Refresh, Mist Ball, Zen Headbutt, Recover, Psycho Shift, Charm, Psychic, Heal Pulse, Reflect Type, Guard Split, Dragon Pulse, Healing Wish
Type: Dragon-Psychic
Height: 4' 07"   **Weight:** 88.2 lbs.
Region: Hoenn

LEGENDARY POKÉMON

DOES NOT EVOLVE

LATIOS
EON POKÉMON

An extremely intelligent Pokémon, Latios can fly faster than a plane.

Pronounced: LAT-ee-ose
Possible Moves: Psywave, Heal Block, Helping Hand, Safeguard, DragonBreath, Protect, Refresh, Luster Purge, Zen Headbutt, Recover, Psycho Shift, Dragon Dance, Psychic, Heal Pulse, Telekinesis, Power Split, Dragon Pulse, Memento
Type: Dragon-Psychic
Height: 6' 07"
Weight: 132.3 lbs.
Region: Hoenn

LEGENDARY POKÉMON

DOES NOT EVOLVE

LEAFEON
VERDANT POKÉMON

Leafeon is always surrounded by clear air, and, like a plant, it uses photosynthesis.

Pronounced: LEEF-ee-on
Possible Moves: Tail Whip, Tackle, Helping Hand, Sand-Attack, Razor Leaf, Quick Attack, Synthesis, Magical Leaf, Giga Drain, Last Resort, GrassWhistle, Sunny Day, Leaf Blade, Swords Dance
Type: Grass
Height: 3' 03"　　**Weight:** 56.2 lbs.
Region: Sinnoh

EEVEE ➤ LEAFEON

LEAVANNY
NURTURING POKÉMON

Using sticky silk and the cutters on its arms, Leavanny weaves leaves into clothing for any small Pokémon it meets. It also uses fermenting leaves to keep its Eggs warm, and it turns leaves into wrappings for Sewaddle.

Pronounced: lee-VAN-nee
Possible Moves: False Swipe, Tackle, String Shot, Bug Bite, Razor Leaf, Struggle Bug, Slash, Helping Hand, Leaf Blade, X-Scissor, Entrainment, Swords Dance, Leaf Storm
Type: Bug-Grass
Height: 3' 11"
Weight: 45.2 lbs.
Region: Unova

SEWADDLE ➤ SWADLOON ➤ LEAVANNY

LEDIAN
FIVE STAR POKÉMON

Using starlight for energy, the patterns on Ledian's back will become bigger or smaller depending on the amount of energy it stores.

Pronounced: LEH-dee-an
Possible Moves: Tackle, Supersonic, Comet Punch, Light Screen, Reflect, Safeguard, Mach Punch, Baton Pass, Silver Wind, Agility, Swift, Double-Edge, Bug Buzz
Type: Bug-Flying
Height: 4' 07"   **Weight:** 78.5 lbs.
Region: Johto

LEDYBA

LEDIAN

LEDYBA
FIVE STAR POKÉMON

Ledyba is so timid it will only move with a swarm of others. It communicates with other Ledyba by using its scent.

Pronounced: LEH-dee-bah
Possible Moves: Tackle, Supersonic, Comet Punch, Light Screen, Reflect, Safeguard, Mach Punch, Baton Pass, Silver Wind, Agility, Swift, Double-Edge, Bug Buzz
Type: Bug-Flying
Height: 3' 03"
Weight: 23.8 lbs.
Region: Johto

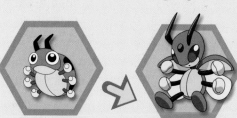

LEDYBA

LEDIAN

LICKILICKY
LICKING POKÉMON

Lickilicky battles by coiling foes in its large and long tongue, leaving them soaked with drool!

Pronounced: LICK-ee-LICK-ee
Possible Moves: Lick, Supersonic, Defense Curl, Knock Off, Wrap, Stomp, Disable, Slam, Rollout, Chip Away, Me First, Refresh, Screech, Power Whip, Wring Out, Gyro Ball
Type: Normal
Height: 5' 07"
Weight: 308.6 lbs.
Region: Sinnoh

LICKITUNG

LICKILICKY

LICKITUNG
LICKING POKÉMON

Lickitung uses its tongue to fight instead of its hands. Its tongue is covered with a sticky saliva that can grip anything.

Pronounced: LICK-i-tung
Possible Moves: Lick, Supersonic, Defense Curl, Knock Off, Wrap, Stomp, Disable, Slam, Rollout, Chip Away, Me First, Refresh, Screech, Power Whip, Wring Out
Type: Normal
Height: 3' 11"   **Weight:** 144.4 lbs.
Region: Kanto

LICKITUNG

LICKILICKY

LIEPARD
CRUEL POKÉMON

Many Trainers are attracted to this Pokémon's beautiful fur. Liepard appears and disappears without warning, and it can sneak up and surprise its targets.

Pronounced: LY-purd
Possible Moves: Scratch, Growl, Assist, Sand-Attack, Fury Swipes, Pursuit, Torment, Fake Out, Hone Claws, Assurance, Slash, Taunt, Night Slash, Snatch, Nasty Plot, Sucker Punch
Type: Dark
Height: 3' 07"   **Weight:** 82.7 lbs.
Region: Unova

PURRLOIN → LIEPARD

LILEEP
SEA LILY POKÉMON

This Pokémon shares the same origin story as Anorith. Scientists found the fossilized Lileep on the sea floor, and reanimated it.

Pronounced: lill-LEEP
Possible Moves: Astonish, Constrict, Acid, Ingrain, Confuse Ray, Amnesia, Gastro Acid, AncientPower, Energy Ball, Stockpile, Spit Up, Swallow, Wring Out
Type: Rock-Grass
Height: 3' 03"
Weight: 52.5 lbs.
Region: Hoenn

LILEEP → CRADILY

LILLIGANT
FLOWERING POKÉMON

Though Lilligant is popular with celebrities, getting its flower to bloom is a challenge. The garland on Lilligant's head has a relaxing scent, but it withers without good care.

Pronounced: LIL-lih-gunt
Possible Moves: Growth, Leech Seed, Mega Drain, Synthesis, Teeter Dance, Quiver Dance, Petal Dance
Type: Grass
Height: 3' 07"
Weight: 35.9 lbs.
Region: Unova

PETILIL

LILLIGANT

LILLIPUP
PUPPY POKÉMON

The long hair around its face makes it sensitive to every slight change in its surroundings. Though brave against even strong opponents, Lillipup is intelligent and will retreat if at a disadvantage.

Pronounced: LIL-ee-pup
Possible Moves: Leer, Tackle, Odor Sleuth, Bite, Helping Hand, Take Down, Work Up, Crunch, Roar, Retaliate, Reversal, Last Resort, Giga Impact
Type: Normal
Height: 1' 04"
Weight: 9.0 lbs.
Region: Unova

LILLIPUP

HERDIER

STOUTLAND

LINOONE
RUSHING POKÉMON

The trick to avoiding Linoone is to cut right or left if it is chasing you. Although it reaches speeds of up to 60 miles per hour, it can only run in a straight line.

Pronounced: line-NOON
Possible Moves: Switcheroo, Tackle, Growl, Tail Whip, Headbutt, Sand-Attack, Odor Sleuth, Mud Sport, Fury Swipes, Covet, Bestow, Slash, Rest, Belly Drum, Fling
Type: Normal
Height: 1' 08"
Weight: 71.6 lbs.
Region: Hoenn

ZIGZAGOON → LINOONE

LITWICK
CANDLE POKÉMON

Litwick fuels its light with the life energy it absorbs from people and Pokémon. Though it pretends to guide others with this light, it drains the life force of anyone who follows it.

Pronounced: LIT-wik
Possible Moves: Ember, Astonish, Minimize, Smog, Fire Spin, Confuse Ray, Night Shade, Will-O-Wisp, Flame Burst, Imprison, Hex, Memento, Inferno, Curse, Shadow Ball, Pain Split, Overheat
Type: Ghost-Fire   **Height:** 1' 00"   **Weight:** 6.8 lbs.
Region: Unova

LITWICK   LAMPENT   CHANDELURE

LOMBRE
JOLLY POKÉMON

Lombre loves to play with fishermen, often tugging on fishing lines to make people believe they've caught something.

Pronounced: LOM-brey
Possible Moves: Astonish, Growl, Absorb, Nature Power, Fake Out, Fury Swipes, Water Sport, BubbleBeam, Zen Headbutt, Uproar, Hydro Pump
Type: Water-Grass
Height: 3' 11"
Weight: 71.6 lbs.
Region: Hoenn

LOTAD → LOMBRE → LUDICOLO

LOPUNNY
RABBIT POKÉMON

Lopunny will use its ears to cloak itself when it senses danger. It is known to be a very vain Pokémon.

Pronounced: LAH-puh-nee
Possible Moves: Mirror Coat, Magic Coat, Splash, Pound, Defense Curl, Foresight, Endure, Return, Quick Attack, Jump Kick, Baton Pass, Agility, Dizzy Punch, After You, Charm, Entrainment, Bounce, Healing Wish
Type: Normal
Height: 3' 11"   **Weight:** 73.4 lbs.
Region: Sinnoh

BUNEARY →

LOPUNNY

LOTAD
WATER WEED POKÉMON

Lotad looks like a water lily, but this sturdy Pokémon can ferry Pokémon that can't swim.

Pronounced: LOW-tad
Possible Moves: Astonish, Growl, Absorb, Nature Power, Mist, Natural Gift, Mega Drain, BubbleBeam, Zen Headbutt, Rain Dance, Energy Ball
Type: Water-Grass   **Height:** 1' 08"   **Weight:** 5.7 lbs.
Region: Hoenn

LOTAD   LOMBRE   LUDICOLO

LOUDRED
BIG VOICE POKÉMON

To power up, Loudred will stamp its feet although it doesn't need to, since the shock waves generated when it cries are so powerful they can tip over vehicles.

Pronounced: LOUD-red
Possible Moves: Pound, Uproar, Astonish, Howl, Bite, Supersonic, Stomp, Screech, Roar, Synchronoise, Rest, Sleep Talk, Hyper Voice
Type: Normal   **Height:** 3' 03"   **Weight:** 89.3 lbs.
Region: Hoenn

WHISMUR   LOUDRED   EXPLOUD

LUCARIO
AURA POKÉMON

Lucario is able to read thoughts by sensing the auras around others. It can also understand human speech.

Pronounced: loo-CAR-ee-oh
Possible Moves: Dark Pulse, Quick Attack, Foresight, Detect, Metal Claw, Counter, Force Palm, Feint, Bone Rush, Metal Sound, Me First, Quick Guard, Swords Dance, Heal Pulse, Calm Mind, Aura Sphere, Close Combat, Dragon Pulse, ExtremeSpeed
Type: Fighting-Steel
Height: 3' 11"
Weight: 119.0 lbs.
Region: Sinnoh

RIOLU → LUCARIO

LUDICOLO
CAREFREE POKÉMON

Ludicolo's muscles are filled with energy when it hears music, and then it can't help but dance.

Pronounced: LOO-dee-KO-low
Possible Moves: Astonish, Growl, Mega Drain, Nature Power
Type: Water-Grass
Height: 4' 11"
Weight: 121.3 lbs.
Region: Hoenn

LOTAD → LOMBRE → LUDICOLO

LUGIA
DIVING POKÉMON

If Lugia used its wings, it could cause a forty day storm. Thankfully, it rarely emerges from the deep-sea trenches it calls home.

Pronounced: LOO-gee-uh
Possible Moves: Whirlwind, Weather Ball, Gust, Dragon Rush, Extrasensory, Rain Dance, Hydro Pump, Aeroblast, Punishment, AncientPower, Safeguard, Recover, Future Sight, Natural Gift, Calm Mind, Sky Attack
Type: Psychic-Flying
Height: 17' 01"
Weight: 476.2 lbs.
Region: Johto

DOES NOT EVOLVE

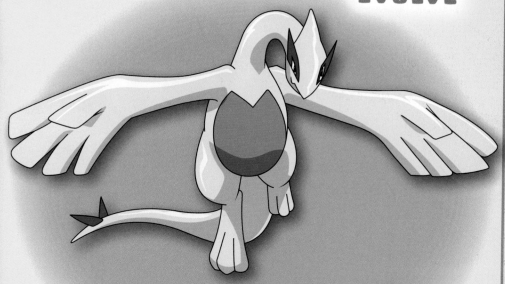

LEGENDARY POKÉMON

LUMINEON
NEON POKÉMON

Lumineon can crawl along seafloors using the fins on its chest. It will flash the patterns on its tail fins to attract prey.

Pronounced: loo-MIN-ee-onn
Possible Moves: Pound, Water Gun, Attract, Rain Dance, Gust, Water Pulse, Captivate, Safeguard, Aqua Ring, Whirlpool, U-turn, Bounce, Silver Wind, Soak
Type: Water
Height: 3' 11"
Weight: 52.9 lbs.
Region: Sinnoh

FINNEON

LUMINEON

LUNATONE
METEORITE POKÉMON

Lunatone will only become active on nights with a full moon—which would explain its crescent shape, and its affinity for everything moon-like.

Pronounced: LOO-nuh-tone
Possible Moves: Tackle, Harden, Confusion, Rock Throw, Hypnosis, Rock Polish, Psywave, Embargo, Cosmic Power, Heal Block, Psychic, Future Sight, Explosion, Magic Room
Type: Rock-Psychic
Height: 3' 03"
Weight: 370.4 lbs.
Region: Hoenn

DOES NOT EVOLVE

LUVDISC
RENDEZVOUS POKÉMON

When a couple finds the warm-sea dwelling Luvdisc, it is said they will enjoy eternal love.

Pronounced: LOVE-disk
Possible Moves: Tackle, Charm, Water Gun, Agility, Take Down, Lucky Chant, Water Pulse, Attract, Flail, Sweet Kiss, Hydro Pump, Aqua Ring, Captivate, Safeguard
Type: Water
Height: 2' 00"
Weight: 19.2 lbs.
Region: Hoenn

DOES NOT EVOLVE

LUXIO
SPARK POKÉMON

Luxio can cause their foes to faint by letting loose with some spectacular high-voltage electricity.

Pronounced: LUCKS-ee-oh
Possible Moves: Tackle, Leer, Charge, Spark, Bite, Roar, Swagger, Thunder Fang, Crunch, Scary Face, Discharge
Type: Electric
Height: 2' 11"
Weight: 67.2 lbs.
Region: Sinnoh

SHINX **LUXIO** **LUXRAY**

LUXRAY
GLEAM EYES POKÉMON

When Luxray's eyes turn gold, it can spot prey hiding anywhere, including those trying to duck behind walls.

Pronounced: LUCKS-ray
Possible Moves: Tackle, Leer, Charge, Spark, Bite, Roar, Swagger, Thunder Fang, Crunch, Scary Face, Discharge, Wild Charge
Type: Electric   **Height:** 4' 07"   **Weight:** 92.6 lbs.
Region: Sinnoh

SHINX **LUXIO** **LUXRAY**

MACHAMP
SUPERPOWER POKÉMON

Machamp's four arms allow it to slam foes at amazing speeds. Its muscles give extra power to its punches.

Pronounced: mah-CHAMP
Possible Moves: Wide Guard, Low Kick, Leer, Focus Energy, Karate Chop, Low Sweep, Foresight, Seismic Toss, Revenge, Vital Throw, Submission, Wake-Up Slap, Cross Chop, Scary Face, DynamicPunch
Type: Fighting
Height: 5' 03"
Weight: 286.6 lbs.
Region: Kanto

MACHOP 〉 MACHOKE 〉 MACHAMP

MACHOKE
SUPERPOWER POKÉMON

Machoke's strength can be out of control, so it wears a belt to help keep it in check.

Pronounced: mah-CHOKE
Possible Moves: Low Kick, Leer, Focus Energy, Karate Chop, Low Sweep, Foresight, Seismic Toss, Revenge, Vital Throw, Submission, Wake-Up Slap, Cross Chop, Scary Face, DynamicPunch
Type: Fighting
Height: 4' 11"
Weight: 155.4 lbs.
Region: Kanto

MACHOP   MACHOKE   MACHAMP

MACHOP
SUPERPOWER POKÉMON

Machop trains in all types of martial arts to keep itself strong.

Pronounced: mah-CHOP
Possible Moves: Low Kick, Leer, Focus Energy, Karate Chop, Low Sweep, Foresight, Seismic Toss, Revenge, Vital Throw, Submission, Wake-Up Slap, Cross Chop, Scary Face, DynamicPunch
Type: Fighting
Height: 2' 07"
Weight: 43.0 lbs.
Region: Kanto

MACHOP   MACHOKE   MACHAMP

MAGBY
LIVE COAL POKÉMON

As long as it's breathing yellow flames, Magby is healthy—even though its body temperature can reach 1,000 degrees Fahrenheit.

Pronounced: MAG-bee
Possible Moves: Smog, Leer, Ember, SmokeScreen, Faint Attack, Fire Spin, Confuse Ray, Flame Burst, Fire Punch, Lava Plume, Flamethrower, Sunny Day, Fire Blast
Type: Fire
Height: 2' 04"
Weight: 47.2 lbs.
Region: Johto

MAGBY > **MAGMAR** > **MAGMORTAR**

MAGCARGO
LAVA POKÉMON

Flames occasionally erupt from Magcargo's shell, which is normal considering its body reaches temperatures of 18,000 degrees Fahrenheit.

Pronounced: mag-CAR-go
Possible Moves: Yawn, Smog, Ember, Rock Throw, Harden, Recover, Flame Burst, AncientPower, Amnesia, Lava Plume, Shell Smash, Rock Slide, Body Slam, Flamethrower, Earth Power
Type: Fire-Rock
Height: 2' 07"
Weight: 121.3 lbs.
Region: Johto

SLUGMA > **MAGCARGO**

MAGIKARP
FISH POKÉMON

Poor Magikarp! It is generally regarded as the weakest Pokémon ever. How it has managed to survive is a mystery.

Pronounced: MAJ-i-karp
Possible Moves: Splash, Tackle, Flail
Type: Water
Height: 2' 11"
Weight: 22.0 lbs.
Region: Kanto

MAGIKARP

GYARADOS

MAGMAR
SPITFIRE POKÉMON

Covered in flames that shimmer like the sun, this Pokémon was born in a volcano.

Pronounced: MAG-mar
Possible Moves: Smog, Leer, Ember, SmokeScreen, Faint Attack, Fire Spin, Confuse Ray, Flame Burst, Fire Punch, Lava Plume, Flamethrower, Sunny Day, Fire Blast
Type: Fire
Height: 4' 03"
Weight: 98.1 lbs.
Region: Kanto

MAGBY

MAGMAR

MAGMORTAR

MAGMORTAR
BLAST POKÉMON

Magmortar can blast fireballs of over 3,600 degrees Fahrenheit from the ends of its arms.

Pronounced: mag-MOR-tur

Possible Moves: ThunderPunch, Smog, Leer, Ember, SmokeScreen, Faint Attack, Fire Spin, Confuse Ray, Flame Burst, Fire Punch, Lava Plume, Flamethrower, Sunny Day, Fire Blast, Hyper Beam

Type: Fire

Height: 5' 03"

Weight: 149.9 lbs.

Region: Sinnoh

MAGBY — MAGMAR — MAGMORTAR

MAGNEMITE
MAGNET POKÉMON

Feeding on electricity, it uses its sides to make electromagnetic waves that enable it to fly.

Pronounced: MAG-nuh-mite

Possible Moves: Metal Sound, Tackle, ThunderShock, Supersonic, SonicBoom, Thunder Wave, Spark, Electro Ball, Lock-On, Magnet Bomb, Screech, Discharge, Mirror Shot, Magnet Rise, Gyro Ball, Zap Cannon

Type: Electric-Steel   **Height:** 1' 00"   **Weight:** 13.2 lbs.

Region: Kanto

MAGNEMITE — MAGNETON — MAGNEZONE

MAGNETON
MAGNET POKÉMON

Look closely—did you know Magneton is three Magnemite stuck together by magnets? A group of these can set off a magnetic storm!

Pronounced: MAG-nuh-tun

Possible Moves: Tri Attack, Metal Sound, Tackle, ThunderShock, Supersonic, SonicBoom, Thunder Wave, Spark, Electro Ball, Lock-On, Magnet Bomb, Screech, Discharge, Mirror Shot, Magnet Rise, Gyro Ball, Zap Cannon

Type: Electric-Steel

Height: 3' 03"

Weight: 132.3 lbs.

Region: Kanto

 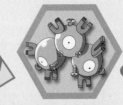 

MAGNEMITE → MAGNETON → MAGNEZONE

MAGNEZONE
MAGNET AREA POKÉMON

With Magnezone, which evolved from exposure to special magnetic fields, you can generate magnetism.

Pronounced: MAG-nuh-zone

Possible Moves: Mirror Coat, Barrier, Metal Sound, Tackle, ThunderShock, Supersonic, SonicBoom, Thunder Wave, Spark, Electro Ball, Lock-On, Magnet Bomb, Screech, Discharge, Mirror Shot, Magnet Rise, Gyro Ball, Zap Cannon

Type: Electric-Steel

Height: 3' 11"

Weight: 396.8 lbs.

Region: Sinnoh

 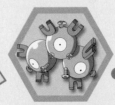 

MAGNEMITE → MAGNETON → MAGNEZONE

MAKUHITA
GUTS POKÉMON

You're likely to find a lot of snapped trees near this Pokémon—it slams into them to toughen up its body.

Pronounced: MAK-oo-HEE-ta

Possible Moves: Tackle, Focus Energy, Sand-Attack, Arm Thrust, Vital Throw, Fake Out, Whirlwind, Knock Off, SmellingSalt, Belly Drum, Force Palm, Seismic Toss, Wake-Up Slap, Endure, Close Combat, Reversal, Heavy Slam

Type: Fighting

Height: 3' 03" **Weight:** 190.5 lbs.

Region: Hoenn

MAKUHITA > HARIYAMA

MAMOSWINE
TWIN TUSK POKÉMON

The Mamoswine population decreased shortly after the ice age. Its tusks are made of ice.

Pronounced: MAMO-swine

Possible Moves: AncientPower, Peck, Odor Sleuth, Mud Sport, Powder Snow, Mud-Slap, Endure, Mud Bomb, Hail, Ice Fang, Take Down, Double Hit, Earthquake, Mist, Blizzard, Scary Face

Type: Ice-Ground

Height: 8' 02" **Weight:** 641.5 lbs. **Region:** Sinnoh

SWINUB > PILOSWINE > MAMOSWINE

MANAPHY
SEAFARING POKÉMON

Because water makes up eighty percent of its body, this Pokémon is greatly affected by weather changes in its environment. It will also swim great distances to return to its birthplace.

Pronounced: man-UH-fee

Possible Moves: Tail Glow, Bubble, Water Sport, Charm, Supersonic, BubbleBeam, Acid Armor, Whirlpool, Water Pulse, Aqua Ring, Dive, Rain Dance, Heart Swap

Type: Water

Height: 1' 00"

Weight: 3.1 lbs.

Region: Sinnoh

DOES
NOT
EVOLVE

MYTHICAL
POKÉMON

MANDIBUZZ
BONE VULTURE POKÉMON

Mandibuzz uses bones to adorn itself and build its nest. It looks for weakened Pokémon from the sky, then swoops down to seize prey in its talons and carry it off to the nest.

Pronounced: MAN-dih-buz

Possible Moves: Gust, Leer, Fury Attack, Pluck, Nasty Plot, Flatter, Faint Attack, Punishment, Defog, Tailwind, Air Slash, Dark Pulse, Embargo, Bone Rush, Whirlwind, Brave Bird, Mirror Move

Type: Dark-Flying   **Height:** 3' 11"
Weight: 87.1 lbs.   **Region:** Unova

VULLABY

MANDIBUZZ

MANECTRIC
DISCHARGE POKÉMON

Manectric creates a lightning-bolt thundercloud by discharging electricity through its mane.

Pronounced: mane-EK-trick

Possible Moves: Fire Fang, Tackle, Thunder Wave, Leer, Howl, Quick Attack, Spark, Odor Sleuth, Bite, Thunder Fang, Roar, Discharge, Charge, Wild Charge, Thunder

Type: Electric

Height: 4' 11"

Weight: 88.6 lbs.

Region: Hoenn

ELECTRIKE   MANECTRIC

MANKEY
PIG MONKEY POKÉMON

Mankey lives with groups of other Mankey on treetops. If one Mankey gets angry, the whole group will follow suit.

Pronounced: MANK-ee
Possible Moves: Covet, Scratch, Low Kick, Leer, Focus Energy, Fury Swipes, Karate Chop, Seismic Toss, Screech, Assurance, Swagger, Cross Chop, Thrash, Punishment, Close Combat, Final Gambit
Type: Fighting
Height: 1' 08"   **Weight:** 61.7 lbs.
Region: Kanto

MANKEY

PRIMEAPE

MANTINE
KITE POKÉMON

These docile Pokémon can be seen swimming in unison when the sea is calm—it almost seems as if they are flying.

Pronounced: MAN-tine
Possible Moves: Psybeam, Bullet Seed, Signal Beam, Tackle, Bubble, Supersonic, BubbleBeam, Headbutt, Agility, Wing Attack, Water Pulse, Take Down, Confuse Ray, Bounce, Aqua Ring, Hydro Pump

Type: Water-Flying
Height: 6' 11"
Weight: 485.0 lbs.
Region: Johto

MANTYKE   MANTINE

MANTYKE
KITE POKÉMON

The patterns on Mantyke's back will be different in every region. It uses the antennae on its head to detect subtle changes in the ocean's currents.

Pronounced: MAN-tike
Possible Moves: Tackle, Bubble, Supersonic, BubbleBeam, Headbutt, Agility, Wing Attack, Water Pulse, Take Down, Confuse Ray, Bounce, Aqua Ring, Hydro Pump
Type: Water-Flying
Height: 3' 03"   **Weight:** 143.3 lbs.
Region: Sinnoh

MANTYKE

MANTINE

MARACTUS
CACTUS POKÉMON

Found in arid regions, Maractus moves in rhythm while making a sound like maracas. It does a lively song and dance to ward off avian Pokémon who are after its flower seeds.

Pronounced: mah-RAK-tus
Possible Moves: Peck, Absorb, Sweet Scent, Growth, Pin Missile, Mega Drain, Synthesis, Cotton Spore, Needle Arm, Giga Drain, Acupressure, Ingrain, Petal Dance, Sucker Punch, Sunny Day, SolarBeam, Cotton Guard, After You
Type: Grass   **Height:** 3' 03"
Weight: 61.7 lbs.   **Region:** Unova

DOES
NOT
EVOLVE

MAREEP
WOOL POKÉMON

Mareep is not prone to being petted, since its fluffy coat immediately doubles in size due to stored static electricity.

Pronounced: mah-REEP
Possible Moves: Tackle, Growl, ThunderShock, Thunder Wave, Cotton Spore, Charge, Electro Ball, Cotton Guard, Discharge, Signal Beam, Light Screen, Power Gem, Thunder
Type: Electric   **Height:** 2' 00"   **Weight:** 17.2 lbs.
Region: Johto

MAREEP   FLAAFFY   AMPHAROS

MARILL
AQUA MOUSE POKÉMON

When it dives underwater, Marill use its oil-filled tail as a float, and eats plants from the river bottom.

Pronounced: MARE-rull
Possible Moves: Tackle, Defense Curl, Tail Whip, Water Gun, Rollout, BubbleBeam, Aqua Ring, Double-Edge, Rain Dance, Aqua Tail, Hydro Pump
Type: Water
Height: 1' 04"
Weight: 18.7 lbs.
Region: Johto

AZURILL   MARILL   AZUMARILL

MAROWAK
BONE KEEPER POKÉMON

Marowak uses bones both as weapons and to tap out signals on boulders.

Pronounced: MAR-row-ack
Possible Moves: Growl, Tail Whip, Bone Club, Headbutt, Leer, Focus Energy, Bonemerang, Rage, False Swipe, Thrash, Fling, Bone Rush, Endeavor, Double-Edge, Retaliate
Type: Ground
Height: 3' 03"
Weight: 99.2 lbs.
Region: Kanto

CUBONE

MAROWAK

MARSHTOMP
MUD FISH POKÉMON

This Pokémon's sure stance will stay sturdy even in shifting mud. It loves to burrow into dirt to sleep.

Pronounced: MARSH-stomp
Possible Moves: Tackle, Growl, Mud-Slap, Water Gun, Bide, Mud Shot, Foresight, Mud Bomb, Take Down, Muddy Water, Protect, Earthquake, Endeavor
Type: Water-Ground
Height: 2' 04"   **Weight:** 61.7 lbs.   **Region:** Hoenn

MUDKIP   MARSHTOMP   SWAMPERT

MASQUERAIN
EYEBALL POKÉMON

Masquerain uses its four eye-patterned wings to fly and hover in any direction.

Pronounced: mas-ker-RAIN
Possible Moves: Ominous Wind, Bubble, Quick Attack, Sweet Scent, Water Sport, Gust, Scary Face, Stun Spore, Silver Wind, Air Slash, Whirlwind, Bug Buzz, Quiver Dance
Type: Bug-Flying
Height: 2' 07"
Weight: 7.9 lbs.
Region: Hoenn

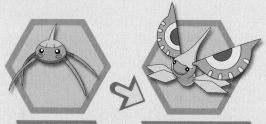

SURSKIT → MASQUERAIN

MAWILE
DECEIVER POKÉMON

The huge set of jaws formed by horns on Mawile's head can chew through iron beams.

Pronounced: MAW-while
Possible Moves: Astonish, Fake Tears, Bite, Sweet Scent, ViceGrip, Faint Attack, Baton Pass, Crunch, Iron Defense, Sucker Punch, Stockpile, Swallow, Spit Up, Iron Head
Type: Steel
Height: 2' 00"   **Weight:** 25.4 lbs.
Region: Hoenn

DOES NOT EVOLVE

MEDICHAM
MEDITATE POKÉMON

Medicham hones its sixth sense with a disciplined routine of daily meditation.

Pronounced: MED-uh-cham
Possible Moves: Fire Punch, ThunderPunch, Ice Punch, Bide, Meditate, Confusion, Detect, Hidden Power, Mind Reader, Feint, Calm Mind, Force Palm, Hi Jump Kick, Psych Up, Acupressure, Power Trick, Reversal, Recover
Type: Fighting-Psychic
Height: 4' 03"   **Weight:** 69.4 lbs.
Region: Hoenn

MEDITITE

MEDICHAM

MEDITITE
MEDITATE POKÉMON

While it never misses its daily yoga workouts, Meditite also likes to temper and sharpen its spirit through fasting.

Pronounced: MED-uh-tite
Possible Moves: Bide, Meditate, Confusion, Detect, Hidden Power, Mind Reader, Feint, Calm Mind, Force Palm, Hi Jump Kick, Psych Up, Acupressure, Power Trick, Reversal, Recover
Type: Fighting-Psychic
Height: 2' 00"
Weight: 24.7 lbs.
Region: Hoenn

MEDITITE   MEDICHAM

MEGANIUM
HERB POKÉMON

Meganium has the ability to bring dead plants and flowers back to life! All it has to do is breathe on them.

Pronounced: meg-GAY-nee-um
Possible Moves: Tackle, Growl, Razor Leaf, PoisonPowder, Synthesis, Reflect, Magical Leaf, Natural Gift, Petal Dance, Sweet Scent, Light Screen, Body Slam, Safeguard, Aromatherapy, SolarBeam
Type: Grass
Height: 5' 11"
Weight: 221.6 lbs.
Region: Johto

CHIKORITA

BAYLEEF

MEGANIUM

MEOWTH
SCRATCH CAT POKÉMON

Meowth is mostly nocturnal. Its eyes will glitter brightly if it sees something shiny.

Pronounced: me-OUTH
Possible Moves: Scratch, Growl, Bite, Fake Out, Fury Swipes, Screech, Faint Attack, Taunt, Pay Day, Slash, Nasty Plot, Assurance, Captivate, Night Slash, Feint
Type: Normal
Height: 1' 04"   **Weight:** 9.3 lbs.
Region: Kanto

MEOWTH

PERSIAN

MESPRIT
EMOTION POKÉMON

Also known as The Being of Emotion, Mesprit is said to have taught humans the nobility of pain, sorrow, and joy. It caused the birth of emotions.

Pronounced: MES-prit
Possible Moves: Rest, Confusion, Imprison, Protect, Swift, Lucky Chant, Future Sight, Charm, Extrasensory, Copycat, Natural Gift, Healing Wish
Type: Psychic
Height: 1' 00"
Weight: 0.7 lbs.
Region: Sinnoh

LEGENDARY POKÉMON

DOES NOT EVOLVE

METAGROSS
IRON LEG POKÉMON

By combining two Metang, the quad-brained Metagross has the smarts of a supercomputer.

Pronounced: MET-uh-gross
Possible Moves: Magnet Rise, Take Down, Metal Claw, Confusion, Scary Face, Pursuit, Bullet Punch, Psychic, Iron Defense, Agility, Hammer Arm, Meteor Mash, Zen Headbutt, Hyper Beam
Type:
Steel-Psychic
Height: 5' 03"
Weight:
1212.5 lbs.
Region: Hoenn

BELDUM → METANG → METAGROSS

METANG
IRON CLAW POKÉMON

Metang's body is so strong that not even a jet plane could scratch it. Its body is formed by the combination of two Beldum.

Pronounced: met-TANG
Possible Moves: Magnet Rise, Take Down, Metal Claw, Confusion, Scary Face, Pursuit, Bullet Punch, Psychic, Iron Defense, Agility, Meteor Mash, Zen Headbutt, Hyper Beam
Type: Steel-Psychic   **Height:** 3' 11"   **Weight:** 446.4 lbs.
Region:
Hoenn

BELDUM → METANG → METAGROSS

METAPOD
COCOON POKÉMON

This Pokémon has the power of patience, using its hardened shell to repel attacks while awaiting its Evolution.

Pronounced: MET-uh-pod
Possible Moves: Harden
Type: Bug
Height: 2' 04"
Weight: 21.8 lbs.
Region: Kanto

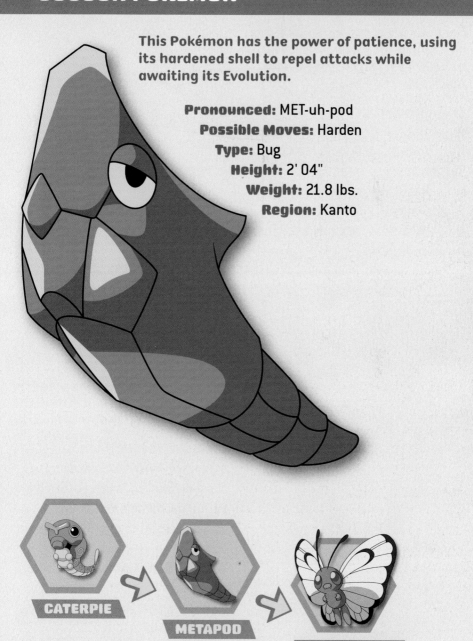

CATERPIE

METAPOD

BUTTERFREE

MEW
NEW SPECIES POKÉMON

Because Mew can learn and use any Pokémon move, it is thought to be ancestrally linked to all Pokémon.

Pronounced: MYU
Possible Moves: Pound, Reflect Type, Transform, Mega Punch, Metronome, Psychic, Barrier, AncientPower, Amnesia, Me First, Baton Pass, Nasty Plot, Aura Sphere
Type: Psychic
Height: 1' 04" **Weight:** 8.8 lbs.
Region: Kanto

MYTHICAL POKÉMON

DOES NOT EVOLVE

MEWTWO
GENETIC POKÉMON

Mewtwo was created when scientists recombined Mew's genes. It has the most savage heart of all Pokémon.

Pronounced: MYU-too
Possible Moves: Confusion, Disable, Barrier, Swift, Future Sight, Psych Up, Miracle Eye, Mist, Psycho Cut, Amnesia, Power Swap, Guard Swap, Psychic, Me First, Recover, Safeguard, Aura Sphere, Psystrike
Type: Psychic
Height: 6' 07"
Weight: 269.0 lbs.
Region: Kanto

LEGENDARY POKÉMON

DOES NOT EVOLVE

MIENFOO
MARTIAL ARTS POKÉMON

This sharp-clawed Pokémon has mastered elegant move combos, dominating battles with flowing, continuous attacks. By concentrating, Mienfoo makes its moves even faster and more precise.

Pronounced: MEEN-FOO
Possible Moves: Pound, Meditate, Detect, Fake Out, DoubleSlap, Swift, Calm Mind, Force Palm, Drain Punch, Jump Kick, U-turn, Quick Guard, Bounce, Hi Jump Kick, Reversal, Aura Sphere
Type: Fighting   **Height:** 2' 11"
Weight: 44.1 lbs.   **Region:** Unova

MIENFOO

MIENSHAO

MIENSHAO
MARTIAL ARTS POKÉMON

Mienshao wields the long fur on its arms like a whip, unleashing attacks too fast to see.

Pronounced: MEEN-SHOW
Possible Moves: Pound, Meditate, Detect, Fake Out, DoubleSlap, Swift, Calm Mind, Force Palm, Drain Punch, Jump Kick, U-turn, Wide Guard, Bounce, Hi Jump Kick, Reversal, Aura Sphere

Type: Fighting
Height: 4' 07"
Weight: 78.3 lbs.
Region: Unova

MIENFOO

MIENSHAO

MIGHTYENA
BITE POKÉMON

This Pokémon chases down its prey in a pack, and is very obedient to a skilled Trainer.

Pronounced: MY-tee-EH-nah
Possible Moves: Tackle, Howl, Sand-Attack, Bite, Odor Sleuth, Roar, Swagger, Assurance, Scary Face, Taunt, Embargo, Take Down, Thief, Sucker Punch
Type: Dark
Height: 3' 03"
Weight: 81.6 lbs.
Region: Hoenn

POOCHYENA → MIGHTYENA

MILOTIC
TENDER POKÉMON

This Pokémon has the ability to calm people, and is widely thought to be the world's most beautiful Pokémon.

Pronounced: MY-low-tic
Possible Moves: Water Gun, Wrap, Water Sport, Refresh, Water Pulse, Twister, Recover, Captivate, Aqua Tail, Rain Dance, Hydro Pump, Attract, Safeguard, Aqua Ring
Type: Water   **Height:** 20' 04"
Weight: 357.1 lbs.   **Region:** Hoenn

FEEBAS → MILOTIC

MILTANK
MILK COW POKÉMON

By drinking Miltank's milk, kids will become healthy adults.

Pronounced: MILL-tank
Possible Moves: Tackle, Growl, Defense Curl, Stomp, Milk Drink, Bide, Rollout, Body Slam, Zen Headbutt, Captivate, Gyro Ball, Heal Bell, Wake-Up Slap
Type: Normal
Height: 3' 11"   **Weight:** 166.4 lbs.
Region: Johto

DOES NOT EVOLVE

MIME JR.
MIME POKÉMON

Mime Jr. can imitate its foes and mesmerize them, allowing it to escape.

Pronounced: mime-JOON-yur
Possible Moves: Tickle, Barrier, Confusion, Copycat, Meditate, Encore, DoubleSlap, Mimic, Light Screen, Reflect, Psybeam, Substitute, Recycle, Trick, Psychic, Role Play, Baton Pass, Safeguard
Type: Psychic
Height: 2' 00"
Weight: 28.7 lbs.
Region: Sinnoh

MIME JR.   MR. MIME

MINCCINO
CHINCHILLA POKÉMON

Always sweeping, always dusting, Minccino likes a tidy habitat and uses its tail as a broom. It also uses its clean, well-groomed tail to rub other Minccino as a greeting.

Pronounced: min-CHEE-noh
Possible Moves: Pound, Growl, Helping Hand, Tickle, DoubleSlap, Encore, Swift, Sing, Tail Slap, Charm, Wake-Up Slap, Echoed Voice, Slam, Captivate, Hyper Voice, Last Resort, After You
Type: Normal   **Height:** 1' 04"
Weight: 12.8 lbs.
Region: Unova

MINCCINO ➔ CINCCINO

MINUN
CHEERING POKÉMON

Minun is a cheerleader Pokémon, like Plusle. If its friends are losing, its body lets off more and more sparks.

Pronounced: MIE-nun
Possible Moves: Growl, Thunder Wave, Quick Attack, Helping Hand, Spark, Encore, Charm, Copycat, Electro Ball, Swift, Fake Tears, Charge, Thunder, Baton Pass, Agility, Trump Card, Nasty Plot, Entrainment
Type: Electric
Height: 1' 04"   **Weight:** 9.3 lbs.
Region: Hoenn

DOES NOT EVOLVE

MISDREAVUS
SCREECH POKÉMON

Misdreavus feeds on fear, which it instills in the unsuspecting with its frightening shrieks.

Pronounced: mis-DREE-vuss
Possible Moves: Growl, Psywave, Spite, Astonish, Confuse Ray, Mean Look, Hex, Psybeam, Pain Split, Payback, Shadow Ball, Perish Song, Grudge, Power Gem
Type: Ghost
Height: 2' 04"
Weight: 2.2 lbs.
Region: Johto

MISDREAVUS

MISMAGIUS

MISMAGIUS
MAGICAL POKÉMON

While most of Mismagius's chants can cause pain and headaches, some of them are known to bring happiness.

Pronounced: mis-MAG-ee-us
Possible Moves: Lucky Chant, Magical Leaf, Growl, Psywave, Spite, Astonish
Type: Ghost
Height: 2' 11"
Weight: 9.7 lbs.
Region: Sinnoh

MISDREAVUS

MISMAGIUS

MOLTRES
FLAME POKÉMON

The appearance of Moltres, a Legendary Pokémon, usually heralds the fact that spring is on its way.

Pronounced: MOLE-trace

Possible Moves: Wing Attack, Ember, Fire Spin, Agility, Endure, AncientPower, Flamethrower, Safeguard, Air Slash, Roost, Heat Wave, SolarBeam, Sky Attack, Sunny Day

Type: Fire-Flying

Height: 6' 07"

Weight: 132.3 lbs.

Region: Kanto

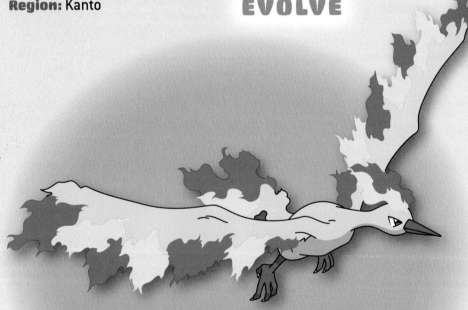

LEGENDARY
POKÉMON

MONFERNO
PLAYFUL POKÉMON

Monferno has been known to use the fire on its tail strategically to make itself appear larger. This helps keep foes at a distance.

Pronounced: mon-FERN-oh
Possible Moves: Scratch, Leer, Ember, Taunt, Mach Punch, Fury Swipes, Flame Wheel, Feint, Torment, Close Combat, Fire Spin, Acrobatics, Slack Off, Flare Blitz
Type: Fire-Fighting
Height: 2' 11"
Weight: 48.5 lbs.
Region: Sinnoh

CHIMCHAR → MONFERNO → INFERNAPE

MOTHIM
MOTH POKÉMON

Mothim are always in search of honey. They're on the go so much that they won't take the time to make nests. Sometimes, this Pokémon will even steal honey from Combee.

Pronounced: MAH-thum

Possible Moves: Tackle, Protect, Bug Bite, Hidden Power, Confusion, Gust, PoisonPowder, Psybeam, Camouflage, Silver Wind, Air Slash, Psychic, Bug Buzz, Quiver Dance

Type: Bug-Flying

Height: 2' 11"

Weight: 51.4 lbs.

Region: Sinnoh

BURMY ♂

MOTHIM

MR. MIME
BARRIER POKÉMON

By using certain pantomime gestures, Mr. Mime can build invisible solid walls.

Pronounced: MIS-ter MIME
Possible Moves: Magical Leaf, Quick Guard, Wide Guard, Power Swap, Guard Swap, Barrier, Confusion, Copycat, Meditate, Encore, DoubleSlap, Mimic, Light Screen, Reflect, Psybeam, Substitute, Recycle, Trick, Psychic, Role Play, Baton Pass, Safeguard
Type: Psychic
Height: 4' 03"
Weight: 120.1 lbs.
Region: Kanto

MIME JR.   MR. MIME

MUDKIP
MUD FISH POKÉMON

Mudkip uses its strength to lift heavy boulders. The fin on top of its head can sense the flow of water.

Pronounced: MUD-kip
Possible Moves: Tackle, Growl, Mud-Slap, Water Gun, Bide, Foresight, Mud Sport, Take Down, Whirlpool, Protect, Hydro Pump, Endeavor
Type: Water   **Height:** 1' 04"   **Weight:** 16.8 lbs.
Region: Hoenn

MUDKIP

MARSHTOMP

SWAMPERT

MUK
SLUDGE POKÉMON

The fluid that comes out of Muk is so toxic it can kill plants and trees instantly.

Pronounced: MUCK
Possible Moves: Poison Gas, Pound, Harden, Mud-Slap, Disable, Minimize, Sludge, Mud Bomb, Fling, Screech, Sludge Bomb, Acid Armor, Sludge Wave, Gunk Shot, Memento
Type: Poison
Height: 3' 11"
Weight: 66.1 lbs.
Region: Kanto

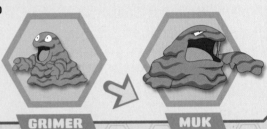

GRIMER > MUK

MUNCHLAX
BIG EATER POKÉMON

Munchlax can swallow its food whole and eats the equivalent of its body weight every day. It hoards food, too. Sometimes, it hides spare food in its long hair, and then forgets it's there.

Pronounced: MUNCH-lacks
Possible Moves: Metronome, Odor Sleuth, Tackle, Defense Curl, Amnesia, Lick, Recycle, Screech, Chip Away, Stockpile, Swallow, Body Slam, Fling, Rollout, Natural Gift, Snatch, Last Resort
Type: Normal
Height: 2' 00"   **Weight:** 231.5 lbs.
Region: Sinnoh

MUNCHLAX > SNORLAX

MUNNA
DREAM EATER POKÉMON

Munna always floats in the air. It eats the dreams of people and Pokémon, and if a dream is eaten by Munna, the dreamer forgets what it was about. When Munna eats a nice dream, it emits a pinkish mist.

Pronounced: MOON-nuh
Possible Moves: Psywave, Defense Curl, Lucky Chant, Yawn, Psybeam, Imprison, Moonlight, Hypnosis, Zen Headbutt, Synchronoise, Nightmare, Future Sight, Calm Mind, Psychic, Dream Eater, Telekinesis, Stored Power
Type: Psychic
Height: 2' 00"
Weight: 51.4 lbs.
Region: Unova

MUNNA MUSHARNA

MURKROW
DARKNESS POKÉMON

Night travelers know to avoid Murkrow. This Pokémon is rumored to bring bad luck to those that it lures into the forests.

Pronounced: MUR-crow
Possible Moves: Peck, Astonish, Pursuit, Haze, Wing Attack, Night Shade, Assurance, Taunt, Faint Attack, Mean Look, Foul Play, Tailwind, Sucker Punch, Torment, Quash
Type: Dark-Flying
Height: 1' 08"
Weight: 4.6 lbs.
Region: Johto

MURKROW   HONCHKROW

MUSHARNA
DROWSING POKÉMON

The mist from Musharna's forehead is filled with the dreams of people and Pokémon. Within this mist, Musharna can create the shapes of things from the dreams it's eaten.

Pronounced: moo-SHAHR-nuh
Possible Moves: Defense Curl, Lucky Chant, Psybeam, Hypnosis
Type: Psychic
Height: 3' 07"
Weight: 133.4 lbs.
Region: Unova

MUNNA

MUSHARNA

NATU
TINY BIRD POKÉMON

Natu is so agile that it can pick food from cacti without hitting buds or spines, even though it seems to skip while it moves.

Pronounced: NAH-too
Possible Moves: Peck, Leer, Night Shade, Teleport, Lucky Chant, Miracle Eye, Me First, Confuse Ray, Wish, Psycho Shift, Future Sight, Stored Power, Ominous Wind, Power Swap, Guard Swap, Psychic
Type: Psychic-Flying
Height: 0' 08"   **Weight:** 4.4 lbs.
Region: Johto

NATU

XATU

NIDOKING
DRILL POKÉMON

Talk about might—the tail on this ferocious Pokémon can snap a telephone pole like a toothpick.

Pronounced: NEE-doe-king
Possible Moves: Peck, Focus Energy, Double Kick, Poison Sting, Chip Away, Thrash, Earth Power, Megahorn
Type: Poison-Ground
Height: 4' 07"   **Weight:** 136.7 lbs.
Region: Kanto

NIDORAN ♂   NIDORINO   NIDOKING

NIDOQUEEN
DRILL POKÉMON

This queen is a fierce protector of its young—it will defend a lair with its life. It is formidable, with iron-hard scales all over its body.

Pronounced: NEE-doe-queen
Possible Moves: Scratch, Tail Whip, Double Kick, Poison Sting, Chip Away, Body Slam, Earth Power, Superpower
Type: Poison-Ground   **Height:** 4' 03"   **Weight:** 132.3 lbs.
Region: Kanto

NIDORAN ♀   NIDORINA   NIDOQUEEN

NIDORAN ♂
POISON PIN POKÉMON

How does a Nidoran ♂ know when prey is around? It raises its ears above the grass line. It keeps enemies away with the toxic horn on its head.

Pronounced: NEE-door-ann
Possible Moves: Leer, Peck, Focus Energy, Double Kick, Poison Sting, Fury Attack, Horn Attack, Helping Hand, Toxic Spikes, Flatter, Poison Jab, Captivate, Horn Drill
Type: Poison
Height: 1' 08"
Weight: 19.8 lbs.
Region: Kanto

NIDORAN ♂   NIDORINO   NIDOKING

NIDORAN ♀
POISON PIN POKÉMON

Nidoran ♀ doesn't like to fight, and it doesn't need to either—one pinprick of its poisonous barbs can be fatal.

Pronounced: NEE-door-ann
Possible Moves: Growl, Scratch, Tail Whip, Double Kick, Poison Sting, Fury Swipes, Bite, Helping Hand, Toxic Spikes, Flatter, Crunch, Captivate, Poison Fang
Type: Poison
Height: 1' 04"
Weight: 15.4 lbs.
Region: Kanto

NIDORAN ♀ > NIDORINA > NIDOQUEEN

NIDORINA
POISON PIN POKÉMON

When Nidorina senses danger, the barbs on its body are raised. You can tell the gender of these Pokémon by the size of the barbs—a Nidorina grows them slower and shorter than a Nidorino.

Pronounced: nee-door-EE-nuh
Possible Moves: Growl, Scratch, Tail Whip, Double Kick, Poison Sting, Fury Swipes, Bite, Helping Hand, Toxic Spikes, Flatter, Crunch, Captivate, Poison Fang
Type: Poison   **Height:** 2' 07"   **Weight:** 44.1 lbs.
Region: Kanto

NIDORAN ♀ > NIDORINA > NIDOQUEEN

NIDORINO
POISON PIN POKÉMON

This Pokémon is an angry one—it stabs out at foes with its poison horn.

Pronounced: nee-door-EE-no
Possible Moves: Leer, Peck, Focus Energy, Double Kick, Poison Sting, Fury Attack, Horn Attack, Helping Hand, Toxic Spikes, Flatter, Poison Jab, Captivate, Horn Drill
Type: Poison
Height: 2' 11"
Weight: 43.0 lbs.
Region: Kanto

NIDORAN ♂   NIDORINO   NIDOKING

NINCADA
TRAINEE POKÉMON

The underground-dwelling Nincada uses the antennae on top of its head (instead of its eyes) to sense its surroundings.

Pronounced: nin-KAH-da
Possible Moves: Scratch, Harden, Leech Life, Sand-Attack, Fury Swipes, Mind Reader, False Swipe, Mud-Slap, Metal Claw, Dig
Type: Bug-Ground
Height: 1' 08"
Weight: 12.1 lbs.
Region: Hoenn

NINCADA

NINJASK   SHEDINJA

NINETALES
FOX POKÉMON

With a life span of a thousand years, its nine tails are said to contain mystic power.

Pronounced: NINE-tails
Possible Moves: Nasty Plot, Ember, Quick Attack, Confuse Ray, Safeguard
Type: Fire
Height: 3' 07"
Weight: 43.9 lbs.
Region: Kanto

VULPIX

NINETALES

NINJASK
NINJA POKÉMON

You can usually find this Pokémon around tree sap, but look fast—it moves so quickly that it is virtually unnoticeable.

Pronounced: NIN-jask
Possible Moves: Bug Bite, Scratch, Harden, Leech Life, Sand-Attack, Fury Swipes, Mind Reader, Double Team, Fury Cutter, Screech, Swords Dance, Slash, Agility, Baton Pass, X-Scissor
Type: Bug-Flying
Height: 2' 07"
Weight: 26.5 lbs.
Region: Hoenn

NINCADA

NINJASK

SHEDINJA

NOCTOWL
OWL POKÉMON

Even in the most minimal levels of light, Noctowl can use its super-sharp eyesight to find objects.

Pronounced: NAHK-towl
Possible Moves: Sky Attack, Tackle, Growl, Foresight, Hypnosis, Peck, Uproar, Reflect, Confusion, Echoed Voice, Take Down, Air Slash, Zen Headbutt, Synchronoise, Extrasensory, Psycho Shift, Roost, Dream Eater
Type: Normal-Flying
Height: 5' 03"
Weight: 89.9 lbs.
Region: Johto

HOOTHOOT   NOCTOWL

NOSEPASS
COMPASS POKÉMON

Because its nose is a magnet, Nosepass will always face north.

Pronounced: NOSE-pass
Possible Moves: Tackle, Harden, Rock Throw, Block, Thunder Wave, Rock Slide, Sandstorm, Rest, Power Gem, Discharge, Stone Edge, Zap Cannon, Lock-On, Earth Power
Type: Rock
Height: 3' 03"
Weight: 213.8 lbs.
Region: Hoenn

NOSEPASS

PROBOPASS

NUMEL
NUMB POKÉMON

Numel's humped back stores extremely hot magma. When it rains, the magma cools and Numel slows to a crawl.

Pronounced: NUM-mull
Possible Moves: Growl, Tackle, Ember, Magnitude, Focus Energy, Flame Burst, Take Down, Amnesia, Lava Plume, Earth Power, Earthquake, Flamethrower, Double-Edge
Type: Fire-Ground
Height: 2' 04"　**Weight:** 52.9 lbs.
Region: Hoenn

NUMEL　CAMERUPT

NUZLEAF
WILY POKÉMON

If you are in the deep forests Nuzleaf inhabits and you hear the sound of its grass flute, you will become uneasy.

Pronounced: NUZ-leaf
Possible Moves: Razor Leaf, Pound, Harden, Growth, Nature Power, Fake Out, Torment, Faint Attack, Razor Wind, Swagger, Extrasensory
Type: Grass-Dark　**Height:** 3' 03"
Weight: 61.7 lbs.
Region: Hoenn

SEEDOT　NUZLEAF　SHIFTRY

OCTILLERY
JET POKÉMON

Octillery uses its suction cups to grip its prey, which it finds among gaps in seafloor boulders.

Pronounced: ock-TILL-er-ree
Possible Moves: Gunk Shot, Rock Blast, Water Gun, Constrict, Psybeam, Aurora Beam, BubbleBeam, Focus Energy, Octazooka, Bullet Seed, Wring Out, Signal Beam, Ice Beam, Hyper Beam, Soak

Type: Water	**Height:** 2' 11"
Weight: 62.8 lbs.	**Region:** Johto

REMORAID

OCTILLERY

ODDISH
WEED POKÉMON

Oddish can plant its feet in the ground during the day, and will use them to sow seeds at night.

Pronounced: ODD-ish
Possible Moves: Absorb, Sweet Scent, Acid, PoisonPowder, Stun Spore, Sleep Powder, Mega Drain, Lucky Chant, Natural Gift, Moonlight, Giga Drain, Petal Dance
Type: Grass-Poison
Height: 1' 08"
Weight: 11.9 lbs.
Region: Kanto

ODDISH

GLOOM

VILEPLUME

BELLOSSOM

OMANYTE
SPIRAL POKÉMON

Scientists revived Omanyte from fossils.

Pronounced: OHM-uh-nite
Possible Moves: Constrict, Withdraw, Bite, Water Gun, Rollout, Leer, Mud Shot, Brine, Protect, Ancient-Power, Tickle, Rock Blast, Shell Smash, Hydro Pump
Type: Rock-Water
Height: 1' 04"
Weight: 16.5 lbs.
Region: Kanto

OMANYTE

OMASTAR

OMASTAR
SPIRAL POKÉMON

Because its shell is so large, this Pokémon was thought to be extinct.

Pronounced: AHM-uh-star
Possible Moves: Constrict, Withdraw, Bite, Water Gun, Rollout, Leer, Mud Shot, Brine, Protect, AncientPower, Spike Cannon, Tickle, Rock Blast, Shell Smash, Hydro Pump

Type: Rock-Water
Height: 3' 03"
Weight: 77.2 lbs.
Region: Kanto

OMANYTE

OMASTAR

ONIX
ROCK SNAKE POKÉMON

Onix can move at 50 miles per hour when burrowing. You can tell where Onix is by the vibrations.

Pronounced: ON-icks

Possible Moves: Mud Sport, Tackle, Harden, Bind, Screech, Rock Throw, Rage, Rock Tomb, Smack Down, Sandstorm, Rock Polish, Slam, Stealth Rock, DragonBreath, Curse, Iron Tail, Sand Tomb, Double-Edge, Stone Edge

Type: Rock-Ground

Height: 28' 10"

Weight: 463.0 lbs.

Region: Kanto

ONIX   STEELIX

OSHAWOTT
SEA OTTER POKÉMON

The detachable scalchop on Oshawott's stomach is made from the same material as claws. Oshawott uses the scalchop like a blade to slash at foes.

Pronounced: AH-shuh-wot

Possible Moves: Tackle, Tail Whip, Water Gun, Water Sport, Focus Energy, Razor Shell, Fury Cutter, Water Pulse, Revenge, Aqua Jet, Encore, Aqua Tail, Retaliate, Swords Dance, Hydro Pump

Type: Water

Height: 1' 08"

Weight: 13.0 lbs.

Region: Unova

OSHAWOTT   DEWOTT   SAMUROTT

PACHIRISU
ELESQUIRREL POKÉMON

Pachirisu lives atop trees and will make electrified fur balls that it hides along with berries it collects. For defense, it shoots electricity from its tail.

Pronounced: patch-ee-REE-su
Possible Moves: Growl, Bide, Quick Attack, Charm, Spark, Endure, Swift, Electro Ball, Sweet Kiss, Thunder Wave, Super Fang, Discharge, Last Resort, Hyper Fang
Type: Electric   **Height:** 1' 04"
Weight: 8.6 lbs.   **Region:** Sinnoh

DOES NOT EVOLVE

PALKIA
SPATIAL POKÉMON

This mythological creature is rumored to live in a gap in the spatial dimension. It has the ability to distort space.

Pronounced: PAL-kee-uh
Possible Moves: DragonBreath, Scary Face, Water Pulse, AncientPower, Slash, Power Gem, Aqua Tail, Dragon Claw, Earth Power, Aura Sphere, Aqua Tail, Spacial Rend, Hydro Pump
Type: Water-Dragon
Height: 13' 09"
Weight: 740.8 lbs.
Region: Sinnoh

LEGENDARY POKÉMON

DOES NOT EVOLVE

PALPITOAD
VIBRATION POKÉMON

Palpitoad can live in water or on land. It creates water waves or ground tremors by vibrating the bumps on its head. It snares prey with a long, sticky tongue.

Pronounced: PAL-pih-tohd
Possible Moves: Bubble, Growl, Supersonic, Round, BubbleBeam, Mud Shot, Aqua Ring, Uproar, Muddy Water, Rain Dance, Flail, Echoed Voice, Hydro Pump, Hyper Voice
Type: Water-Ground
Height: 2' 07"
Weight: 37.5 lbs.
Region: Unova

TYMPOLE → PALPITOAD → SEISMITOAD

PANPOUR
SPRAY POKÉMON

Panpour doesn't do well in dry environments. To keep itself damp, it stores water in its head tuft and uses its tail as a water-sprayer.

Pronounced: PAN-por
Possible Moves: Scratch, Leer, Lick, Water Gun, Fury Swipes, Water Sport, Bite, Scald, Taunt, Fling, Acrobatics, Brine, Recycle, Natural Gift, Crunch
Type: Water
Height: 2' 00"
Weight: 29.8 lbs.
Region: Unova

PANPOUR → SIMIPOUR

PANSAGE
GRASS MONKEY POKÉMON

Pansage lives deep in the forest. The edible leaf on its head has stress-relieving properties, and Pansage shares this leaf with tired-looking Pokémon.

Pronounced: PAN-sayj
Possible Moves: Scratch, Leer, Lick, Vine Whip, Fury Swipes, Leech Seed, Bite, Seed Bomb, Torment, Fling, Acrobatics, Grass Knot, Recycle, Natural Gift, Crunch
Type: Grass
Height: 2' 00"
Weight: 23.1 lbs.
Region: Unova

PANSAGE ➔ SIMISAGE

PANSEAR
HIGH TEMP POKÉMON

Pansear lives in volcanic caverns and uses the tuft on its head to roast berries. The inside of this tuft burns as hot as 600 degrees Fahrenheit if Pansear is angry.

Pronounced: PAN-seer
Possible Moves: Scratch, Leer, Lick, Incinerate, Fury Swipes, Yawn, Bite, Flame Burst, Amnesia, Fling, Acrobatics, Fire Blast, Recycle, Natural Gift, Crunch
Type: Fire
Height: 2' 00"
Weight: 24.3 lbs
Region: Unova

PANSEAR ➔ SIMISEAR

PARAS
MUSHROOM POKÉMON

Paras grows mushrooms on its back, and they grow along with Paras.

Pronounced: PAR-iss
Possible Moves: Scratch, Stun Spore, PoisonPowder, Leech Life, Fury Cutter, Spore, Slash, Growth, Giga Drain, Aromatherapy, Rage Powder, X-Scissor
Type: Bug-Grass
Height: 1' 00"
Weight: 11.9 lbs.
Region: Kanto

PARAS → PARASECT

PARASECT
MUSHROOM POKÉMON

The mushroom on its back eventually outgrows Parasect and scatters poisonous spores.

Pronounced: PAR-i-sect
Possible Moves: Cross Poison, Scratch, Stun Spore, PoisonPowder, Leech Life, Fury Cutter, Spore, Slash, Growth, Giga Drain, Aromatherapy, Rage Powder, X-Scissor
Type: Bug-Grass
Height: 3' 03"
Weight: 65.0 lbs.
Region: Kanto

PARAS → PARASECT

PATRAT
SCOUT POKÉMON

Patrat use their tails to communicate, and they keep watch over their nest in shifts. By storing food in cheek pouches, a Patrat can keep watch for days at a time.

Pronounced: pat-RAT
Possible Moves: Tackle, Leer, Bite, Bide, Detect, Sand-Attack, Crunch, Hypnosis, Super Fang, After You, Work Up, Hyper Fang, Mean Look, Baton Pass, Slam
Type: Normal
Height: 1' 08"   **Weight:** 25.6 lbs.
Region: Unova

PATRAT   WATCHOG

PAWNIARD
SHARP BLADE POKÉMON

Pawniard's body is made of blades. If its blades are dull from battling, it sharpens them on stones by the river. It fights under orders from Bisharp, clinging to prey and digging in its blades.

Pronounced: PAWN-yard
Possible Moves: Scratch, Leer, Fury Cutter, Torment, Faint Attack, Scary Face, Metal Claw, Slash, Assurance, Metal Sound, Embargo, Iron Defense, Night Slash, Iron Head, Swords Dance, Guillotine
Type: Dark-Steel
Height: 1' 08"
Weight: 22.5 lbs.
Region: Unova

PAWNIARD   BISHARP

PELIPPER
WATER BIRD POKÉMON

Pelipper will gather up prey in its mouth by dipping its large bill in the water. Pelipper also delivers mail in its bill to other Pokémon.

Pronounced: PEL-ip-purr
Possible Moves: Soak, Growl, Water Gun, Water Sport, Wing Attack, Supersonic, Mist, Water Pulse, Payback, Protect, Roost, Stockpile, Swallow, Spit Up, Fling, Tailwind, Hydro Pump, Hurricane
Type: Water-Flying
Height: 3' 11"   **Weight:** 61.7 lbs.
Region: Hoenn

WINGULL

PELIPPER

PERSIAN
CLASSY CAT POKÉMON

Persian is a very snobby Pokémon. The jewel on its head is usually the topic of conversation among its fans.

Pronounced: PURR-shin
Possible Moves: Switcheroo, Scratch, Growl, Bite, Fake Out, Fury Swipes, Screech, Faint Attack, Taunt, Power Gem, Slash, Nasty Plot, Assurance, Captivate, Night Slash, Feint
Type: Normal
Height: 3' 03"   **Weight:** 70.5 lbs.
Region: Kanto

MEOWTH

PERSIAN

PETILIL
BULB POKÉMON

The leaves on Petilil's head are very bitter, but reinvigorate a tired body if eaten. Since Petilil favors damp, nutrient-rich soil, its habitat is also a good place to grow plants.

Pronounced: PEH-tih-lil
Possible Moves: Absorb, Growth, Leech Seed, Sleep Powder, Mega Drain, Synthesis, Magical Leaf, Stun Spore, Giga Drain, Aromatherapy, Helping Hand, Energy Ball, Entrainment, Sunny Day, After You, Leaf Storm

Type: Grass
Weight: 14.6 lbs.
Height: 1' 08"
Region: Unova

PETILIL

LILLIGANT

PHANPY
LONG NOSE POKÉMON

Diminutive and cute, Phanpy is still capable of lifting an adult onto its back.

Pronounced: FAN-pee
Possible Moves: Odor Sleuth, Tackle, Growl, Defense Curl, Flail, Take Down, Rollout, Natural Gift, Slam, Endure, Charm, Last Resort, Double-Edge

Type: Ground
Height: 1' 08"
Weight: 73.9 lbs.
Region: Johto

PHANPY   DONPHAN

PHIONE
SEA DRIFTER POKÉMON

See that small bubble on Phione's head? This Pokémon inflates that sac to drift on the surface in warm seas and look for food. Phione always returns to the place where it was born.

Pronounced: fee-OWN-ay
Possible Moves: Bubble, Water Sport, Charm, Supersonic, BubbleBeam, Acid Armor, Whirlpool, Water Pulse, Aqua Ring, Dive, Rain Dance
Type: Water
Height: 1' 04"
Weight: 6.8 lbs.
Region: Sinnoh

MYTHICAL POKÉMON

DOES NOT EVOLVE

PICHU
TINY MOUSE POKÉMON

Pichu can only store small amounts of electricity in its cheeks, but it does play with others by touching tails and discharging power. Ouch!

Pronounced: PEE-choo
Possible Moves: ThunderShock, Charm, Tail Whip, Thunder Wave, Sweet Kiss, Nasty Plot
Type: Electric
Height: 1' 00"
Weight: 4.4 lbs.
Region: Johto

PICHU > **PIKACHU** > **RAICHU**

PIDGEOT
BIRD POKÉMON

Pidgeot commands the winds by whipping them up with its wings, bending even stout trees.

Pronounced: pid-JEE-ot
Possible Moves: Tackle, Sand-Attack, Gust, Quick Attack, Whirlwind, Twister, FeatherDance, Agility, Wing Attack, Roost, Tailwind, Mirror Move, Air Slash, Hurricane
Type: Normal-Flying   **Height:** 4' 11"   **Weight:** 87.1 lbs.
Region: Kanto

PIDGEY > **PIDGEOTTO** > **PIDGEOT**

PIDGEOTTO
BIRD POKÉMON

This Pokémon is very territorial, taking down prey with razor-sharp claws.

Pronounced: pid-JYO-toe
Possible Moves: Tackle, Sand-Attack, Gust, Quick Attack, Whirlwind, Twister, FeatherDance, Agility, Wing Attack, Roost, Tailwind, Mirror Move, Air Slash, Hurricane
Type: Normal-Flying
Height: 3' 07"
Weight: 66.1 lbs.
Region: Kanto

PIDGEY → PIDGEOTTO → PIDGEOT

PIDGEY
TINY BIRD POKÉMON

Pidgey is a flyer, not a fighter—but it will defend itself with ferocity when attacked.

Pronounced: PID-jee
Possible Moves: Tackle, Sand-Attack, Gust, Quick Attack, Whirlwind, Twister, FeatherDance, Agility, Wing Attack, Roost, Tailwind, Mirror Move, Air Slash, Hurricane
Type: Normal-Flying   **Height:** 1' 00"   **Weight:** 4.0 lbs.
Region: Kanto

PIDGEY → PIDGEOTTO → PIDGEOT

PIDOVE
TINY PIGEON POKÉMON

This city Pokémon is used to people, and many Pidove flock to parks and plazas. Pidove does its best to carry out its Trainer's orders, but doesn't always understand complicated commands.

Pronounced: pih-DUV

Possible Moves: Gust, Growl, Leer, Quick Attack, Air Cutter, Roost, Detect, Taunt, Air Slash, Razor Wind, FeatherDance, Swagger, Facade, Tailwind, Sky Attack

Type: Normal-Flying

Height: 1' 00"

Weight: 4.6 lbs.

Region: Unova

PIDOVE   TRANQUILL   UNFEZANT

PIGNITE
FIRE PIG POKÉMON

Anything it eats becomes fuel for the fire in its stomach. This fire burns hottest when Pignite is angry, making its moves faster and sharper. It gives off smoke when it is in trouble.

Pronounced: pig-NYTE

Possible Moves: Tackle, Tail Whip, Ember, Odor Sleuth, Defense Curl, Flame Charge, Arm Thrust, Smog, Rollout, Take Down, Heat Crash, Assurance, Flamethrower, Head Smash, Roar, Flare Blitz

Type: Fire-Fighting   **Height:** 3' 03"   **Weight:** 122.4 lbs.

Region: Unova

TEPIG   PIGNITE   EMBOAR

PIKACHU
MOUSE POKÉMON

This forest-dwelling Pokémon stores electricity in the pouches of its cheeks. From time to time, it will use an Electric-type move to charge up a fellow Pikachu that is injured or weak.

Pronounced: PEEK-uh-chew
Possible Moves: Growl, ThunderShock, Tail Whip, Thunder Wave, Quick Attack, Electro Ball, Double Team, Slam, Thunderbolt, Feint, Agility, Discharge, Light Screen, Thunder
Type: Electric
Height: 1' 04"
Weight: 13.2 lbs.
Region: Kanto

PICHU → PIKACHU → RAICHU

PILOSWINE
SWINE POKÉMON

Piloswine uses its sensitive nose to check its surroundings because it can't see through its hairy coat.

Pronounced: PILE-oh-swine

Possible Moves: AncientPower, Peck, Odor Sleuth, Mud Sport, Powder Snow, Mud-Slap, Endure, Mud Bomb, Icy Wind, Ice Fang, Take Down, Fury Attack, Earthquake, Mist, Blizzard, Amnesia

Type: Ice-Ground

Height: 3' 07"

Weight: 123.0 lbs.

Region: Johto

SWINUB > PILOSWINE > MAMOSWINE

PINECO
BAGWORM POKÉMON

Its pinecone-shaped shell protects it from other Pokémon that try to peck it by mistake.

Pronounced: PINE-co

Possible Moves: Tackle, Protect, Selfdestruct, Bug Bite, Take Down, Rapid Spin, Bide, Natural Gift, Spikes, Payback, Explosion, Iron Defense, Gyro Ball, Double-Edge

Type: Bug

Height: 2' 00"

Weight: 15.9 lbs.

Region: Johto

PINECO

FORRETRESS

PINSIR
STAG BEETLE POKÉMON

Pinsir can rip its prey in half with its pincers, and usually tosses what it can't tear—and tosses it far!

Pronounced: PIN-sir
Possible Moves: ViceGrip, Focus Energy, Bind, Seismic Toss, Harden, Revenge, Brick Break, Vital Throw, X-Scissor, Thrash, Swords Dance, Submission, Guillotine, Superpower
Type: Bug
Height: 4' 11"   **Weight:** 121.3 lbs.
Region: Kanto

DOES NOT EVOLVE

PIPLUP
PENGUIN POKÉMON

Piplup can dive in icy northern waters for ten minutes at a time. Seems like a lot of trouble, but Piplup is too proud to accept food from humans.

Pronounced: PIP-plup
Possible Moves: Pound, Growl, Bubble, Water Sport, Peck, BubbleBeam, Bide, Fury Attack, Brine, Whirlpool, Mist, Drill Peck, Hydro Pump
Type: Water   **Height:** 1' 04"   **Weight:** 11.5 lbs.
Region: Sinnoh

PIPLUP → PRINPLUP → EMPOLEON

PLUSLE
CHEERING POKÉMON

Plusle is the cheerleader of Pokémon, cheering on friends with pom-poms made of sparks. It drains power from telephone poles.

Pronounced: PLUS-ull
Possible Moves: Growl, Thunder Wave, Quick Attack, Helping Hand, Spark, Encore, Fake Tears, Copycat, Electro Ball, Swift, Charge, Thunder, Baton Pass, Agility, Last Resort, Nasty Plot, Entrainment
Type: Electric
Height: 1' 04"   **Weight:** 9.3 lbs.
Region: Hoenn

DOES
NOT
EVOLVE

POLITOED
FROG POKÉMON

This natural leader rallies others to its cause. When it cries, Poliwag seem to obey it.

Pronounced: POL-ee-toad
Possible Moves: BubbleBeam, Hypnosis, DoubleSlap, Perish Song, Swagger, Bounce, Hyper Voice
Type: Water
Height: 3' 07"
Weight: 74.7 lbs.
Region: Johto

POLIWAG   POLIWHIRL   POLITOED

POLIWAG
TADPOLE POKÉMON

Poliwag's skin is so transparent that you can see its organs, and it has a hard time functioning on its new feet.

Pronounced: POL-ee-wag
Possible Moves: Water Sport, Bubble, Hypnosis, Water Gun, DoubleSlap, Rain Dance, Body Slam, BubbleBeam, Mud Shot, Belly Drum, Wake-Up Slap, Hydro Pump, Mud Bomb
Type: Water
Height: 2' 00"
Weight: 27.3 lbs.
Region: Kanto

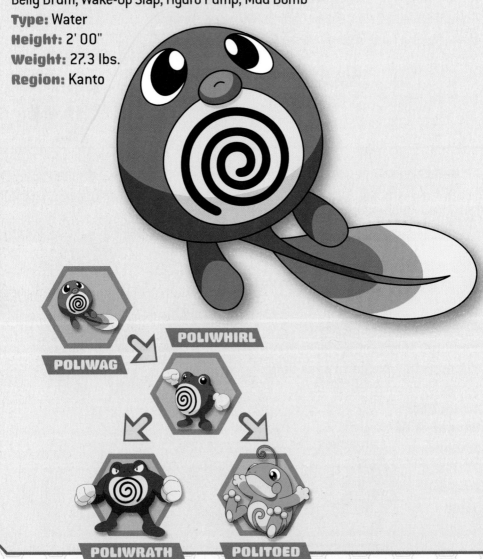

POLIWAG

POLIWHIRL

POLIWRATH

POLITOED

POLIWHIRL
TADPOLE POKÉMON

One can become sleepy by staring at the pattern on Poliwhirl's belly.

Pronounced: POL-ee-wurl
Possible Moves: Water Sport, Bubble, Hypnosis, Water Gun, DoubleSlap, Rain Dance, Body Slam, BubbleBeam, Mud Shot, Belly Drum, Wake-Up Slap, Hydro Pump, Mud Bomb
Type: Water
Height: 3' 03"
Weight: 44.1 lbs.
Region: Kanto

POLIWAG

POLIWHIRL

POLIWRATH

POLITOED

POLIWRATH
TADPOLE POKÉMON

Having great muscles, this Pokémon can swim for long periods of time, and frequents the warmer oceans.

Pronounced: POL-ee-rath
Possible Moves: BubbleBeam, Hypnosis, DoubleSlap, Submission, DynamicPunch, Mind Reader, Circle Throw
Type: Water-Fighting   **Height:** 4' 03"   **Weight:** 119.0 lbs.
Region: Kanto

POLIWAG   POLIWHIRL

POLIWRATH

PONYTA
FIRE HORSE POKÉMON

This stunning Pokémon has a fiery mane and tail that grow out right after birth. It spends its life roaming the hills and valleys where it lives.

Pronounced: PO-nee-tuh

Possible Moves: Growl, Tackle, Tail Whip, Ember, Flame Wheel, Stomp, Flame Charge, Fire Spin, Take Down, Inferno, Agility, Fire Blast, Bounce, Flare Blitz

Type: Fire

Height: 3' 03"

Weight: 66.1 lbs.

Region: Kanto

PONYTA

RAPIDASH

POOCHYENA
BITE POKÉMON

Poochyena never gives up, chasing down foes until they are utterly exhausted.

Pronounced: POO-chee-EH-nah

Possible Moves: Tackle, Howl, Sand-Attack, Bite, Odor Sleuth, Roar, Swagger, Assurance, Scary Face, Taunt, Embargo, Take Down, Sucker Punch, Crunch

Type: Dark

Height: 1' 08"

Weight: 30.0 lbs.

Region: Hoenn

POOCHYENA

MIGHTYENA

PORYGON
VIRTUAL POKÉMON

This Pokémon can travel through electronic space and was the first artificially created Pokémon.

Pronounced: POR-ee-gon

Possible Moves: Conversion 2, Tackle, Conversion, Sharpen, Psybeam, Agility, Recover, Magnet Rise, Signal Beam, Recycle, Discharge, Lock-On, Tri Attack, Magic Coat, Zap Cannon

Type: Normal
Height: 2' 07"
Weight: 80.5 lbs.
Region: Kanto

PORYGON → PORYGON2 → PORYGON-Z

PORYGON2
VIRTUAL POKÉMON

Porygon2 can actually work in space thanks to planetary development software loaded into it.

Pronounced: POR-ee-gon TOO

Possible Moves: Conversion 2, Tackle, Conversion, Defense Curl, Psybeam, Agility, Recover, Magnet Rise, Signal Beam, Recycle, Discharge, Lock-On, Tri Attack, Magic Coat, Zap Cannon, Hyper Beam

Type: Normal   **Height:** 2' 00"   **Weight:** 71.6 lbs.
Region: Johto

PORYGON → PORYGON2 → PORYGON-Z

PORYGON-Z
VIRTUAL POKÉMON

The additional software that was loaded into Porygon-Z to make it better actually caused it to act in odd and unexpected ways.

Pronounced: POR-ee-gon ZEE

Possible Moves: Trick Room, Conversion 2, Tackle, Conversion, Nasty Plot, Psybeam, Agility, Recover, Magnet Rise, Signal Beam, Embargo, Discharge, Lock-On, Tri Attack, Magic Coat, Zap Cannon, Hyper Beam

Type: Normal
Height: 2' 11"
Weight: 75.0 lbs.
Region: Sinnoh

PORYGON → PORYGON2 → PORYGON-Z

PRIMEAPE
PIG MONKEY POKÉMON

If you look into its eyes, your choices are flight or fight. Either way, Primeape will deliver a ferocious beating.

Pronounced: PRIME-ape

Possible Moves: Fling, Scratch, Low Kick, Leer, Focus Energy, Fury Swipes, Karate Chop, Seismic Toss, Screech, Assurance, Rage, Swagger, Cross Chop, Thrash, Punishment, Close Combat, Final Gambit

Type: Fighting
Weight: 70.5 lbs.
Height: 3' 03"
Region: Kanto

MANKEY → PRIMEAPE

PRINPLUP
PENGUIN POKÉMON

Prinplup looks for prey in icy waters and will use its wings to break the thickest of trees. It's a loner Pokémon, because each one believes it is the most important one among its kind.

Pronounced: PRIN-plup
Possible Moves: Tackle, Growl, Bubble, Water Sport, Peck, Metal Claw, BubbleBeam, Bide, Fury Attack, Brine, Whirlpool, Mist, Drill Peck, Hydro Pump
Type: Water
Height: 2' 07"
Weight: 50.7 lbs.
Region: Sinnoh

PIPLUP   PRINPLUP   EMPOLEON

PROBOPASS
COMPASS POKÉMON

You can feel the magnetism from this Pokémon on all fronts. It controls three small units called Mini-Noses.

Pronounced: PRO-bo-pass
Possible Moves: Magnet Rise, Gravity, Tackle, Iron Defense, Magnet Bomb, Block, Thunder Wave, Rock Slide, Sandstorm, Rest, Power Gem, Discharge, Stone Edge, Zap Cannon, Lock-On, Earth Power
Type: Rock-Steel
Height: 4' 07"
Weight: 749.6 lbs.
Region: Sinnoh

NOSEPASS   PROBOPASS

PSYDUCK
DUCK POKÉMON

When its headaches become unbearable, it will use weird powers—but it never remembers them later.

Pronounced: SYE-duck
Possible Moves: Water Sport, Scratch, Tail Whip, Water Gun, Disable, Confusion, Water Pulse, Fury Swipes, Screech, Soak, Psych Up, Zen Headbutt, Amnesia, Hydro Pump, Wonder Room
Type: Water
Height: 2' 07"
Weight: 43.2 lbs.
Region: Kanto

PSYDUCK

GOLDUCK

PUPITAR
HARD SHELL POKÉMON

By building up gases in its body, Pupitar can shoot itself up like a rocket.

Pronounced: PUE-puh-tar
Possible Moves: Bite, Leer, Sandstorm, Screech, Chip Away, Rock Slide, Scary Face, Thrash, Dark Pulse, Payback, Crunch, Earthquake, Stone Edge, Hyper Beam
Type: Rock-Ground   **Height:** 3' 11"   **Weight:** 335.1 lbs.
Region: Johto

LARVITAR   PUPITAR   TYRANITAR

PURRLOIN
DEVIOUS POKÉMON

Though Purrloin can attack with sharp claws, its cute act is a ruse to make opponents drop their guard. Purrloin then steals the target's items for fun, but the victims can't help but forgive it.

Pronounced: PUR-loyn

Possible Moves: Scratch, Growl, Assist, Sand-Attack, Fury Swipes, Pursuit, Torment, Fake Out, Hone Claws, Assurance, Slash, Captivate, Night Slash, Snatch, Nasty Plot, Sucker Punch

Type: Dark   **Height:** 1' 04"
Weight: 22.3 lbs.   **Region:** Unova

PURRLOIN

LIEPARD

PURUGLY
TIGER CAT POKÉMON

Purugly will make itself appear bulkier by squeezing its two tails around its waist. It is known to take over nests belonging to other Pokémon.

Pronounced: purr-UG-lee

Possible Moves: Fake Out, Scratch, Growl, Hypnosis, Faint Attack, Fury Swipes, Charm, Assist, Captivate, Slash, Swagger, Body Slam, Attract, Hone Claws

Type: Normal
Height: 3' 03"
Weight: 96.6 lbs.
Region: Sinnoh

GLAMEOW

PURUGLY

QUAGSIRE
WATER FISH POKÉMON

Quagsire is a sluggard that waits for prey to enter its mouth. It doesn't even care if it knocks its head on boats or river rocks.

Pronounced: KWAG-sire
Possible Moves: Water Gun, Tail Whip, Mud Sport, Mud Shot, Slam, Mud Bomb, Amnesia, Yawn, Earthquake, Rain Dance, Mist, Haze, Muddy Water
Type: Water-Ground
Height: 4' 07"
Weight: 165.3 lbs.
Region: Johto

WOOPER QUAGSIRE

QUILAVA
VOLCANO POKÉMON

When Quilava gets ready to fight, the flames around it will burn more intently, intimidating even the most stalwart foes.

Pronounced: kwil-LA-va
Possible Moves: Tackle, Leer, SmokeScreen, Ember, Quick Attack, Flame Wheel, Defense Curl, Swift, Flame Charge, Lava Plume, Flamethrower, Inferno, Rollout, Double-Edge, Eruption
Type: Fire
Height: 2' 11"
Weight: 41.9 lbs.
Region: Johto

CYNDAQUIL QUILAVA TYPHLOSION

QWILFISH
BALLOON POKÉMON

Although not a very good swimmer due to its corpulent form, Qwilfish is still capable of using its poison spines to defeat its foes.

Pronounced: KWIL-fish

Possible Moves: Spikes, Tackle, Poison Sting, Harden, Minimize, Water Gun, Rollout, Toxic Spikes, Stockpile, Spit Up, Revenge, Brine, Pin Missile, Take Down, Aqua Tail, Poison Jab, Destiny Bond, Hydro Pump

Type: Water-Poison

Height: 1' 08"

Weight: 8.6 lbs.

Region: Johto

DOES NOT EVOLVE

RAICHU
MOUSE POKÉMON

Raichu becomes aggressive if too much electricity is stored in its body. It can release 100,000 volts at a time.

Pronounced: RYE-chew
Possible Moves: ThunderShock, Tail Whip, Quick Attack, Thunderbolt
Type: Electric
Height: 2' 07"
Weight: 66.1 lbs.
Region: Kanto

PICHU

PIKACHU

RAICHU

RAIKOU
THUNDER POKÉMON

Using the rain clouds on its back, Raikou can shoot thunderbolts.

Pronounced: RYE-coo
Possible Moves: Bite, Leer, ThunderShock, Roar, Quick Attack, Spark, Reflect, Crunch, Thunder Fang, Discharge, Extrasensory, Rain Dance, Calm Mind, Thunder
Type: Electric
Height: 6' 03"
Weight: 392.4 lbs.
Region: Johto

LEGENDARY POKÉMON

DOES NOT EVOLVE

RALTS
FEELING POKÉMON

Cheerful people are more likely to see Ralts, which can sense emotions using the horn on its head.

Pronounced: RALTS

Possible Moves: Growl, Confusion, Double Team, Teleport, Lucky Chant, Magical Leaf, Heal Pulse, Calm Mind, Psychic, Imprison, Future Sight, Charm, Hypnosis, Dream Eater, Stored Power

Type: Psychic

Height: 1' 04"

Weight: 14.6 lbs.

Region: Hoenn

RALTS

⬇

KIRLIA

GARDEVOIR   GALLADE

RAMPARDOS
HEAD BUTT POKÉMON

Rampardos can take down forests with a headbutt that has enough power to knock over even the sturdiest of objects.

Pronounced: ram-PAR-dose
Possible Moves: Headbutt, Leer, Focus Energy, Pursuit, Take Down, Scary Face, Assurance, Chip Away, Endeavor, AncientPower, Zen Headbutt, Screech, Head Smash
Type: Rock
Height: 5' 03"
Weight: 226.0 lbs.
Region: Sinnoh

CRANIDOS → RAMPARDOS

RAPIDASH
FIRE HORSE POKÉMON

A very fast Pokémon, Rapidash can run at nearly 150 miles per hour. This speed causes its mane to sparkle, enhancing its beautiful appearance.

Pronounced: RAP-i-dash
Possible Moves: Poison Jab, Megahorn, Growl, Quick Attack, Tail Whip, Ember, Flame Wheel, Stomp, Flame Charge, Fire Spin, Take Down, Inferno, Agility, Fury Attack, Fire Blast, Bounce, Flare Blitz
Type: Fire
Height: 5' 07"
Weight: 209.4 lbs.
Region: Kanto

PONYTA → RAPIDASH

RATICATE
MOUSE POKÉMON

The teeth on this Pokémon aren't just for decoration. It whittles its fangs by gnawing on hard material, and its teeth have the power to gnaw through cinderblock walls.

Pronounced: RAT-i-kate
Possible Moves: Swords Dance, Tackle, Tail Whip, Quick Attack, Focus Energy, Bite, Pursuit, Hyper Fang, Sucker Punch, Scary Face, Crunch, Assurance, Super Fang, Double-Edge, Endeavor
Type: Normal   **Height:** 2' 04"
Weight: 40.8 lbs.   **Region:** Kanto

RATTATA

RATICATE

RATTATA
MOUSE POKÉMON

Don't let its small size fool you. Rattata is a survivor, able to live in almost any environment or extreme.

Pronounced: ruh-TA-tah
Possible Moves: Tackle, Tail Whip, Quick Attack, Focus Energy, Bite, Pursuit, Hyper Fang, Sucker Punch, Crunch, Assurance, Super Fang, Double-Edge, Endeavor

Type: Normal
Height: 1' 00"
Weight: 7.7 lbs.
Region: Kanto

RATTATA   RATICATE

RAYQUAZA
SKY HIGH POKÉMON

Rayquaza lives high above the ozone layer and is rarely seen by anyone.

Pronounced: ray-KWAZ-uh
Possible Moves: Twister, Scary Face, Crunch, Hyper Voice, Rest, Air Slash, AncientPower, Outrage, Dragon Dance, Fly, ExtremeSpeed, Hyper Beam, Dragon Pulse
Type: Dragon-Flying
Height: 23' 00"
Weight: 455.2 lbs.
Region: Hoenn

DOES NOT EVOLVE

LEGENDARY POKÉMON

REGICE
ICEBERG POKÉMON

Regice can control air measured at -328 degrees Fahrenheit, and its body is encased in ice from the ice age.

Pronounced: REDGE-ice
Possible Moves: Explosion, Stomp, Icy Wind, Curse, Superpower, AncientPower, Amnesia, Charge Beam, Lock-On, Zap Cannon, Ice Beam, Hammer Arm, Hyper Beam
Type: Ice
Height: 5' 11"
Weight: 385.8 lbs.
Region: Hoenn

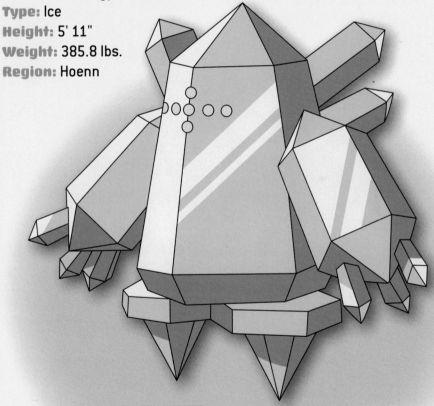

LEGENDARY
POKÉMON

DOES
NOT
EVOLVE

REGIGIGAS
COLOSSAL POKÉMON

According to legend, this mighty Pokémon towed continents with ropes. Some believe it formed Pokémon that resemble it out of a special ice mountain, magma, and rocks.

Pronounced: REDGE-ee-gee-gus
Possible Moves: Fire Punch, Ice Punch, ThunderPunch, Dizzy Punch, Knock Off, Confuse Ray, Foresight, Revenge, Wide Guard, Zen Headbutt, Payback, Crush Grip, Heavy Slam, Giga Impact
Type: Normal
Height: 12' 02"
Weight: 925.9 lbs.
Region: Sinnoh

DOES NOT EVOLVE

LEGENDARY
POKÉMON

REGIROCK
ROCK PEAK POKÉMON

Regirock can repair itself in any battle by picking up rocks and attaching them to itself. Its entire body is made up of rocks.

Pronounced: REDGE-ee-rock

Possible Moves: Explosion, Stomp, Rock Throw, Curse, Superpower, AncientPower, Iron Defense, Charge Beam, Lock-On, Zap Cannon, Stone Edge, Hammer Arm, Hyper Beam

Type: Rock

Height: 5' 07"

Weight: 507.1 lbs.

Region: Hoenn

DOES NOT EVOLVE

LEGENDARY POKÉMON

REGISTEEL
IRON POKÉMON

Registeel's body has been tempered underground for tens of thousands of years, so its body cannot be scratched.

Pronounced: REDGE-ee-steel

Possible Moves: Explosion, Stomp, Metal Claw, Curse, Superpower, AncientPower, Iron Defense, Amnesia, Charge Beam, Lock-On, Zap Cannon, Iron Head, Flash Cannon, Hammer Arm, Hyper Beam

Type: Steel

Height: 6' 03"

Weight: 451.9 lbs.

Region: Hoenn

DOES NOT EVOLVE

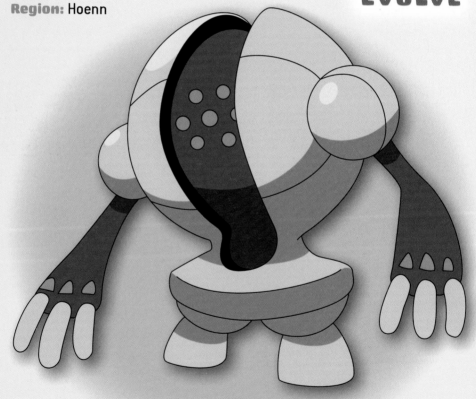

LEGENDARY POKÉMON

RELICANTH
LONGEVITY POKÉMON

This rare Pokémon was discovered during a deep-sea exploration. It has remained unchanged for over one hundred million years.

Pronounced: REL-uh-canth
Possible Moves: Tackle, Harden, Water Gun, Rock Tomb, Yawn, Take Down, Mud Sport, AncientPower, Double-Edge, Dive, Rest, Hydro Pump, Head Smash
Type: Water-Rock
Height: 3' 03"   **Weight:** 51.6 lbs.
Region: Hoenn

DOES NOT EVOLVE

REMORAID
JET POKÉMON

Remoraid clings to Mantine to feed on their food scraps. It can also shoot down flying prey with forceful squirts from its mouth.

Pronounced: REM-oh-rade
Possible Moves: Water Gun, Lock-On, Psybeam, Aurora Beam, BubbleBeam, Focus Energy, Bullet Seed, Water Pulse, Signal Beam, Ice Beam, Hyper Beam, Soak
Type: Water
Height: 2' 00"
Weight: 26.5 lbs.
Region: Johto

REMORAID → OCTILLERY

RESHIRAM
VAST WHITE POKÉMON

Reshiram is mentioned in myths. The flame from its tail can sear everything around it, and when that tail flares, the heat stirs the atmosphere and alters weather worldwide.

Pronounced: RESH-i-ram
Possible Moves: Fire Fang, Dragon Rage, Imprison, AncientPower, Flamethrower, DragonBreath, Slash, Extrasensory, Fusion Flare, Dragon Pulse, Imprison, Crunch, Fire Blast, Outrage, Hyper Voice, Blue Flare
Type: Dragon-Fire
Height: 10' 06"
Weight: 727.5 lbs.
Region: Unova

**DOES
NOT
EVOLVE**

**LEGENDARY
POKÉMON**

REUNICLUS
MULTIPLYING POKÉMON

Reuniclus controls arms with a grip strong enough to crush rock. When it shakes hands with another Reuniclus, a network is created between their brains. This network boosts their psychic power.

Pronounced: ree-yoo-NEE-klus
Possible Moves: Psywave, Reflect, Rollout, Snatch, Hidden Power, Light Screen, Charm, Recover, Psyshock, Endeavor, Future Sight, Pain Split, Psychic, Dizzy Punch, Skill Swap, Heal Block, Wonder Room
Type: Psychic
Height: 3' 03"
Weight: 44.3 lbs.
Region: Unova

SOLOSIS ➔ DUOSION ➔ REUNICLUS

RHYDON
DRILL POKÉMON

Rhydon can use the horn on its head to barrel through thick rock. It is slightly smarter than Rhyhorn.

Pronounced: RYE-don
Possible Moves: Horn Attack, Tail Whip, Stomp, Fury Attack, Scary Face, Rock Blast, Bulldoze, Chip Away, Take Down, Hammer Arm, Drill Run, Stone Edge, Earthquake, Horn Drill, Megahorn
Type: Ground-Rock   **Height:** 6' 03"   **Weight:** 264.6 lbs.
Region: Kanto

 ➔  ➔

RHYHORN   RHYDON   RHYPERIOR

RHYHORN
SPIKES POKÉMON

Covered in thick hide and able to take down buildings, this Pokémon is not known for its smarts.

Pronounced: RYE-horn
Possible Moves: Horn Attack, Tail Whip, Stomp, Fury Attack, Scary Face, Rock Blast, Bulldoze, Chip Away, Take Down, Drill Run, Stone Edge, Earthquake, Horn Drill, Megahorn
Type: Ground-Rock
Height: 3' 03"
Weight: 253.5 lbs.
Region: Kanto

RHYHORN | RHYDON | RHYPERIOR

RHYPERIOR
DRILL POKÉMON

Rhyperior uses its muscles to shoot rocks (and sometimes Geodude) through holes in its palms.

Pronounced: RYE-peer-ee-urr
Possible Moves: Poison Jab, Horn Attack, Tail Whip, Stomp, Fury Attack, Scary Face, Rock Blast, Chip Away, Take Down, Hammer Arm, Drill Run, Stone Edge, Earthquake, Horn Drill, Megahorn, Rock Wrecker
Type: Ground-Rock   **Height:** 7' 10"   **Weight:** 623.5 lbs.
Region: Sinnoh

RHYHORN | RHYDON | RHYPERIOR

RIOLU
EMANATION POKÉMON

Riolu is very agile. It may look small, but it's extremely powerful. You can gauge its emotion from the aura that projects from its body.

Pronounced: ree-OH-loo
Possible Moves: Quick Attack, Foresight, Endure, Counter, Force Palm, Feint, Reversal, Screech, Copycat, Nasty Plot, Final Gambit
Type: Fighting   **Height:** 2' 04"
Weight: 44.5 lbs.
Region: Sinnoh

RIOLU

LUCARIO

ROGGENROLA
MANTLE POKÉMON

First discovered a hundred years ago in an earthquake fissure, Roggenrola has a body hard as steel from being compressed underground. Each Roggenrola has a hexagonal ear and an internal energy core.

Pronounced: rah-gen-ROH-lah
Possible Moves: Tackle, Harden, Sand-Attack, Headbutt, Rock Blast, Mud-Slap, Iron Defense, Smack Down, Rock Slide, Stealth Rock, Sandstorm, Stone Edge, Explosion
Type: Rock   **Height:** 1' 04"   **Weight:** 39.7 lbs.
Region: Unova

ROGGENROLA

BOLDORE

GIGALITH

ROSELIA
THORN POKÉMON

The flowers on Roselia's arms have toxic thorns. When raised on clean drinking water, they are known to grow beautifully colored flowers.

Pronounced: roh-ZEH-lee-uh
Possible Moves: Absorb, Growth, Poison Sting, Stun Spore, Mega Drain, Leech Seed, Magical Leaf, GrassWhistle, Giga Drain, Toxic Spikes, Sweet Scent, Ingrain, Toxic, Petal Dance, Aromatherapy, Synthesis
Type: Grass-Poison
Height: 1' 00"
Weight: 4.4 lbs.
Region: Hoenn

BUDEW > ROSELIA > ROSERADE

ROSERADE
BOUQUET POKÉMON

Roserade will hide the whips in its arms until it is ready to attack its foes. It attracts its prey by emitting a sweet-smelling aroma.

Pronounced: ROSE-raid
Possible Moves: Weather Ball, Poison Sting, Mega Drain, Magical Leaf, Sweet Scent
Type: Grass-Poison   **Height:** 2' 11"
Weight: 32.0 lbs.   **Region:** Sinnoh

BUDEW > ROSELIA > ROSERADE

ROTOM
PLASMA POKÉMON

This destructive little Pokémon gets into electronic devices and causes lots of damage, which is easy for Rotom since it is composed of plasma.

Pronounced: ROW-tom
Possible Moves: Trick, Astonish, ThunderShock, Confuse Ray, Uproar, Double Team, Shock Wave, Ominous Wind, Substitute, Electro Ball, Hex, Charge, Discharge
Type: Electric-Ghost
Height: 1' 00"   **Weight:** 0.7 lbs.
Region: Sinnoh

DOES NOT EVOLVE

RUFFLET
EAGLET POKÉMON

Rufflet bravely and fearlessly challenges any opponent, no matter how powerful, and it grows stronger from frequent battles. It crushes berries in its talons.

Pronounced: RUF-lit
Possible Moves: Peck, Leer, Fury Attack, Wing Attack, Hone Claws, Scary Face, Aerial Ace, Slash, Defog, Tailwind, Air Slash, Crush Claw, Sky Drop, Whirlwind, Brave Bird, Thrash
Type: Normal-Flying
Height: 1' 08"
Weight: 23.1 lbs.
Region: Unova

RUFFLET → BRAVIARY

259

SABLEYE
DARKNESS POKÉMON

Sableye's eyes have been transformed into gemstones as a result of its steady diet of gems. It loves the darkness of caves.

Pronounced: SAY-bull-eye
Possible Moves: Leer, Scratch, Foresight, Night Shade, Astonish, Fury Swipes, Fake Out, Detect, Shadow Sneak, Knock Off, Faint Attack, Punishment, Shadow Claw, Power Gem, Confuse Ray, Foul Play, Zen Headbutt, Shadow Ball, Mean Look
Type: Dark-Ghost
Height: 1' 08"   **Weight:** 24.3 lbs.
Region: Hoenn

DOES NOT EVOLVE

SALAMENCE
DRAGON POKÉMON

Because its pre-evolved form, Bagon, always dreamed of flying, Salamence's cellular structure changed: It grew wings and is able to fly.

Pronounced: SAL-uh-mence
Possible Moves: Fire Fang, Thunder Fang, Rage, Bite, Leer, Headbutt, Focus Energy, Ember, Protect, DragonBreath, Zen Headbutt, Scary Face, Fly, Crunch, Dragon Claw, Double-Edge, Dragon Tail
Type: Dragon-Flying   **Height:** 4' 11"   **Weight:** 226.2 lbs.
Region: Hoenn

BAGON   SHELGON   SALAMENCE

SAMUROTT
FORMIDABLE POKÉMON

Samurott's cry intimidates foes, and its glare silences them. Its huge blade, drawn from the armor on its forelegs, can take down an opponent in one hit.

Pronounced: SAM-uh-rot
Possible Moves: Megahorn, Tackle, Tail Whip, Water Gun, Water Sport, Focus Energy, Razor Shell, Fury Cutter, Water Pulse, Revenge, Aqua Jet, Slash, Encore, Aqua Tail, Retaliate, Swords Dance, Hydro Pump
Type: Water
Height: 4' 11"
Weight: 208.6 lbs.
Region: Unova

OSHAWOTT → DEWOTT → SAMUROTT

SANDILE
DESERT CROC POKÉMON

Sandile lives buried in the sun-warmed sand that keeps its body temperature from dropping. Only its nose and eyes are exposed, but a dark membrane protects its eyes from the sun.

Pronounced: SAN-dyle
Possible Moves: Leer, Rage, Bite, Sand-Attack, Torment, Sand Tomb, Assurance, Mud-Slap, Embargo, Swagger, Crunch, Dig, Scary Face, Foul Play, Sandstorm, Earthquake, Thrash
Type: Ground-Dark
Height: 2' 04"
Weight: 33.5 lbs.
Region: Unova

SANDILE

KROKOROK

KROOKODILE

SANDSHREW
MOUSE POKÉMON

This Pokémon curls into a defensive ball when attacked, and survives in mostly arid areas.

Pronounced: SAND-shroo
Possible Moves: Scratch, Defense Curl, Sand-Attack, Poison Sting, Rapid Spin, Swift, Fury Swipes, Rollout, Fury Cutter, Sand Tomb, Slash, Gyro Ball, Sandstorm
Type: Ground
Height: 2' 00"   **Weight:** 26.5 lbs.
Region: Kanto

SANDSHREW

SANDSLASH

SANDSLASH
MOUSE POKÉMON

Sandslash uses the sharp spines on its back to damage foes, curling into a ball and rolling into them when attacked.

Pronounced: SAND-slash

Possible Moves: Scratch, Defense Curl, Sand-Attack, Poison Sting, Rapid Spin, Swift, Fury Swipes, Rollout, Crush Claw, Fury Cutter, Sand Tomb, Slash, Gyro Ball, Sandstorm

Type: Ground

Height: 3' 03"   **Weight:** 65.0 lbs.

Region: Kanto

SANDSHREW

SANDSLASH

SAWK
KARATE POKÉMON

When Sawk trains in the mountains, the sound of its punches hitting boulders and trees can be heard far away—and if its training is disturbed, it gets angry! By tying its belt, it psyches itself up and makes its punches more powerful.

Pronounced: SAWK

Possible Moves: Rock Smash, Leer, Bide, Focus Energy, Double Kick, Low Sweep, Counter, Karate Chop, Brick Break, Bulk Up, Retaliate, Endure, Quick Guard, Close Combat, Reversal

Type: Fighting

Height: 4' 07"

Weight: 112.4 lbs.

Region: Unova

DOES NOT EVOLVE

SAWSBUCK
SEASON POKÉMON

People track the changing seasons by looking at Sawsbuck's horns—not only does Sawsbuck migrate with the seasons, the plants on its horns vary with the seasons as well. The leader of a herd has impressive horns.

Pronounced: SAWZ-buk
Possible Moves: Megahorn, Tackle, Camouflage, Growl, Sand-Attack, Double Kick, Leech Seed, Faint Attack, Take Down, Jump Kick, Aromatherapy, Energy Ball, Charm, Horn Leech, Nature Power, Double-Edge, SolarBeam
Type: Normal-Grass
Height: 6' 03"
Weight: 203.9 lbs.
Region: Unova

Spring Form

Winter Form

Summer Form

Autumn Form

DEERLING

SAWSBUCK

SCEPTILE
FOREST POKÉMON

Unmatched in jungle combat, Sceptile can take down trees using the razor-sharp leaves on its arms.

Pronounced: SEP-tile
Possible Moves: Night Slash, Pound, Leer, Absorb, Quick Attack, X-Scissor, Pursuit, Screech, Leaf Blade, Agility, Slam, Detect, False Swipe, Leaf Storm
Type: Grass
Height: 5' 07"
Weight: 115.1 lbs.
Region: Hoenn

TREECKO > GROVYLE > SCEPTILE

SCIZOR
PINCER POKÉMON

Scizor intimidates its foes by raising its pincers, which have a distinctive eye-shaped pattern on them.

Pronounced: SI-zor
Possible Moves: Bullet Punch, Quick Attack, Leer, Focus Energy, Pursuit, False Swipe, Agility, Metal Claw, Fury Cutter, Slash, Razor Wind, Iron Defense, X-Scissor, Night Slash, Double Hit, Iron Head, Swords Dance, Feint
Type: Bug-Steel
Height: 5' 11"
Weight: 260.1 lbs.
Region: Johto

SCYTHER > SCIZOR

SCOLIPEDE
MEGAPEDE POKÉMON

This aggressive Pokémon poisons targets by grabbing them with the claws around its neck. When it pursues a foe, it moves swiftly and attacks with its horns.

Pronounced: SKOH-lih-peed
Possible Moves: Megahorn, Defense Curl, Rollout, Poison Sting, Screech, Pursuit, Protect, Poison Tail, Bug Bite, Venoshock, Baton Pass, Agility, Steamroller, Toxic, Rock Climb, Double-Edge
Type: Bug-Poison
Height: 8' 02"
Weight: 442.0 lbs.
Region: Unova

VENIPEDE → WHIRLIPEDE → SCOLIPEDE

SCRAFTY
HOODLUM POKÉMON

Scrafty spits acidic liquid and uses kicking attacks to smash concrete blocks. A group of Scrafty, led by the one with the biggest crest, will attack anyone who enters their territory.

Pronounced: SKRAF-tee
Possible Moves: Leer, Low Kick, Sand-Attack, Faint Attack, Headbutt, Swagger, Brick Break, Payback, Chip Away, Hi Jump Kick, Scary Face, Crunch, Facade, Rock Climb, Focus Punch, Head Smash
Type: Dark-Fighting   **Height:** 3' 07"
Weight: 66.1 lbs.   **Region:** Unova

SCRAGGY → SCRAFTY

SCRAGGY
SHEDDING POKÉMON

Scraggy's skull is extremely thick. This Pokémon headbutts anyone who makes eye contact with it. It can shield itself by pulling its rubbery skin up to its neck.

Pronounced: SKRAG-ee
Possible Moves: Leer, Low Kick, Sand-Attack, Faint Attack, Headbutt, Swagger, Brick Break, Payback, Chip Away, Hi Jump Kick, Scary Face, Crunch, Facade, Rock Climb, Focus Punch, Head Smash
Type: Dark-Fighting
Height: 2' 00"   **Weight:** 26.0 lbs.
Region: Unova

SCRAGGY   SCRAFTY

SCYTHER
MANTIS POKÉMON

It is almost impossible to avoid Scyther's razor-sharp scythes because it moves like a ninja.

Pronounced: SYE-ther
Possible Moves: Vacuum Wave, Quick Attack, Leer, Focus Energy, Pursuit, False Swipe, Agility, Wing Attack, Fury Cutter, Slash, Razor Wind, Double Team, X-Scissor, Night Slash, Double Hit, Air Slash, Swords Dance, Feint
Type: Bug-Flying
Height: 4' 11"
Weight: 123.5 lbs.
Region: Kanto

SCYTHER   SCIZOR

SEADRA
DRAGON POKÉMON

Located in its fins and bones are ingredients used to make medicine—but its spine is used purely for protection.

Pronounced: SEE-druh
Possible Moves: Bubble, SmokeScreen, Leer, Water Gun, Focus Energy, BubbleBeam, Agility, Twister, Brine, Hydro Pump, Dragon Dance, Dragon Pulse
Type: Water
Height: 3' 11"
Weight: 55.1 lbs.
Region: Kanto

HORSEA → SEADRA →  KINGDRA

SEAKING
GOLDFISH POKÉMON

Seaking lives in boulders that it hollows out by using its horn. It will protect its Eggs with its life.

Pronounced: SEE-king
Possible Moves: Poison Jab, Peck, Tail Whip, Water Sport, Supersonic, Horn Attack, Water Pulse, Flail, Aqua Ring, Fury Attack, Waterfall, Horn Drill, Agility, Soak, Megahorn
Type: Water
Height: 4' 03"   **Weight:** 86.0 lbs.
Region: Kanto

GOLDEEN → SEAKING

SEALEO
BALL ROLL POKÉMON

Sealeo can learn different smells and textures by constantly spinning things on its nose.

Pronounced: SEEL-ee-oh
Possible Moves: Powder Snow, Growl, Water Gun, Encore, Ice Ball, Body Slam, Aurora Beam, Hail, Swagger, Rest, Snore, Blizzard, Sheer Cold
Type: Ice-Water
Height: 3' 07"
Weight: 193.1 lbs.
Region: Hoenn

SPHEAL → SEALEO → WALREIN

SEEDOT
ACORN POKÉMON

It has fun by dangling from tree branches and pretending to be an acorn, then scaring unsuspecting Pokémon.

Pronounced: SEE-dot
Possible Moves: Bide, Harden, Growth, Nature Power, Synthesis, Sunny Day, Explosion
Type: Grass
Height: 1' 08"
Weight: 8.8 lbs.
Region: Hoenn

SEEDOT → NUZLEAF → SHIFTRY

SEEL
SEA LION POKÉMON

The point on Seel's head is used to break ice while swimming below icebergs.

Pronounced: SEEL
Possible Moves: Headbutt, Growl, Water Sport, Icy Wind, Encore, Ice Shard, Rest, Aqua Ring, Aurora Beam, Aqua Jet, Brine, Take Down, Dive, Aqua Tail, Ice Beam, Safeguard, Hail
Type: Water
Height: 3' 07"
Weight: 198.4 lbs.
Region: Kanto

SEEL

DEWGONG

SEISMITOAD
VIBRATION POKÉMON

Seismitoad battles using vibrations: It powers up punches by vibrating the bumps on its fists, and it can smash a boulder with one blow. The bumps on its head shoot a paralyzing liquid.

Pronounced: SYZ-mih-tohd
Possible Moves: Bubble, Growl, Supersonic, Round, BubbleBeam, Mud Shot, Aqua Ring, Uproar, Muddy Water, Rain Dance, Acid, Flail, Drain Punch, Echoed Voice, Hydro Pump, Hyper Voice
Type: Water-Ground
Height: 4' 11"
Weight: 136.7 lbs.
Region: Unova

TYMPOLE

PALPITOAD

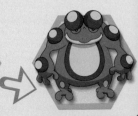

SEISMITOAD

SENTRET
SCOUT POKÉMON

Cautious by nature, Sentret will stand on its tail to scan wide areas for foes.

Pronounced: SEN-tret

Possible Moves: Scratch, Foresight, Defense Curl, Quick Attack, Fury Swipes, Helping Hand, Follow Me, Slam, Rest, Sucker Punch, Amnesia, Baton Pass, Me First, Hyper Voice

Type: Normal

Height: 2' 07"

Weight: 13.2 lbs.

Region: Johto

SENTRET → FURRET

SERPERIOR
REGAL POKÉMON

Serperior absorbs solar energy and magnifies it. When Serperior rears its head, its glare alone is enough to halt an opponent. Serperior battle at full force only against the toughest foes.

Pronounced: sur-PEER-ee-ur

Possible Moves: Tackle, Leer, Vine Whip, Wrap, Growth, Leaf Tornado, Leech Seed, Mega Drain, Slam, Leaf Blade, Coil, Giga Drain, Wring Out, Gastro Acid, Leaf Storm

Type: Grass   **Height:** 10' 10"   **Weight:** 138.9 lbs.

Region: Unova

SNIVY → SERVINE → SERPERIOR

SERVINE
GRASS SNAKE POKÉMON

Servine almost glides across the ground, and foes are baffled by its quick moves. It can slip into the shadow of thick vegetation to avoid attacks. It has superb technique when attacking with a vine whip.

Pronounced: SUR-vine
Possible Moves: Tackle, Leer, Vine Whip, Wrap, Growth, Leaf Tornado, Leech Seed, Mega Drain, Slam, Leaf Blade, Coil, Giga Drain, Wring Out, Gastro Acid, Leaf Storm
Type: Grass
Height: 2' 07"
Weight: 35.3 lbs.
Region: Unova

SNIVY → SERVINE → SERPERIOR

SEVIPER
FANG SNAKE POKÉMON

Seviper uses rocks to sharpen its tail for battle. Its greatest rival is Zangoose.

Pronounced: seh-VIE-per
Possible Moves: Wrap, Lick, Bite, Poison Tail, Screech, Glare, Crunch, Poison Fang, Swagger, Haze, Night Slash, Poison Jab, Venoshock, Wring Out, Coil
Type: Poison
Height: 8' 10"   **Weight:** 115.7 lbs.
Region: Hoenn

DOES
NOT
EVOLVE

SEWADDLE
SEWING POKÉMON

It sleeps with its head hidden in its hood. To make its own clothes, it chews up leaves and sews them together with a sticky thread from its mouth. Leavanny also make clothes to dress newly hatched Sewaddle.

Pronounced: seh-WAH-dul
Possible Moves: Tackle, String Shot, Bug Bite, Razor Leaf, Struggle Bug, Endure, Bug Buzz, Flail
Type: Bug-Grass
Height: 1' 00"
Weight: 5.5 lbs.
Region: Unova

SEWADDLE ❯ SWADLOON ❯ LEAVANNY

SHARPEDO
BRUTAL POKÉMON

Sharpedo have been clocked swimming at 75 mph, and their fangs, which can rip through sheet iron, are one of the reasons that this Pokémon is known as the Bully of the Sea.

Pronounced: shar-PEE-do
Possible Moves: Feint, Leer, Bite, Rage, Focus Energy, Scary Face, Ice Fang, Screech, Swagger, Assurance, Crunch, Slash, Aqua Jet, Taunt, Agility, Skull Bash, Night Slash
Type: Water-Dark
Height: 5' 11"
Weight: 195.8 lbs.
Region: Hoenn

CARVANHA ❯ SHARPEDO

273

SHAYMIN LAND FORME
GRATITUDE POKÉMON

Shaymin Land Forme has the power to clean its environment. It absorbs toxins into its body, then purifies them and turns them into light and water.

Pronounced: SHAY-min
Possible Moves: Growth, Magical Leaf, Leech Seed, Synthesis, Sweet Scent, Natural Gift, Worry Seed, Aromatherapy, Energy Ball, Sweet Kiss, Healing Wish, Seed Flare
Type: Grass
Height: 0' 08"
Weight: 4.6 lbs.
Region: Sinnoh

DOES NOT EVOLVE

MYTHICAL POKÉMON

SHAYMIN SKY FORME
GRATITUDE POKÉMON

Shaymin has the power to clean the environment in this forme, too. Once it has transformed, Shaymin Sky Forme flies off to find a new home.

Pronounced: SHAY-min
Possible Moves: Growth, Magical Leaf, Leech Seed, Quick Attack, Sweet Scent, Natural Gift, Worry Seed, Air Slash, Energy Ball, Sweet Kiss, Leaf Storm, Seed Flare
Type: Grass-Flying
Height: 1' 04"
Weight: 11.5 lbs.
Region: Sinnoh

DOES NOT EVOLVE

MYTHICAL POKÉMON

SHEDINJA
SHED POKÉMON

Shedinja came to life from a discarded shell; it is said that if you look into the crack on its back, it can steal your soul.

Pronounced: sheh-DIN-ja
Possible Moves: Scratch, Harden, Leech Life, Sand-Attack, Fury Swipes, Mind Reader, Spite, Confuse Ray, Shadow Sneak, Grudge, Heal Block, Shadow Ball
Type: Bug-Ghost
Height: 2' 07"
Weight: 2.6 lbs.
Region: Hoenn

NINCADA

NINJASK

SHEDINJA

SHELGON
ENDURANCE POKÉMON

Shelgon's shell acts like a cocoon and will peel off the day it evolves.

Pronounced: SHELL-gon
Possible Moves: Rage, Bite, Leer, Headbutt, Focus Energy, Ember, Protect, DragonBreath, Zen Headbutt, Scary Face, Crunch, Dragon Claw, Double-Edge
Type: Dragon
Height: 3' 07"
Weight: 243.6 lbs.
Region: Hoenn

BAGON

SHELGON

SALAMENCE

SHELLDER
BIVALVE POKÉMON

By opening and closing its two shells it can swim backward, and its large tongue always hangs out.

Pronounced: SHELL-der
Possible Moves: Tackle, Withdraw, Supersonic, Icicle Spear, Protect, Leer, Clamp, Ice Shard, Razor Shell, Aurora Beam, Whirlpool, Brine, Iron Defense, Ice Beam, Shell Smash, Hydro Pump
Type: Water
Height: 1' 00"
Weight: 8.8 lbs.
Region: Kanto

SHELLDER

CLOYSTER

SHELLOS EAST SEA
SEA SLUG POKÉMON

Like Gastrodon, Shellos will look quite different depending upon where it lives.

Pronounced: SHELL-oss
Possible Moves: Mud-Slap, Mud Sport, Harden, Water Pulse, Mud Bomb, Hidden Power, Rain Dance, Body Slam, Muddy Water, Recover
Type: Water
Height: 1' 00"
Weight: 13.9 lbs.
Region: Sinnoh

SHELLOS
(EAST SEA)

GASTRODON
(EAST SEA)

SHELLOS WEST SEA
SEA SLUG POKÉMON

Like Gastrodon, Shellos will look quite different depending upon where it lives.

Pronounced: SHELL-oss
Possible Moves: Mud-Slap, Mud Sport, Harden, Water Pulse, Mud Bomb, Hidden Power, Rain Dance, Body Slam, Muddy Water, Recover
Type: Water
Height: 1' 00"
Weight: 13.9 lbs.
Region: Sinnoh

SHELLOS
(WEST SEA)

GASTRODON
(WEST SEA)

SHELMET
SNAIL POKÉMON

Shelmet defends itself by shutting the lid of its shell and spitting a sticky, poisonous liquid. It evolves when both it and a Karrablast are bathed in electric-like energy.

Pronounced: SHELL-met
Possible Moves: Leech Life, Acid, Bide, Curse, Struggle Bug, Mega Drain, Yawn, Protect, Acid Armor, Giga Drain, Body Slam, Bug Buzz, Recover, Guard Swap, Final Gambit
Type: Bug   **Height:** 1' 04"
Weight: 17.0 lbs.   **Region:** Unova

SHELMET

ACCELGOR

SHIELDON
SHIELD POKÉMON

Shieldon will polish its face constantly by rubbing it against tree trunks. It is said that it lived in jungles around one hundred million years ago.

Pronounced: SHEEL-donn
Possible Moves: Tackle, Protect, Taunt, Metal Sound, Take Down, Iron Defense, Swagger, AncientPower, Endure, Metal Burst, Iron Head, Heavy Slam
Type: Rock-Steel
Height: 1' 08"
Weight: 125.7 lbs.
Region: Sinnoh

SHIELDON

BASTIODON

SHIFTRY
WICKED POKÉMON

Shiftry uses its leafy fan to whip up winds of one hundred feet per second.

Pronounced: SHIFF-tree
Possible Moves: Faint Attack, Whirlwind, Nasty Plot, Razor Leaf, Leaf Tornado, Leaf Storm
Type: Grass-Dark
Height: 4' 03"   **Weight:** 131.4 lbs.
Region: Hoenn

SEEDOT ➔ NUZLEAF ➔ SHIFTRY

SHINX
FLASH POKÉMON

When it senses danger, this Pokémon can temporarily blind its foes by creating a dazzling light show with its electrified fur.

Pronounced: SHINKS
Possible Moves: Tackle, Leer, Charge, Spark, Bite, Roar, Swagger, Thunder Fang, Crunch, Scary Face, Discharge, Wild Charge
Type: Electric
Height: 1' 08"
Weight: 20.9 lbs.
Region: Sinnoh

SHINX ➔ LUXIO ➔ LUXRAY

SHROOMISH
MUSHROOM POKÉMON

If you inhale the poison that Shroomish emits from the top of its head, you will be wracked with pain.

Pronounced: SHROOM-ish
Possible Moves: Absorb, Tackle, Stun Spore, Leech Seed, Mega Drain, Headbutt, PoisonPowder, Worry Seed, Growth, Giga Drain, Seed Bomb, Spore
Type: Grass
Height: 1' 04"   **Weight:** 9.9 lbs.
Region: Hoenn

SHROOMISH

BRELOOM

SHUCKLE
MOLD POKÉMON

Shuckle stores berries in its shell, which eventually ferment into delicious juice.

Pronounced: SHUCK-kull
Possible Moves: Withdraw, Constrict, Bide, Struggle Bug, Encore, Wrap, Safeguard, Rest, Gastro Acid, Rollout, Power Trick, Bug Bite, Power Split, Guard Split
Type: Bug-Rock
Height: 2' 00"   **Weight:** 45.2 lbs.
Region: Johto

DOES NOT EVOLVE

SHUPPET
PUPPET POKÉMON

Shuppet thrives on vengeful emotions, and will often hide in the houses of people who want revenge on someone or something.

Pronounced: SHUP-pett
Possible Moves: Knock Off, Screech, Night Shade, Curse, Spite, Shadow Sneak, Will-O-Wisp, Faint Attack, Hex, Shadow Ball, Sucker Punch, Embargo, Snatch, Grudge, Trick
Type: Ghost
Height: 2' 00"
Weight: 5.1 lbs.
Region: Hoenn

SHUPPET

BANETTE

SIGILYPH
AVIANOID POKÉMON

Clinging to memories of its time as guardian of an ancient city, a Sigilyph always flies the same route and uses psychic power to attack foes who enter its territory.

Pronounced: SIH-jih-liff
Possible Moves: Gust, Miracle Eye, Hypnosis, Psywave, Tailwind, Whirlwind, Psybeam, Air Cutter, Light Screen, Reflect, Synchronoise, Mirror Move, Gravity, Air Slash, Psychic, Cosmic Power, Sky Attack
Type: Psychic-Flying   **Height:** 4' 07"
Weight: 30.9 lbs.   **Region:** Unova

DOES NOT EVOLVE

SILCOON
COCOON POKÉMON

Silcoon will stay motionless until it evolves, and anchors itself by using silk from its body to wrap itself up in twigs.

Pronounced: sill-COON
Possible Moves: Harden
Type: Bug
Height: 2' 00"
Weight: 22.0 lbs.
Region: Hoenn

WURMPLE   SILCOON   BEAUTIFLY

SIMIPOUR
GEYSER POKÉMON

Simipour stores water in its head tufts. When it's running low, it siphons up water with its tail. This tail also shoots out water at pressures high enough to blast apart a concrete wall.

Pronounced: SIH-mee-por
Possible Moves: Leer, Lick, Fury Swipes, Scald
Type: Water
Height: 3' 03"
Weight: 63.9 lbs.
Region: Unova

PANPOUR   SIMIPOUR

SIMISAGE
THORN MONKEY POKÉMON

This short-tempered Pokémon fights with wild swings of its thorn-covered tail. The leaves growing on its head are extremely bitter.

Pronounced: SIH-mee-sayj
Possible Moves: Leer, Lick, Fury Swipes, Seed Bomb
Type: Grass
Height: 3' 07"
Weight: 67.2 lbs.
Region: Unova

PANSAGE

SIMISAGE

SIMISEAR
EMBER POKÉMON

Simisear has a taste for sweets, which fuel the fire inside it. It burns foes by scattering embers from its head and tail.

Pronounced: SIH-mee-seer
Possible Moves: Leer, Lick, Fury Swipes, Flame Burst
Type: Fire
Height: 3' 03"
Weight: 61.7 lbs.
Region: Unova

PANSEAR

SIMISEAR

SKARMORY
ARMOR BIRD POKÉMON

Even though Skarmory's body is covered in iron armor, it can fly at over 180 mph.

Pronounced: SKAR-more-ree
Possible Moves: Leer, Peck, Sand-Attack, Swift, Agility, Fury Attack, Feint, Air Cutter, Spikes, Metal Sound, Steel Wing, Autotomize, Air Slash, Slash, Night Slash
Type: Steel-Flying
Height: 5' 07"
Weight: 111.3 lbs.
Region: Johto

DOES NOT EVOLVE

SKIPLOOM
COTTONWEED POKÉMON

Skiploom will float in the sky to absorb as much sunlight as it can, and will bloom when the weather is warm.

Pronounced: SKIP-loom
Possible Moves: Splash, Synthesis, Tail Whip, Tackle, PoisonPowder, Stun Spore, Sleep Powder, Bullet Seed, Leech Seed, Mega Drain, Acrobatics, Rage Powder, Cotton Spore, U-turn, Worry Seed, Giga Drain, Bounce, Memento
Type: Grass-Flying   **Height:** 2' 00"   **Weight:** 2.2 lbs.
Region: Johto

HOPPIP   SKIPLOOM   JUMPLUFF

SKITTY
KITTEN POKÉMON

Skitty will run in circles chasing its own tail. It will look for any excuse to chase moving objects—or Pokémon.

Pronounced: SKIT-tee
Possible Moves: Fake Out, Growl, Tail Whip, Tackle, Foresight, Attract, Sing, DoubleSlap, Copycat, Assist, Charm, Faint Attack, Wake-Up Slap, Covet, Heal Bell, Double-Edge, Captivate
Type: Normal
Height: 2' 00"   **Weight:** 24.3 lbs.
Region: Hoenn

SKITTY

DELCATTY

SKORUPI
SCORPION POKÉMON

Skorupi buries itself in sand to surprise its prey. Once its prey is in its claws, Skorupi injects it with poison.

Pronounced: sco-ROO-pee
Possible Moves: Bite, Poison Sting, Leer, Knock Off, Pin Missile, Acupressure, Scary Face, Toxic Spikes, Bug Bite, Poison Fang, Hone Claws, Venoshock, Crunch, Cross Poison
Type: Poison-Bug
Height: 2' 07"   **Weight:** 26.5 lbs.
Region: Sinnoh

SKORUPI

DRAPION

SKUNTANK
SKUNK POKÉMON

Skuntank is able to spray its stench hundreds of feet away, and the longer it lingers, the worse it will smell.

Pronounced: SKUN-tank
Possible Moves: Scratch, Focus Energy, Poison Gas, Screech, Fury Swipes, SmokeScreen, Feint, Slash, Toxic, Acid Spray, Flamethrower, Night Slash, Memento, Explosion
Type: Poison-Dark
Height: 3' 03"   **Weight:** 83.8 lbs.
Region: Sinnoh

STUNKY

SKUNTANK

SLAKING
LAZY POKÉMON

Although dubbed The World's Laziest Pokémon, Slaking is actually storing energy for attacks.

Pronounced: SLAH-king
Possible Moves: Scratch, Yawn, Encore, Slack Off, Faint Attack, Amnesia, Covet, Swagger, Chip Away, Counter, Flail, Fling, Punishment, Hammer Arm
Type: Normal   **Height:** 6' 07"   **Weight:** 287.7 lbs.
Region: Hoenn

SLAKOTH

VIGOROTH

SLAKING

SLAKOTH
SLACKER POKÉMON

Just looking at Slakoth can make you sleepy, and no wonder—it spends all day lounging around.

Pronounced: SLAH-koth
Possible Moves: Scratch, Yawn, Encore, Slack Off, Faint Attack, Amnesia, Covet, Chip Away, Counter, Flail
Type: Normal
Height: 2' 07"
Weight: 52.9 lbs.
Region: Hoenn

SLAKOTH VIGOROTH ⟩ SLAKING

SLOWBRO
HERMIT CRAB POKÉMON

The Shellder on its tail will bite down to encourage Slowbro, who is usually a little dim.

Pronounced: SLOW-bro
Possible Moves: Curse, Yawn, Tackle, Growl, Water Gun, Confusion, Disable, Headbutt, Water Pulse, Zen Headbutt, Slack Off, Withdraw, Amnesia, Psychic, Rain Dance, Psych Up, Heal Pulse
Type: Water-Psychic
Height: 5' 03"   **Weight:** 173.1 lbs.
Region: Kanto

SLOWPOKE

SLOWBRO   SLOWKING

SLOWKING
ROYAL POKÉMON

Unlike Slowbro and Slowpoke, when bitten by the Shellder on its head, Slowking's intelligence rises to that of well-known scientists.

Pronounced: SLOW-king
Possible Moves: Power Gem, Hidden Power, Curse, Yawn, Tackle, Growl, Water Gun, Confusion, Disable, Headbutt, Water Pulse, Zen Headbutt, Nasty Plot, Swagger, Psychic, Trump Card, Psych Up, Heal Pulse
Type: Water-Psychic
Height: 6' 07"
Weight: 175.3 lbs.
Region: Johto

SLOWPOKE

SLOWBRO

SLOWKING

SLOWPOKE
DOPEY POKÉMON

Even though it's very slow, it has figured out how to use its tail (which doesn't register pain) to fish.

Pronounced: SLOW-poke
Possible Moves: Curse, Yawn, Tackle, Growl, Water Gun, Confusion, Disable, Headbutt, Water Pulse, Zen Headbutt, Slack Off, Amnesia, Psychic, Rain Dance, Psych Up, Heal Pulse
Type: Water-Psychic
Height: 3' 11"
Weight: 79.4 lbs.
Region: Kanto

SLOWPOKE

SLOWBRO

SLOWKING

SLUGMA
LAVA POKÉMON

This Pokémon needs to move constantly or the magma in its body will cool and harden.

Pronounced: SLUG-ma
Possible Moves: Yawn, Smog, Ember, Rock Throw, Harden, Recover, Flame Burst, AncientPower, Amnesia, Lava Plume, Rock Slide, Body Slam, Flamethrower, Earth Power
Type: Fire
Height: 2' 04"
Weight: 77.2 lbs.
Region: Johto

SLUGMA ➔ MAGCARGO

SMEARGLE
PAINTER POKÉMON

Using its tail like a paintbrush to claim its territory, Smeargle is capable of over five thousand different marks.

Pronounced: SMEAR-gull
Possible Moves: Sketch
Type: Normal
Height: 3' 11"
Weight: 127.9 lbs.
Region: Johto

DOES NOT EVOLVE

SMOOCHUM
KISS POKÉMON

Smoochum's lips will remember all the good and bad things it likes and dislikes.

Pronounced: SMOO-chum
Possible Moves: Pound, Lick, Sweet Kiss, Powder Snow, Confusion, Sing, Heart Stamp, Mean Look, Fake Tears, Lucky Chant, Avalanche, Psychic, Copycat, Perish Song, Blizzard
Type: Ice-Psychic
Height: 1' 04"   **Weight:** 13.2 lbs.
Region: Johto

SMOOCHUM

JYNX

SNEASEL
SHARP CLAW POKÉMON

Using its hooked claws to defeat its prey, Sneasel will stop at nothing—not until the prey is incapable of moving.

Pronounced: SNEE-zul
Possible Moves: Scratch, Leer, Taunt, Quick Attack, Screech, Faint Attack, Fury Swipes, Agility, Icy Wind, Hone Claws, Slash, Beat Up, Metal Claw, Ice Shard
Type: Dark-Ice
Height: 2' 11"
Weight: 61.7 lbs.
Region: Johto

SNEASEL

WEAVILE

SNIVY
GRASS SNAKE POKÉMON

Calm and intelligent, Snivy speeds up when exposed to lots of sunlight. By bathing its tail in solar rays, it can photosynthesize. But if it feels unwell, its tail droops.

Pronounced: SNY-vee
Possible Moves: Tackle, Leer, Vine Whip, Wrap, Growth, Leaf Tornado, Leech Seed, Mega Drain, Slam, Leaf Blade, Coil, Giga Drain, Wring Out, Gastro Acid, Leaf Storm
Type: Grass
Height: 2' 00"
Weight: 17.9 lbs.
Region: Unova

SNIVY → SERVINE → SERPERIOR

SNORLAX
SLEEPING POKÉMON

Snorlax will eat anything—even rotten food—and feasts all day, stopping only to sleep.

Pronounced: SNORE-lacks
Possible Moves: Tackle, Defense Curl, Amnesia, Lick, Belly Drum, Yawn, Chip Away, Rest, Snore, Sleep Talk, Body Slam, Block, Rollout, Crunch, Heavy Slam, Giga Impact
Type: Normal
Height: 6' 11"
Weight: 1014.1 lbs.
Region: Kanto

MUNCHLAX

SNORLAX

SNORUNT
SNOW HAT POKÉMON

If a Snorunt appears at a home, it is said that the house will prosper. It lives in snowy areas.

SNORUNT

Pronounced: SNOW-runt
Possible Moves: Powder Snow, Leer, Double Team, Bite, Icy Wind, Headbutt, Protect, Ice Fang, Crunch, Ice Shard, Hail, Blizzard
Type: Ice
Height: 2' 04"
Weight: 37.0 lbs.
Region: Hoenn

GLALIE

FROSLASS

SNOVER
FROST TREE POKÉMON

Having only had minor contact with humans, Snover tends to be curious. It lives on snowy mountains and grows berries around its belly every spring.

Pronounced: SNOW-vurr
Possible Moves: Powder Snow, Leer, Razor Leaf, Icy Wind, GrassWhistle, Swagger, Mist, Ice Shard, Ingrain, Wood Hammer, Blizzard, Sheer Cold
Type: Grass-Ice
Height: 3' 03"
Weight: 111.3 lbs.
Region: Sinnoh

SNOVER   ABOMASNOW

SNUBBULL
FAIRY POKÉMON

Although considered cute by some women, most small creatures will flee from its scary face.

Pronounced: SNUB-bull
Possible Moves: Ice Fang, Fire Fang, Thunder Fang, Tackle, Scary Face, Tail Whip, Charm, Bite, Lick, Headbutt, Roar, Rage, Take Down, Payback, Crunch
Type: Normal
Height: 2' 00"   **Weight:** 17.2 lbs.
Region: Johto

SNUBBULL

GRANBULL

SOLOSIS
CELL POKÉMON

Solosis can survive in any environment, since its body is enveloped in a special liquid. It communicates with other Solosis by telepathy, and it uses psychic power to drive off foes.

Pronounced: soh-LOH-sis

Possible Moves: Psywave, Reflect, Rollout, Snatch, Hidden Power, Light Screen, Charm, Recover, Psyshock, Endeavor, Future Sight, Pain Split, Psychic, Skill Swap, Heal Block, Wonder Room

Type: Psychic
Height: 1' 00"
Weight: 2.2 lbs.
Region: Unova

SOLOSIS ➔ DUOSION ➔ REUNICLUS

SOLROCK
METEORITE POKÉMON

Unlike the moonish Lunatone, Solrock is rumored to be more sun-oriented, and gives off a sunlight-like glow while spinning.

Pronounced: SOL-rock

Possible Moves: Tackle, Harden, Confusion, Rock Throw, Fire Spin, Rock Polish, Psywave, Embargo, Cosmic Power, Heal Block, Rock Slide, SolarBeam, Explosion, Wonder Room

Type: Rock-Psychic
Height: 3' 11"   **Weight:** 339.5 lbs.
Region: Hoenn

DOES NOT EVOLVE

SPEAROW
TINY BIRD POKÉMON

Fast and furious, Spearow can spot prey in the grass and use its strong beak to pick it out.

Pronounced: SPEER-oh
Possible Moves: Peck, Growl, Leer, Fury Attack, Pursuit, Aerial Ace, Mirror Move, Agility, Assurance, Roost, Drill Peck
Type: Normal-Flying
Height: 1' 00"   **Weight:** 4.4 lbs.
Region: Kanto

SPEAROW

FEAROW

SPHEAL
CLAP POKÉMON

Because Spheal's body is shaped like a ball, it can roll across frozen ice floes to reach the shore.

Pronounced: SFEEL
Possible Moves: Defense Curl, Powder Snow, Growl, Water Gun, Encore, Ice Ball, Body Slam, Aurora Beam, Hail, Rest, Snore, Blizzard, Sheer Cold
Type: Ice-Water   **Height:** 2' 07"   **Weight:** 87.1 lbs.
Region: Hoenn

SPHEAL

SEALEO

WALREIN

SPINARAK
STRING SPIT POKÉMON

Using strong, thin silk to capture its prey, Spinarak will wait motionlessly for hours on end for its prey to arrive.

Pronounced: SPIN-uh-rack

Possible Moves: Poison Sting, String Shot, Scary Face, Constrict, Leech Life, Night Shade, Shadow Sneak, Fury Swipes, Sucker Punch, Spider Web, Agility, Pin Missile, Psychic, Poison Jab, Cross Poison

Type: Bug-Poison

Height: 1' 08"   **Weight:** 18.7 lbs.

Region: Johto

SPINARAK

ARIADOS

SPINDA
SPOT PANDA POKÉMON

The way this Pokémon walks—by teetering back and forth—makes it a difficult target to hit. Every Spinda has a unique pattern of spots.

Pronounced: SPIN-dah

Possible Moves: Tackle, Uproar, Copycat, Faint Attack, Psybeam, Hypnosis, Dizzy Punch, Sucker Punch, Teeter Dance, Psych Up, Double-Edge, Flail, Thrash

Type: Normal

Height: 3' 07"

Weight: 11.0 lbs.

Region: Hoenn

DOES NOT EVOLVE

SPIRITOMB
FORBIDDEN POKÉMON

Spiritomb, which is a combination of over one hundred different spirits, was punished half a century ago by being bound to something called an Odd Keystone.

Pronounced: SPIRI-toom
Possible Moves: Curse, Pursuit, Confuse Ray, Spite, Shadow Sneak, Faint Attack, Hypnosis, Dream Eater, Ominous Wind, Sucker Punch, Nasty Plot, Memento, Dark Pulse
Type: Ghost-Dark
Height: 3' 03"
Weight: 238.1 lbs.
Region: Sinnoh

DOES
NOT
EVOLVE

SPOINK

GRUMPIG

SPOINK
BOUNCE POKÉMON

Spoink bounces constantly on its spring-like tail, which also keeps its heart beating.

Pronounced: SPOINK
Possible Moves: Splash, Psywave, Odor Sleuth, Psybeam, Psych Up, Confuse Ray, Magic Coat, Zen Headbutt, Rest, Snore, Psyshock, Payback, Psychic, Power Gem, Bounce
Type: Psychic
Height: 2' 04"   **Weight:** 67.5 lbs.
Region: Hoenn

SQUIRTLE
TINY TURTLE POKÉMON

Striking regularly with spouts of water, Squirtle can be tricky to see, since it hides within its shell a lot.

Pronounced: SKWIR-tuhl

Possible Moves: Tackle, Tail Whip, Bubble, Withdraw, Water Gun, Bite, Rapid Spin, Protect, Water Pulse, Aqua Tail, Skull Bash, Iron Defense, Rain Dance, Hydro Pump

Type: Water

Height: 1' 08"

Weight: 19.8 lbs.

Region: Kanto

SQUIRTLE → WARTORTLE → BLASTOISE

STANTLER
BIG HORN POKÉMON

You can easily become entranced by the patterns on the majestic antlers of this Pokémon.

Pronounced: STAN-tler
Possible Moves: Tackle, Leer, Astonish, Hypnosis, Stomp, Sand-Attack, Take Down, Confuse Ray, Calm Mind, Role Play, Zen Headbutt, Jump Kick, Imprison, Captivate, Me First
Type: Normal
Height: 4' 07"   **Weight:** 157.0 lbs.
Region: Johto

DOES NOT EVOLVE

STARAPTOR
PREDATOR POKÉMON

Since it has strong legs and wings, Staraptor thinks nothing of challenging foes bigger than itself.

Pronounced: star-RAPT-orr
Possible Moves: Tackle, Growl, Quick Attack, Wing Attack, Double Team, Endeavor, Whirlwind, Aerial Ace, Take Down, Close Combat, Agility, Brave Bird, Final Gambit
Type: Normal-Flying   **Height:** 3' 11"   **Weight:** 54.9 lbs.
Region: Sinnoh

STARLY ➔ STARAVIA ➔ STARAPTOR

STARAVIA
STARLING POKÉMON

While searching for Bug-type Pokémon, Staravia will fly around in flocks. But if they meet up with another flock, a territorial battle will erupt.

Pronounced: star-AY-vee-ah

Possible Moves: Tackle, Growl, Quick Attack, Wing Attack, Double Team, Endeavor, Whirlwind, Aerial Ace, Take Down, Agility, Brave Bird, Final Gambit

Type: Normal-Flying

Height: 2' 00"

Weight: 34.2 lbs.

Region: Sinnoh

STARLY   STARAVIA   STARAPTOR

STARLY
STARLING POKÉMON

Though small, Starly can flap their wings with great power. They always travel en masse, because they are small enough to be vulnerable on their own.

Pronounced: STAR-lee

Possible Moves: Tackle, Growl, Quick Attack, Wing Attack, Double Team, Endeavor, Whirlwind, Aerial Ace, Take Down, Agility, Brave Bird, Final Gambit

Type: Normal-Flying   **Height:** 1' 00"   **Weight:** 4.4 lbs.

Region: Sinnoh

STARLY   STARAVIA   STARAPTOR

STARMIE
MYSTERIOUS POKÉMON

The red core in the center of Starmie can send mysterious radio signals into the night sky.

Pronounced: STAR-me
Possible Moves: Water Gun, Rapid Spin, Recover, Swift, Confuse Ray
Type: Water-Psychic
Height: 3' 07"
Weight: 176.4 lbs.
Region: Kanto

STARYU

STARMIE

STARYU
STAR SHAPE POKÉMON

If it is torn or damaged in battle, the rest of Staryu can grow back—as long as the red core of its body (which flashes at midnight) stays intact.

Pronounced: STAR-you
Possible Moves: Tackle, Harden, Water Gun, Rapid Spin, Recover, Camouflage, Swift, BubbleBeam, Minimize, Gyro Ball, Light Screen, Reflect Type, Power Gem, Cosmic Power, Hydro Pump
Type: Water
Height: 2' 07"   **Weight:** 76.1 lbs.
Region: Kanto

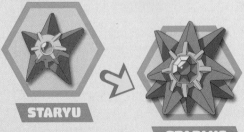

STARYU

STARMIE

STEELIX
IRON SNAKE POKÉMON

Steelix has a body that is harder than any metal. It can chew through boulders and see in the dark.

Pronounced: STEE-licks

Possible Moves: Thunder Fang, Ice Fang, Fire Fang, Mud Sport, Tackle, Harden, Bind, Screech, Rock Throw, Rage, Rock Tomb, Smack Down, Sandstorm, Autotomize, Slam, Stealth Rock, DragonBreath, Curse, Iron Tail, Crunch, Double-Edge, Stone Edge

Type: Steel-Ground

Height: 30' 02"   **Weight:** 881.8 lbs.

Region: Johto

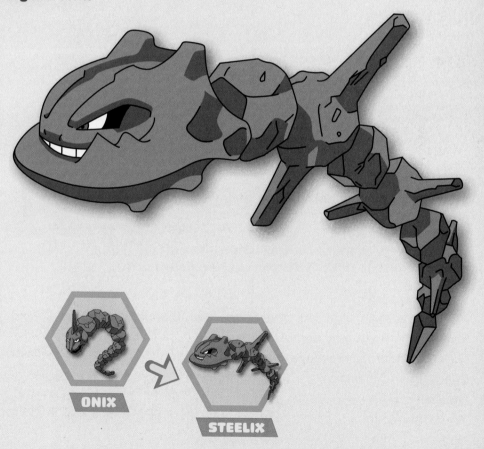

ONIX → STEELIX

STOUTLAND
BIG-HEARTED POKÉMON

Stoutland's shaggy fur coat shields it from the cold. This wise Pokémon is excellent at rescuing people trapped by mountain blizzards or stranded at sea.

Pronounced: STOWT-lund
Possible Moves: Ice Fang, Fire Fang, Thunder Fang, Leer, Tackle, Odor Sleuth, Bite, Helping Hand, Take Down, Work Up, Crunch, Roar, Retaliate, Reversal, Last Resort, Giga Impact
Type: Normal
Height: 3' 11"
Weight: 134.5 lbs.
Region: Unova

| LILLIPUP | HERDIER | STOUTLAND |

STUNFISK
TRAP POKÉMON

Stunfisk's skin is so hard, it can shrug off being stepped on by a sumo wrestler. Hidden in mud along the seashore, Stunfisk waits for prey to make contact, then gives off an electrical jolt. It smiles when discharging electricity.

Pronounced: STUN-fisk
Possible Moves: Mud-Slap, Mud Sport, Bide, ThunderShock, Mud Shot, Camouflage, Mud Bomb, Discharge, Endure, Bounce, Muddy Water, Thunderbolt, Revenge, Flail, Fissure
Type: Ground-Electric
Height: 2' 04"
Weight: 24.3 lbs.
Region: Unova

DOES NOT EVOLVE

STUNKY
SKUNK POKÉMON

To keep away foes, Stunky will spray a noxious stench from its rear. One word comes to mind—ewwwwww!

Pronounced: STUNK-ee
Possible Moves: Scratch, Focus Energy, Poison Gas, Screech, Fury Swipes, SmokeScreen, Feint, Slash, Toxic, Acid Spray, Night Slash, Memento, Explosion
Type: Poison-Dark
Height: 1' 04"   **Weight:** 42.3 lbs.
Region: Sinnoh

STUNKY → SKUNTANK

SUDOWOODO
IMITATION POKÉMON

Despite its stalwart wooden appearance, Sudowoodo is more closely related to rocks and stones than trees—which would explain why it seems to disappear when it rains.

Pronounced: SOO-doe-WOO-doe
Possible Moves: Wood Hammer, Copycat, Flail, Low Kick, Rock Throw, Mimic, Block, Faint Attack, Rock Tomb, Rock Slide, Slam, Sucker Punch, Double-Edge, Hammer Arm
Type: Rock
Height: 3' 11"
Weight: 83.8 lbs.
Region: Johto

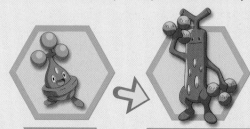

BONSLY → SUDOWOODO

SUICUNE
AURORA POKÉMON

Suicune will dash around the world on the north winds, purifying foul waters.

Pronounced: SWEE-koon

Possible Moves: Bite, Leer, BubbleBeam, Rain Dance, Gust, Aurora Beam, Mist, Mirror Coat, Ice Fang, Tailwind, Extrasensory, Hydro Pump, Calm Mind, Blizzard

Type: Water

Height: 6' 07"

Weight: 412.3 lbs.

Region: Johto

DOES NOT EVOLVE

LEGENDARY POKÉMON

SUNFLORA
SUN POKÉMON

Sunflora uses warm sunlight for energy, and will constantly travel to find it.

Pronounced: SUN-FLOR-a
Possible Moves: Absorb, Pound, Growth, Mega Drain, Ingrain, GrassWhistle, Leech Seed, Bullet Seed, Worry Seed, Razor Leaf, Petal Dance, Sunny Day, SolarBeam, Leaf Storm
Type: Grass
Height: 2' 07"   **Weight:** 18.7 lbs.
Region: Johto

SUNKERN → SUNFLORA

SUNKERN
SEED POKÉMON

The Sunkern population will explode the year after a cold summer.

Pronounced: SUN-kurn
Possible Moves: Absorb, Growth, Mega Drain, Ingrain, GrassWhistle, Leech Seed, Endeavor, Worry Seed, Razor Leaf, Synthesis, Sunny Day, Giga Drain, Seed Bomb
Type: Grass
Height: 1' 00"
Weight: 4.0 lbs.
Region: Johto

SUNKERN → SUNFLORA

SURSKIT
POND SKATER POKÉMON

Surskit emits a sweet scent from the tip of its head. It looks like it's skating on water.

Pronounced: SUR-skit
Possible Moves: Bubble, Quick Attack, Sweet Scent, Water Sport, BubbleBeam, Agility, Mist, Haze, Baton Pass
Type: Bug-Water
Height: 1' 08"
Weight: 3.7 lbs.
Region: Hoenn

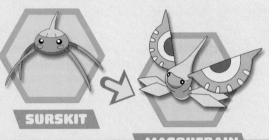

SURSKIT

MASQUERAIN

SWABLU
COTTON BIRD POKÉMON

With wings that resemble cotton, Swablu can sit atop someone's head and look like a cotton hat.

Pronounced: SWAH-blue
Possible Moves: Peck, Growl, Astonish, Sing, Fury Attack, Safeguard, Mist, Take Down, Natural Gift, Mirror Move, Cotton Guard, Refresh, Dragon Pulse, Perish Song
Type: Normal-Flying
Height: 1' 04"   **Weight:** 2.6 lbs.
Region: Hoenn

SWABLU

ALTARIA

SWADLOON
LEAF-WRAPPED POKÉMON

It wraps itself in leaves to keep away the cold. Swadloon forests have lush foliage, because Swadloon turn fallen leaves into fertilizing nutrients.

Pronounced: swahd-LOON
Possible Moves: GrassWhistle, Tackle, String Shot, Bug Bite, Razor Leaf, Protect
Type: Bug-Grass
Height: 1' 08"
Weight: 16.1 lbs.
Region: Unova

SEWADDLE

>

SWADLOON

>

LEAVANNY

SWALOT
POISON BAG POKÉMON

For protection, Swalot exudes toxic fluid from its follicles, and can swallow anything whole.

Pronounced: SWAH-lot
Possible Moves: Pound, Yawn, Poison Gas, Sludge, Amnesia, Encore, Body Slam, Toxic, Acid Spray, Stockpile, Spit Up, Swallow, Sludge Bomb, Gastro Acid, Wring Out, Gunk Shot
Type: Poison
Height: 5' 07"
Weight: 176.4 lbs.
Region: Hoenn

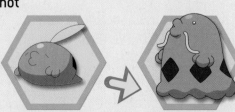
GULPIN

>

SWALOT

SWAMPERT
MUD FISH POKÉMON

Swampert uses its thick arms to swat down foes, and can even fight while towing a large ship.

Pronounced: SWAM-pert
Possible Moves: Tackle, Growl, Mud-Slap, Water Gun, Bide, Mud Shot, Foresight, Mud Bomb, Take Down, Muddy Water, Protect, Earthquake, Endeavor, Hammer Arm
Type: Water-Ground
Height: 4' 11"
Weight: 180.6 lbs.
Region: Hoenn

MUDKIP → MARSHTOMP → SWAMPERT

SWANNA
WHITE BIRD POKÉMON

It can whip its neck around to deliver powerful attacks with its bill. At dusk, a Swanna flock dances with the flock's leader in the middle.

Pronounced: SWAH-nuh
Possible Moves: Water Gun, Water Sport, Defog, Wing Attack, Water Pulse, Aerial Ace, BubbleBeam, Feather-Dance, Aqua Ring, Air Slash, Roost, Rain Dance, Tailwind, Brave Bird, Hurricane
Type: Water-Flying   **Height:** 4' 03"
Weight: 53.4 lbs.   **Region:** Unova

DUCKLETT → SWANNA

SWELLOW
SWALLOW POKÉMON

After circling the skies for hours, Swellow will dive directly at its prey.

Pronounced: SWELL-low
Possible Moves: Pluck, Peck, Growl, Focus Energy, Quick Attack, Wing Attack, Double Team, Endeavor, Aerial Ace, Agility, Air Slash
Type: Normal-Flying
Height: 2' 04"
Weight: 43.7 lbs.
Region: Hoenn

TAILLOW

SWELLOW

SWINUB
PIG POKÉMON

While digging under dead grass for mushrooms to eat, Swinub also chances upon hot springs.

Pronounced: SWY-nub
Possible Moves: Tackle, Odor Sleuth, Mud Sport, Powder Snow, Mud-Slap, Endure, Mud Bomb, Icy Wind, Ice Shard, Take Down, Earthquake, Mist, Blizzard, Amnesia
Type: Ice-Ground   **Height:** 1' 04"   **Weight:** 14.3 lbs.
Region: Johto

SWINUB

PILOSWINE

MAMOSWINE

SWOOBAT
COURTING POKÉMON

Swoobat uses its nose to emit sound waves at different frequencies, some of which are strong enough to destroy rock. When a courting male Swoobat gives off ultrasonic waves, it improves the mood of anyone within range.

Pronounced: SWOO-bat
Possible Moves: Confusion, Odor Sleuth, Gust, Assurance, Heart Stamp, Imprison, Air Cutter, Attract, Amnesia, Calm Mind, Air Slash, Future Sight, Psychic, Endeavor
Type: Psychic-Flying
Height: 2' 11"
Weight: 23.1 lbs.
Region: Unova

WOOBAT

SWOOBAT

TAILLOW
TINYSWALLOW POKÉMON

Taillow will bravely take on the toughest foes, and will always look for warm climates in which to live.

Pronounced: TAY-low
Possible Moves: Peck, Growl, Focus Energy, Quick Attack, Wing Attack, Double Team, Endeavor, Aerial Ace, Agility, Air Slash
Type: Normal-Flying
Height: 1' 00"
Weight: 5.1 lbs.
Region: Hoenn

TAILLOW → SWELLOW

TANGELA
VINE POKÉMON

No one has yet seen Tangela's face because it is covered in blue vines.

Pronounced: TANG-guh-luh
Possible Moves: Ingrain, Constrict, Sleep Powder, Absorb, Growth, PoisonPowder, Vine Whip, Bind, Mega Drain, Stun Spore, Knock Off, AncientPower, Natural Gift, Slam, Tickle, Wring Out, Power Whip
Type: Grass
Height: 3' 03"
Weight: 77.2 lbs.
Region: Kanto

TANGELA → TANGROWTH

TANGROWTH
VINE POKÉMON

Tangrowth doesn't care if predators take an arm or two. Its arms are made of vines, and they have enough to go around.

Pronounced: TANG-growth
Possible Moves: Ingrain, Constrict, Sleep Powder, Absorb, Growth, PoisonPowder, Vine Whip, Bind, Mega Drain, Stun Spore, AncientPower, Knock Off, Natural Gift, Slam, Tickle, Wring Out, Power Whip, Block
Type: Grass
Height: 6' 07"
Weight: 283.5 lbs.
Region: Sinnoh

TANGELA → TANGROWTH

TAUROS
WILD BULL POKÉMON

Very violent by nature, Tauros will attack a foe by charging head-on.

Pronounced: TOR-ose
Possible Moves: Tackle, Tail Whip, Rage, Horn Attack, Scary Face, Pursuit, Rest, Payback, Work Up, Zen Headbutt, Take Down, Swagger, Thrash, Giga Impact
Type: Normal
Height: 4' 07"   **Weight:** 194.9 lbs.
Region: Kanto

DOES
NOT
EVOLVE

TEDDIURSA
LITTLE BEAR POKÉMON

Teddiursa eats honey that soaks through its paws. Every set of paws has a different taste.

Pronounced: TED-dy-UR-sa
Possible Moves: Covet, Scratch, Leer, Lick, Fake Tears, Fury Swipes, Faint Attack, Sweet Scent, Slash, Charm, Rest, Snore, Thrash, Fling
Type: Normal
Height: 2' 00"
Weight: 19.4 lbs.
Region: Johto

TEDDIURSA

URSARING

TENTACOOL
JELLYFISH POKÉMON

Made mostly of water, it uses beams from its eyes. Unfortunately, many fishermen have fallen prey to its poisonous barbs.

Pronounced: TENT-uh-cool
Possible Moves: Poison Sting, Supersonic, Constrict, Acid, Toxic Spikes, BubbleBeam, Wrap, Acid Spray, Barrier, Water Pulse, Poison Jab, Screech, Hex, Hydro Pump, Sludge Wave, Wring Out
Type: Water-Poison
Height: 2' 11"
Weight: 100.3 lbs.
Region: Kanto

TENTACOOL TENTACRUEL

TENTACRUEL
JELLYFISH POKÉMON

After weakening its prey with poison, Tentacruel uses its tentacles to hold its victims.

Pronounced: TENT-uh-crool
Possible Moves: Poison Sting, Supersonic, Constrict, Acid, Toxic Spikes, BubbleBeam, Wrap, Acid Spray, Barrier, Water Pulse, Poison Jab, Screech, Hex, Hydro Pump, Sludge Wave, Wring Out
Type: Water-Poison
Height: 5' 03"   **Weight:** 121.3 lbs.
Region: Kanto

TENTACOOL TENTACRUEL

TEPIG
FIRE PIG POKÉMON

Tepig can blow fire from its nose, either to launch fireballs or to roast berries for food. But if it catches a cold, it blows out black smoke instead.

Pronounced: TEH-pig
Possible Moves: Tackle, Tail Whip, Ember, Odor Sleuth, Defense Curl, Flame Charge, Smog, Rollout, Take Down, Heat Crash, Assurance, Flamethrower, Head Smash, Roar, Flare Blitz
Type: Fire
Height: 1' 08"
Weight: 21.8 lbs.
Region: Unova

TEPIG   PIGNITE   EMBOAR

TERRAKION
CAVERN POKÉMON

Strong enough to break through a huge castle wall in a single mighty charge, Terrakion is spoken of in legends.

Pronounced: tur-RAK-ee-un
Possible Moves: Quick Attack, Leer, Double Kick, Smack Down, Take Down, Helping Hand, Retaliate, Rock Slide, Sacred Sword, Swords Dance, Quick Guard, Work Up, Stone Edge, Close Combat
Type: Rock-Fighting
Height: 6' 03"
Weight: 573.2 lbs.
Region: Unova

LEGENDARY POKÉMON

DOES NOT EVOLVE

THROH
JUDO POKÉMON

Throh tries to toss any foe that's larger than itself. This Pokémon always travels in a pack of five. A wild Throh weaves its own belt out of vines, and tightening that belt makes it stronger.

Pronounced: THROH
Possible Moves: Bind, Leer, Bide, Focus Energy, Seismic Toss, Vital Throw, Revenge, Storm Throw, Body Slam, Bulk Up, Circle Throw, Endure, Wide Guard, Superpower, Reversal
Type: Fighting   **Height:** 4' 03"
Weight: 122.4 lbs.   **Region:** Unova

DOES NOT EVOLVE

THUNDURUS
BOLT STRIKE POKÉMON

Thundurus flies through the Unova region, firing huge lightning bolts from the spikes on its tail and leaving charred landscapes in its wake.

Pronounced: THUN-duh-rus

Possible Moves: Uproar, Astonish, ThunderShock, Swagger, Bite, Revenge, Shock Wave, Heal Block, Agility, Discharge, Crunch, Charge, Nasty Plot, Thunder, Dark Pulse, Hammer Arm, Thrash

Type: Electric-Flying

Height: 4' 11"

Weight: 134.5 lbs.

Region: Unova

DOES
NOT
EVOLVE

LEGENDARY
POKÉMON

TIMBURR
MUSCULAR POKÉMON

Timburr shows up at construction sites and helps with the work. It always carries a squared-off log that it can swing like a weapon.

Pronounced: TIM-bur
Possible Moves: Pound, Leer, Focus Energy, Bide, Low Kick, Rock Throw, Wake-Up Slap, Chip Away, Bulk Up, Rock Slide, DynamicPunch, Scary Face, Hammer Arm, Stone Edge, Focus Punch, Superpower
Type: Fighting
Height: 2' 00"
Weight: 27.6 lbs.
Region: Unova

TIMBURR

GURDURR

CONKELDURR

TIRTOUGA
PROTOTURTLE POKÉMON

Restored from a fossil, Tirtouga lived in the oceans about a hundred million years ago and can dive to depths of a half mile or more. It may have hunted prey on land as well.

Pronounced: teer-TOO-guh
Possible Moves: Bide, Withdraw, Water Gun, Rollout, Bite, Protect, Aqua Jet, AncientPower, Crunch, Wide Guard, Brine, Smack Down, Curse, Shell Smash, Aqua Tail, Rock Slide, Rain Dance, Hydro Pump
Type: Water-Rock   **Height:** 2' 04"
Weight: 36.4 lbs.   **Region:** Unova

TIRTOUGA

CARRACOSTA

TOGEKISS
JUBILEE POKÉMON

This Pokémon does not like to appear where there is trouble, which would explain why it's rarely seen.

Pronounced: TOE-geh-kiss
Possible Moves: Sky Attack, ExtremeSpeed, Aura Sphere, Air Slash
Type: Normal-Flying
Height: 4' 11"
Weight: 83.8 lbs.
Region: Sinnoh

TOGEPI → TOGETIC → TOGEKISS

TOGEPI
SPIKE BALL POKÉMON

Where does Togepi's limitless joy come from? The secret is said to be contained in its hard shell.

Pronounced: TOE-geh-pee
Possible Moves: Growl, Charm, Metronome, Sweet Kiss, Yawn, Encore, Follow Me, Bestow, Wish, AncientPower, Safeguard, Baton Pass, Double-Edge, Last Resort, After You
Type: Normal
Height: 1' 00"
Weight: 3.3 lbs.
Region: Johto

TOGEPI   TOGETIC   TOGEKISS

TOGETIC
HAPPINESS POKÉMON

When people are kind and good-natured, you may find Togetic spreading a glowing down known as Joy Dust.

Pronounced: TOE-geh-tick
Possible Moves: Magical Leaf, Growl, Charm, Metronome, Sweet Kiss, Yawn, Encore, Follow Me, Bestow, Wish, AncientPower, Safeguard, Baton Pass, Double-Edge, Last Resort, After You
Type: Normal-Flying
Height: 2' 00"
Weight: 7.1 lbs.
Region: Johto

TOGEPI   TOGETIC   TOGEKISS

TORCHIC
CHICK POKÉMON

Torchic feels very warm to the touch thanks to the fire burning inside of it. It can throw fireballs that are 1,800 degrees Fahrenheit.

Pronounced: TOR-chick
Possible Moves: Scratch, Growl, Focus Energy, Ember, Peck, Sand-Attack, Fire Spin, Quick Attack, Slash, Mirror Move, Flamethrower
Type: Fire
Height: 1' 04"
Weight: 5.5 lbs.
Region: Hoenn

| TORCHIC | COMBUSKEN | BLAZIKEN |

TORKOAL
COAL POKÉMON

When in danger, this Pokémon will blow out black soot generated from burning the coal it stores inside its shell.

Pronounced: TOR-coal
Possible Moves: Ember, Smog, Withdraw, Curse, Fire Spin, SmokeScreen, Rapid Spin, Flamethrower, Body Slam, Protect, Lava Plume, Iron Defense, Amnesia, Flail, Heat Wave, Inferno, Shell Smash
Type: Fire
Height: 1' 08"   **Weight:** 177.2 lbs.
Region: Hoenn

DOES NOT EVOLVE

TORNADUS
CYCLONE POKÉMON

With its lower half shrouded in a cloud of energy, Tornadus zooms through the air at 200 miles per hour. Its wind can blow away a house, or it can create powerful storms with the energy expelled from its tail.

Pronounced: tohr-NAY-dus
Possible Moves: Uproar, Astonish, Gust, Swagger, Bite, Revenge, Air Cutter, Extrasensory, Agility, Air Slash, Crunch, Tailwind, Rain Dance, Hurricane, Dark Pulse, Hammer Arm, Thrash
Type: Flying
Height: 4' 11"
Weight: 138.9 lbs.
Region: Unova

LEGENDARY
POKÉMON

DOES
NOT
EVOLVE

TORTERRA
CONTINENT POKÉMON

You can sometimes see smaller Pokémon living on the backs of Torterra and building nests. When in groups, Torterra have been mistaken for moving forests.

Pronounced: tor-TERR-uh

Possible Moves: Wood Hammer, Tackle, Withdraw, Absorb, Razor Leaf, Curse, Bite, Mega Drain, Earthquake, Leech Seed, Synthesis, Crunch, Giga Drain, Leaf Storm

Type: Grass-Ground

Height: 7' 03"

Weight: 683.4 lbs.

Region: Sinnoh

TURTWIG   GROTLE   TORTERRA

TOTODILE
BIG JAW POKÉMON

Prone to bite anything with its strong jaws, even Totodile's Trainer must be very careful when handling it.

Pronounced: TOE-toe-dyle

Possible Moves: Scratch, Leer, Water Gun, Rage, Bite, Scary Face, Ice Fang, Flail, Crunch, Chip Away, Slash, Screech, Thrash, Aqua Tail, Superpower, Hydro Pump

Type: Water

Height: 2' 00"   **Weight:** 20.9 lbs.

Region: Johto

TOTODILE   CROCONAW   FERALIGATR

TOXICROAK
TOXIC MOUTH POKÉMON

Toxicroak will build up poison in its fingers, and even one scratch can be fatal.

Pronounced: TOCKS-eh-croak
Possible Moves: Astonish, Mud-Slap, Poison Sting, Taunt, Pursuit, Faint Attack, Revenge, Swagger, Mud Bomb, Sucker Punch, Venoshock, Nasty Plot, Poison Jab, Sludge Bomb, Flatter
Type: Poison-Fighting
Height: 4' 03"
Weight: 97.9 lbs.
Region: Sinnoh

CROAGUNK

TOXICROAK

TRANQUILL
WILD PIGEON POKÉMON

If Tranquill is separated from its Trainer, it can still find its way back, regardless of distance. Wild Tranquill live deep in the forest, and many believe that their home is a peaceful place with no war.

Pronounced: TRAN-kwil
Possible Moves: Gust, Growl, Leer, Quick Attack, Air Cutter, Roost, Detect, Taunt, Air Slash, Razor Wind, FeatherDance, Swagger, Facade, Tailwind, Sky Attack
Type: Normal-Flying
Height: 2' 00"
Weight: 33.1 lbs.
Region: Unova

PIDOVE

TRANQUILL

UNFEZANT

TRAPINCH
ANT PIT POKÉMON

Trapinch live in the desert and capture their prey by waiting at the bottom of sand pits they build as traps.

Pronounced: TRAP-pinch
Possible Moves: Bite, Sand-Attack, Faint Attack, Sand Tomb, Crunch, Dig, Sandstorm, Hyper Beam, Earth Power, Earthquake, Feint, Fissure
Type: Ground
Height: 2' 04"
Weight: 33.1 lbs.
Region: Hoenn

TRAPINCH   VIBRAVA   FLYGON

TREECKO
WOOD GECKO POKÉMON

Treecko can walk on walls and ceilings by using the tiny spikes in its feet.

Pronounced: TREE-ko
Possible Moves: Pound, Leer, Absorb, Quick Attack, Pursuit, Screech, Mega Drain, Agility, Slam, Detect, Giga Drain, Energy Ball
Type: Grass
Height: 1' 08"　　**Weight:** 11.0 lbs.
Region: Hoenn

TREECKO   GROVYLE   SCEPTILE

TROPIUS
FRUIT POKÉMON

Tropius packs away so much fruit, it actually has fruit growing from its neck.

Pronounced: TROH-pee-us
Possible Moves: Leer, Gust, Growth, Razor Leaf, Stomp, Sweet Scent, Whirlwind, Magical Leaf, Body Slam, Synthesis, Leaf Tornado, Air Slash, Bestow, SolarBeam, Natural Gift, Leaf Storm
Type: Grass-Flying
Height: 6' 07"
Weight: 220.5 lbs.
Region: Hoenn

DOES NOT EVOLVE

TRUBBISH
TRASH BAG POKÉMON

Trubbish likes unsanitary environments, and new Trubbish are created from a chemical reaction of industrial waste and garbage bags. The gas it belches leaves a person unconscious for a week if inhaled.

Pronounced: TRUB-bish
Possible Moves: Pound, Poison Gas, Recycle, Toxic Spikes, Acid Spray, DoubleSlap, Sludge, Stockpile, Swallow, Take Down, Sludge Bomb, Clear Smog, Toxic, Amnesia, Gunk Shot, Explosion
Type: Poison
Weight: 68.3 lbs.
Height: 2' 00"
Region: Unova

TRUBBISH

GARBODOR

TURTWIG
TINY LEAF POKÉMON

Turtwig tends to make its home near lakes. When it drinks water the shell on its back will harden.

Pronounced: TUR-twig
Possible Moves: Tackle, Withdraw, Absorb, Razor Leaf, Curse, Bite, Mega Drain, Leech Seed, Synthesis, Crunch, Giga Drain, Leaf Storm
Type: Grass
Height: 1' 04"
Weight: 22.5 lbs.
Region: Sinnoh

TURTWIG

GROTLE

TORTERRA

TYMPOLE
TADPOLE POKÉMON

Tympole generates sounds beyond human hearing range by vibrating its cheeks. To warn others of danger, it makes a high-pitched noise.

Pronounced: TIM-pohl
Possible Moves: Bubble, Growl, Supersonic, Round, BubbleBeam, Mud Shot, Aqua Ring, Uproar, Muddy Water, Rain Dance, Flail, Echoed Voice, Hydro Pump, Hyper Voice
Type: Water   **Height:** 1' 08"   **Weight:** 9.9 lbs.
Region: Unova

TYMPOLE

PALPITOAD

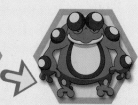

SEISMITOAD

TYNAMO
ELEFISH POKÉMON

If threatened, Tynamo releases electricity from its electricity-generating organ. A single one doesn't have much power, but it travels in schools, and a large group together can be as powerful as lightning.

Pronounced: TY-nuh-moh
Possible Moves: Tackle, Thunder Wave, Spark, Charge Beam
Type: Electric
Height: 0' 08"
Weight: 0.7 lbs.
Region: Unova

TYNAMO — EELEKTRIK — EELEKTROSS

TYPHLOSION
VOLCANO POKÉMON

Typhlosion creates walls of shimmering heat to hide behind, then blasts foes with intense fiery attacks.

Pronounced: tie-FLOW-zhun
Possible Moves: Gyro Ball, Tackle, Leer, SmokeScreen, Ember, Quick Attack, Flame Wheel, Defense Curl, Swift, Flame Charge, Lava Plume, Flamethrower, Inferno, Rollout, Double-Edge, Eruption
Type: Fire
Height: 5' 07"
Weight: 175.3 lbs.
Region: Johto

CYNDAQUIL — QUILAVA — TYPHLOSION

TYRANITAR
ARMOR POKÉMON

Tyranitar can take down mountains and bury rivers if it gets too angry.

Pronounced: tie-RAN-uh-tar
Possible Moves: Thunder Fang, Ice Fang, Fire Fang, Bite, Leer, Sandstorm, Screech, Chip Away, Rock Slide, Scary Face, Thrash, Dark Pulse, Payback, Crunch, Earthquake, Stone Edge, Hyper Beam, Giga Impact
Type: Dark-Ground
Height: 6' 07"
Weight: 445.3 lbs.
Region: Johto

LARVITAR ➡ PUPITAR ➡ TYRANITAR

TYROGUE
SCUFFLE POKÉMON

Tyrogue is a hothead with a very short temper. It thinks nothing of going against foes that are bigger and stronger.

Pronounced: tie-ROAG
Possible Moves: Tackle, Helping Hand, Fake Out, Foresight
Type: Fighting
Height: 2' 04"
Weight: 46.3 lbs.
Region: Johto

TYROGUE

HITMONLEE

HITMONCHAN

HITMONTOP

UMBREON
MOONLIGHT POKÉMON

Umbreon evolved when moonlight changed Eevee's genetic structure.

Pronounced: UMM-bree-on
Possible Moves: Tail Whip, Tackle, Helping Hand, Sand-Attack, Pursuit, Quick Attack, Confuse Ray, Faint Attack, Assurance, Last Resort, Mean Look, Screech, Moonlight, Guard Swap
Type: Dark   **Height:** 3' 03"
Weight: 59.5 lbs.   **Region:** Johto

EEVEE → UMBREON

UNFEZANT
PROUD POKÉMON

Unfezant won't bond with anyone but its Trainer. A male Unfezant can be recognized by its head plumage, which it swings around to threaten foes. Female Unfezant are better fliers than the males.

Pronounced: un-FEZ-ent
Possible Moves: Gust, Growl, Leer, Quick Attack, Air Cutter, Roost, Detect, Taunt, Air Slash, Razor Wind, FeatherDance, Swagger, Facade, Tailwind, Sky Attack
Type: Normal-Flying
Height: 3' 11"
Weight: 63.9 lbs.
Region: Unova

PIDOVE → TRANQUILL → UNFEZANT

UNOWN
SYMBOL POKÉMON

Using telepathy to communicate, these alphabet-shaped Pokémon can be found stuck on walls. It is unknown which came first—these Pokémon, or human language.

Pronounced: un-KNOWN
Possible Moves: Hidden Power
Type: Psychic
Height: 1' 08"
Weight: 11.0 lbs.
Region: Johto

DOES NOT EVOLVE

URSARING
HIBERNATOR POKÉMON

Ursaring is very territorial, and will often mark trees that have tasty berries or fruits.

Pronounced: UR-sa-ring
Possible Moves: Covet, Scratch, Leer, Lick, Fake Tears, Fury Swipes, Faint Attack, Sweet Scent, Slash, Scary Face, Rest, Snore, Thrash, Hammer Arm
Type: Normal
Height: 5' 11"
Weight: 277.3 lbs.
Region: Johto

TEDDIURSA → URSARING

UXIE
KNOWLEDGE POKÉMON

Also known as The Being of Knowledge, Uxie is rumored to have given humans the intelligence they needed to improve the quality of their lives.

Pronounced: YUKE-see
Possible Moves: Rest, Confusion, Imprison, Endure, Swift, Yawn, Future Sight, Amnesia, Extrasensory, Flail, Natural Gift, Memento
Type: Psychic
Height: 1' 00"
Weight: 0.7 lbs.
Region: Sinnoh

DOES NOT EVOLVE

LEGENDARY POKÉMON

VANILLISH
ICY SNOW POKÉMON

Vanillish creates many small ice particles and hides among them to conceal itself from foes. It dwells in snowy mountains but migrated to southern areas during an ancient ice age.

Pronounced: vuh-NIHL-lish

Possible Moves: Icicle Spear, Harden, Astonish, Uproar, Icy Wind, Mist, Avalanche, Taunt, Mirror Shot, Acid Armor, Ice Beam, Hail, Mirror Coat, Blizzard, Sheer Cold

Type: Ice

Height: 3' 07"

Weight: 90.4 lbs.

Region: Unova

VANILLITE → VANILLISH → VANILLUXE

VANILLITE
FRESH SNOW POKÉMON

Formed from icicles bathed in morning sunlight, Vanillite's breath is as cold as -58 degrees Fahrenheit. It sleeps buried in snow. It causes snow to fall around itself by creating snow crystals.

Pronounced: vuh-NIHL-lyte

Possible Moves: Icicle Spear, Harden, Astonish, Uproar, Icy Wind, Mist, Avalanche, Taunt, Mirror Shot, Acid Armor, Ice Beam, Hail, Mirror Coat, Blizzard, Sheer Cold

Type: Ice

Height: 1' 04"

Weight: 12.6 lbs.

Region: Unova

VANILLITE → VANILLISH → VANILLUXE

VANILLUXE
SNOWSTORM POKÉMON

Vanilluxe creates snow clouds inside its body and attacks foes with fierce blizzards. If both heads get angry at the same time, it creates a blizzard that buries everything around it.

Pronounced: vuh-NIHL-lux

Possible Moves: Weather Ball, Icicle Spear, Harden, Astonish, Uproar, Icy Wind, Mist, Avalanche, Taunt, Mirror Shot, Acid Armor, Ice Beam, Hail, Mirror Coat, Blizzard, Sheer Cold

Type: Ice
Height: 4' 03"
Weight: 126.8 lbs.
Region: Unova

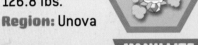

VANILLITE   VANILLISH   VANILLUXE

VAPOREON
BUBBLE JET POKÉMON

Vaporeon has adapted so well to living an aquatic life that it can't be seen while in water.

Pronounced: vay-POR-ee-on

Possible Moves: Tail Whip, Tackle, Helping Hand, Sand-Attack, Water Gun, Quick Attack, Bite, Aurora Beam, Aqua Ring, Last Resort, Haze, Acid Armor, Hydro Pump, Muddy Water

Type: Water
Height: 3' 03"   **Weight:** 63.9 lbs.
Region: Kanto

EEVEE   VAPOREON

VENIPEDE
CENTIPEDE POKÉMON

This aggressive Pokémon's poisonous bite can paralyze even the large avian Pokémon that hunt it. The feelers on its head and tail keep it aware of its surroundings.

Pronounced: VEHN-ih-peed
Possible Moves: Defense Curl, Rollout, Poison Sting, Screech, Pursuit, Protect, Poison Tail, Bug Bite, Venoshock, Agility, Steamroller, Toxic, Rock Climb, Double-Edge
Type: Bug-Poison
Height: 1' 04"
Weight: 11.7 lbs.
Region: Unova

VENIPEDE > WHIRLIPEDE > SCOLIPEDE

VENOMOTH
POISON MOTH POKÉMON

Toxic dust-like scales fall from Venomoth's wings—this Pokémon is not one for petting.

Pronounced: VENN-oh-moth
Possible Moves: Silver Wind, Tackle, Disable, Foresight, Supersonic, Confusion, PoisonPowder, Leech Life, Stun Spore, Psybeam, Sleep Powder, Gust, Signal Beam, Zen Headbutt, Poison Fang, Psychic, Bug Buzz, Quiver Dance
Type: Bug-Poison
Height: 4' 11"
Weight: 27.6 lbs.
Region: Kanto

VENONAT > VENOMOTH

VENONAT
INSECT POKÉMON

Venonat's big eyes are made up of tiny little eyes, and at nighttime it is drawn to light.

Pronounced: VENN-oh-nat
Possible Moves: Tackle, Disable, Foresight, Supersonic, Confusion, PoisonPowder, Leech Life, Stun Spore, Psybeam, Sleep Powder, Signal Beam, Zen Headbutt, Poison Fang, Psychic
Type: Bug-Poison
Height: 3' 03"   **Weight:** 66.1 lbs.
Region: Kanto

VENONAT   VENOMOTH

VENUSAUR
SEED POKÉMON

The flower on this Pokémon's back gains a stronger smell after rainy days.

Pronounced: VEE-nuh-sore
Possible Moves: Tackle, Growl, Leech Seed, Vine Whip, PoisonPowder, Sleep Powder, Take Down, Razor Leaf, Sweet Scent, Growth, Double-Edge, Petal Dance, Worry Seed, Synthesis, SolarBeam
Type: Grass-Poison   **Height:** 6' 07"   **Weight:** 220.5 lbs.
Region: Kanto

BULBASAUR   IVYSAUR   VENUSAUR

VESPIQUEN
BEEHIVE POKÉMON

There is only one Vespiquen in a colony and its stomach acts like a honeycomb for grubs. The grubs will strike at any foe that appears.

Pronounced: VES-pa-kwen
Possible Moves: Sweet Scent, Gust, Poison Sting, Confuse Ray, Fury Cutter, Defend Order, Pursuit, Fury Swipes, Power Gem, Heal Order, Toxic, Slash, Captivate, Attack Order, Swagger, Destiny Bond
Type: Bug-Flying   **Height:** 3' 11"
Weight: 84.9 lbs.   **Region:** Sinnoh

COMBEE → VESPIQUEN

VIBRAVA
VIBRATION POKÉMON

By using ultrasonic waves and flapping its wings rapidly, Vibrava can cause headaches in some people.

Pronounced: VY-brah-va
Possible Moves: SonicBoom, Sand-Attack, Faint Attack, Sand Tomb, Supersonic, DragonBreath, Screech, Sandstorm, Hyper Beam
Type: Ground-Dragon   **Height:** 3' 07"   **Weight:** 33.7 lbs.
Region:
Hoenn

TRAPINCH → VIBRAVA → FLYGON

VICTINI
VICTORY POKÉMON

Victini is the Pokémon that brings victory, and it's said that the Trainer with Victini always wins. It generates an endless supply of energy to share.

Pronounced: vik-TEE-nee
Possible Moves: Searing Shot, Focus Energy, Confusion, Incinerate, Quick Attack, Endure, Headbutt, Flame Charge, Reversal, Flame Burst, Zen Headbutt, Inferno, Double-Edge, Flare Blitz, Final Gambit, Stored Power, Overheat
Type: Psychic-Fire
Height: 1' 04"
Weight: 8.8 lbs.
Region: Unova

DOES NOT EVOLVE

MYTHICAL POKÉMON

VICTREEBEL
FLYCATCHER POKÉMON

The fluid in Victreebel's mouth smells like honey, but is really a toxic acid.

Pronounced: VICK-tree-bell
Possible Moves: Stockpile, Swallow, Spit Up, Vine Whip, Sleep Powder, Sweet Scent, Razor Leaf, Leaf Tornado, Leaf Storm, Leaf Blade
Type: Grass-Poison
Height: 5' 07"
Weight: 34.2 lbs.
Region: Kanto

BELLSPROUT > **WEEPINBELL** > **VICTREEBEL**

VIGOROTH
WILD MONKEY POKÉMON

Vigoroth's heartbeat is so elevated, it can't sit still for one minute.

Pronounced: VIG-er-roth
Possible Moves: Scratch, Focus Energy, Encore, Uproar, Fury Swipes, Endure, Slash, Counter, Chip Away, Focus Punch, Reversal
Type: Normal
Height: 4' 07"   **Weight:** 102.5 lbs.
Region: Hoenn

SLAKOTH > **VIGOROTH** > **SLAKING**

VILEPLUME
FLOWER POKÉMON

Vileplume's petals are so large that it spreads allergenic pollen over a wide area as it walks.

Pronounced: VILE-ploom
Possible Moves: Mega Drain, Aromatherapy, Stun Spore, PoisonPowder, Petal Dance, SolarBeam
Type: Grass-Poison
Height: 3' 11"
Weight: 41.0 lbs.
Region: Kanto

ODDISH > GLOOM > VILEPLUME

VIRIZION
GRASSLAND POKÉMON

Virizion's horns are as sharp as blades. Moving like a whirlwind, it quickly cuts and confounds its opponents. Legends are still told about this Pokémon, which battled humans to protect its friends.

Pronounced: vih-RY-zee-un
Possible Moves: Quick Attack, Leer, Double Kick, Magical Leaf, Take Down, Helping Hand, Retaliate, Giga Drain, Sacred Sword, Swords Dance, Quick Guard, Work Up, Leaf Blade, Close Combat
Type: Grass-Fighting **Height:** 6' 07"
Weight: 440.9 lbs. **Region:** Unova

LEGENDARY POKÉMON

DOES NOT EVOLVE

VOLBEAT
FIREFLY POKÉMON

Volbeat loves the sweet aroma that Illumise generates. It communicates with others by lighting up its rear at night.

Pronounced: VOLL-beat
Possible Moves: Flash, Tackle, Double Team, Confuse Ray, Moonlight, Quick Attack, Tail Glow, Signal Beam, Protect, Helping Hand, Zen Headbutt, Bug Buzz, Double-Edge
Type: Bug
Height: 2' 04"   **Weight:** 39.0 lbs.
Region: Hoenn

DOES NOT EVOLVE

VOLCARONA
SUN POKÉMON

When Volcarona battles, its six wings scatter ember scales that turn the immediate area into a sea of flames. Volcarona's fire replaced the sun in a time when volcanic ash darkened the atmosphere, or so it is said.

Pronounced: vol-kah-ROH-nuh
Possible Moves: Ember, String Shot, Leech Life, Gust, Fire Spin, Whirlwind, Silver Wind, Quiver Dance, Heat Wave, Bug Buzz, Rage Powder, Hurricane, Fiery Dance
Type: Bug-Fire
Height: 5' 03"
Weight: 101.4 lbs.
Region: Unova

LARVESTA   VOLCARONA

VOLTORB
BALL POKÉMON

Although it looks as harmless as a standard Poké Ball, these Pokémon can explode or electrocute on contact.

Pronounced: VOL-torb
Possible Moves: Charge, Tackle, SonicBoom, Spark, Rollout, Screech, Charge Beam, Light Screen, Electro Ball, Selfdestruct, Swift, Magnet Rise, Gyro Ball, Explosion, Mirror Coat
Type: Electric
Height: 1' 08"
Weight: 22.9 lbs.
Region: Kanto

VOLTORB

ELECTRODE

VULLABY
DIAPERED POKÉMON

Vullaby finds suitable bones and uses them to shield its rear, then discards them when it's ready to evolve. Unable to fly since its wings are too small, it pursues weak Pokémon.

Pronounced: VUL-luh-bye
Possible Moves: Gust, Leer, Fury Attack, Pluck, Nasty Plot, Flatter, Faint Attack, Punishment, Defog, Tailwind, Air Slash, Dark Pulse, Embargo, Whirlwind, Brave Bird, Mirror Move
Type: Dark-Flying   **Height:** 1' 08"
Weight: 19.8 lbs.   **Region:** Unova

VULLABY

MANDIBUZZ

VULPIX
FOX POKÉMON

As it grows, Vulpix's tail will split to make more tails. It can control balls of fire.

Pronounced: VULL-picks
Possible Moves: Ember, Tail Whip, Roar, Quick Attack, Fire Spin, Confuse Ray, Imprison, Flame Burst, Safeguard, Will-O-Wisp, Payback, Flamethrower, Captivate, Inferno, Grudge, Extrasensory, Fire Blast
Type: Fire
Height: 2' 00"
Weight: 21.8 lbs.
Region: Kanto

VULPIX

NINETALES

WAILMER
BALL WHALE POKÉMON

Wailmer likes to beach itself so that it can bounce like a ball and play. It also spouts water from its nose.

Pronounced: WAIL-murr
Possible Moves: Splash, Growl, Water Gun, Rollout, Whirlpool, Astonish, Water Pulse, Mist, Rest, Brine, Water Spout, Amnesia, Dive, Bounce, Hydro Pump, Heavy Slam
Type: Water
Height: 6' 07"
Weight: 286.6 lbs.
Region: Hoenn

WAILMER → WAILORD

WAILORD
FLOAT WHALE POKÉMON

This massive Pokémon is the biggest of them all. It can dive to depths of up to ten thousand feet.

Pronounced: WAIL-lord
Possible Moves: Splash, Growl, Water Gun, Rollout, Whirlpool, Astonish, Water Pulse, Mist, Rest, Brine, Water Spout, Amnesia, Dive, Bounce, Hydro Pump, Heavy Slam
Type: Water   **Height:** 47' 07"
Weight: 877.4 lbs.
Region: Hoenn

WAILMER → WAILORD

WALREIN
ICE BREAK POKÉMON

The thick blubber on Walrein's body provides protection. It can easily crack icy surfaces with its big strong tusks.

Pronounced: WAL-rain

Possible Moves: Crunch, Powder Snow, Growl, Water Gun, Encore, Ice Ball, Body Slam, Aurora Beam, Hail, Swagger, Rest, Snore, Ice Fang, Blizzard, Sheer Cold

Type: Ice-Water

Height: 4' 07"

Weight: 332.0 lbs.

Region: Hoenn

SPHEAL   >   SEALEO   >   WALREIN

WARTORTLE
TURTLE POKÉMON

It can live for almost ten thousand years. Its furry tail is popular as a symbol of longevity.

Pronounced: WAR-TOR-tle

Possible Moves: Tackle, Tail Whip, Bubble, Withdraw, Water Gun, Bite, Rapid Spin, Protect, Water Pulse, Aqua Tail, Skull Bash, Iron Defense, Rain Dance, Hydro Pump

Type: Water   **Height:** 3' 03"   **Weight:** 49.6 lbs.

Region: Kanto

SQUIRTLE   >   WARTORTLE   >   BLASTOISE

WATCHOG
LOOKOUT POKÉMON

Watchog threatens predators by making the pattern on its body shine. Its eyesight is so keen, it can see in the dark. If it sees an enemy, it raises its tail and spits berry seeds stored in its cheek pouches.

Pronounced: WAH-chawg
Possible Moves: Tackle, Leer, Bite, Low Kick, Bide, Detect, Sand-Attack, Crunch, Hypnosis, Confuse Ray, Super Fang, After You, Psych Up, Hyper Fang, Mean Look, Baton Pass, Slam
Type: Normal
Height: 3' 07"
Weight: 59.5 lbs.
Region: Unova

PATRAT

WATCHOG

WEAVILE
SHARP CLAW POKÉMON

Weavile send signals to one another by carving them in frost-covered trees and ice.

Pronounced: WEE-vile
Possible Moves: Embargo, Revenge, Assurance, Scratch, Leer, Taunt, Quick Attack, Screech, Faint Attack, Fury Swipes, Nasty Plot, Icy Wind, Hone Claws, Night Slash, Fling, Metal Claw, Dark Pulse
Type: Dark-Ice
Height: 3' 07"   **Weight:** 75.0 lbs.
Region: Sinnoh

SNEASEL

WEAVILE

WEEDLE
HAIRY BUG POKÉMON

Weedle is voracious, eating its weight in leaves every day. Its only defense mechanism is the large needle on its head.

Pronounced: WEE-dull
Possible Moves: Poison Sting, String Shot, Bug Bite
Type: Bug-Poison
Height: 1' 00"
Weight: 7.1 lbs.
Region: Kanto

WEEDLE

KAKUNA

BEEDRILL

WEEPINBELL
FLYCATCHER POKÉMON

This Pokémon looks like a plant, but be careful! It emits a toxic powder to capture prey.

Pronounced: WEEP-in-bell
Possible Moves: Vine Whip, Growth, Wrap, Sleep Powder, PoisonPowder, Stun Spore, Acid, Knock Off, Sweet Scent, Gastro Acid, Razor Leaf, Slam, Wring Out
Type: Grass-Poison   **Height:** 3' 03"
Weight: 14.1 lbs.
Region: Kanto

BELLSPROUT   WEEPINBELL   VICTREEBEL

WEEZING
POISON GAS POKÉMON

This Pokémon grows by feeding on the gases emitted by garbage. Finding a triplet Weezing is very rare.

Pronounced: WEEZE-ing
Possible Moves: Poison Gas, Tackle, Smog, SmokeScreen, Assurance, Clear Smog, Selfdestruct, Sludge, Haze, Double Hit, Explosion, Sludge Bomb, Destiny Bond, Memento
Type: Poison
Height: 3' 11"   **Weight:** 20.9 lbs.
Region: Kanto

KOFFING

WEEZING

WHIMSICOTT
WINDVEILED POKÉMON

Whimsicott rides on whirlwinds and, just like the wind, it can slip through even the smallest crack. It sneaks into houses to cause mischief and leaves behind white balls of fluff.

Pronounced: WHIM-zih-kot
Possible Moves: Growth, Leech Seed, Mega Drain, Cotton Spore, Gust, Tailwind, Hurricane
Type: Grass
Height: 2' 04"   **Weight:** 14.6 lbs.
Region: Unova

COTTONEE

WHIMSICOTT

WHIRLIPEDE
CURLIPEDE POKÉMON

Encased in a hard shell, Whirlipede rarely moves unless attacked. It can spin like a wheel and smash into its foes.

Pronounced: WHIR-lih-peed

Possible Moves: Defense Curl, Rollout, Poison Sting, Screech, Pursuit, Protect, Poison Tail, Iron Defense, Bug Bite, Venoshock, Agility, Steamroller, Toxic, Rock Climb, Double-Edge

Type: Bug-Poison

Height: 3' 11"

Weight: 129.0 lbs.

Region: Unova

VENIPEDE   WHIRLIPEDE   SCOLIPEDE

WHISCASH
WHISKERS POKÉMON

Because Whiscash can create tremors in the ocean by whipping about, it has developed the ability to predict real earthquakes.

Pronounced: WISS-cash

Possible Moves: Zen Headbutt, Tickle, Mud-Slap, Mud Sport, Water Sport, Water Gun, Mud Bomb, Amnesia, Water Pulse, Magnitude, Rest, Snore, Aqua Tail, Earthquake, Future Sight, Fissure

Type: Water-Ground

Height: 2' 11"

Weight: 52.0 lbs.

Region: Hoenn

BARBOACH   WHISCASH

WHISMUR
WHISPER POKÉMON

Whismur shrieks as loud as a jet plane when it is scared, although when it cries, humans can barely hear it.

Pronounced: WHIS-mur
Possible Moves: Pound, Uproar, Astonish, Howl, Supersonic, Stomp, Screech, Roar, Synchronoise, Rest, Sleep Talk, Hyper Voice
Type: Normal
Height: 2' 00"
Weight: 35.9 lbs.
Region: Hoenn

WHISMUR → LOUDRED → EXPLOUD

WIGGLYTUFF
BALLOON POKÉMON

By inhaling air, Wigglytuff can expand its body, and its fur feels soothing to the touch.

Pronounced: WIG-lee-tuff
Possible Moves: Sing, Disable, Defense Curl, DoubleSlap
Type: Normal   **Height:** 3' 03"
Weight: 26.5 lbs.
Region: Kanto

IGGLYBUFF → JIGGLYPUFF → WIGGLYTUFF

WINGULL
SEAGULL POKÉMON

Wingull can soar to great heights by riding the updrafts from the steep cliffs where it nests.

Pronounced: WING-gull
Possible Moves: Growl, Water Gun, Supersonic, Wing Attack, Mist, Water Pulse, Quick Attack, Roost, Pursuit, Agility, Aerial Ace, Air Slash, Hurricane
Type: Water-Flying
Height: 2' 00"
Weight: 20.9 lbs.
Region: Hoenn

WINGULL → PELIPPER

WOBBUFFET
PATIENT POKÉMON

Some think that Wobbuffet's tail hides a secret, which is why it tries to keep it hidden.

Pronounced: WAH-buf-fett
Possible Moves: Counter, Mirror Coat, Safeguard, Destiny Bond
Type: Psychic
Height: 4' 03"
Weight: 62.8 lbs.
Region: Johto

WYNAUT → WOBBUFFET

WOOBAT
BAT POKÉMON

Woobat lives in dark caves and forests, and it senses its surroundings using ultrasonic waves from its nose. When it wants to sleep, the suction of its nostrils helps it cling to a cavern wall. Woobat leaves a heart-shaped mark where it was attached.

Pronounced: WOO-bat

Possible Moves: Confusion, Odor Sleuth, Gust, Assurance, Heart Stamp, Imprison, Air Cutter, Attract, Amnesia, Calm Mind, Air Slash, Future Sight, Psychic, Endeavor

Type: Psychic-Flying

Height: 1' 04"

Weight: 4.6 lbs.

Region: Unova

WOOBAT → SWOOBAT

WOOPER
WATER FISH POKÉMON

This shore-scavenger comes out when the temperature drops, and usually lives half-buried in the mud of riverbanks.

Pronounced: WOOP-pur

Possible Moves: Water Gun, Tail Whip, Mud Sport, Mud Shot, Slam, Mud Bomb, Amnesia, Yawn, Earthquake, Rain Dance, Mist, Haze, Muddy Water

Type: Water-Ground

Height: 1' 04"   **Weight:** 18.7 lbs.

Region: Johto

WOOPER

QUAGSIRE

WORMADAM PLANT CLOAK
BAGWORM POKÉMON

Depending on where Wormadam evolved, its appearance can be different. When it evolved from Burmy, its cloak became a part of its body.

Pronounced: WURR-mah-dam
Possible Moves: Tackle, Protect, Bug Bite, Hidden Power, Confusion, Razor Leaf, Growth, Psybeam, Captivate, Flail, Attract, Psychic, Leaf Storm
Type: Bug-Grass
Height: 1'08" **Weight:** 14.3 lbs.
Region: Sinnoh

BURMY → WORMADAM

WORMADAM SANDY CLOAK
BAGWORM POKÉMON

If you want a Bug- and Ground-type Wormadam, make sure your Burmy has a Sandy Cloak! Once Burmy evolves, there's no going back.

Pronounced: WURR-mah-dam
Possible Moves: Tackle, Protect, Bug Bite, Hidden Power, Confusion, Rock Blast, Harden, Psybeam, Captivate, Flail, Attract, Psychic, Fissure
Type: Bug-Ground
Height: 1'08"
Weight: 14.3 lbs.
Region: Sinnoh

BURMY → WORMADAM

WORMADAM TRASH CLOAK
BAGWORM POKÉMON

Looking for a Wormadam with awesome Steel-type moves? You'll need to evolve a Burmy with a Trash Cloak.

Pronounced: WURR-mah-dam
Possible Moves: Tackle, Protect, Bug Bite, Hidden Power, Confusion, Mirror Shot, Metal Sound, Psybeam, Captivate, Flail, Attract, Psychic, Iron Head
Type: Bug-Steel
Height: 1' 08"   **Weight:** 14.3 lbs.
Region: Sinnoh

BURMY ➤ WORMADAM

WURMPLE
WORM POKÉMON

Wurmple uses its spiked back to protect itself, mainly from its chief predator, Swellow.

Pronounced: WERM-pull
Possible Moves: Tackle, String Shot, Poison Sting, Bug Bite
Type: Bug
Height: 1'00"   **Weight:** 7.9 lbs.
Region: Hoenn

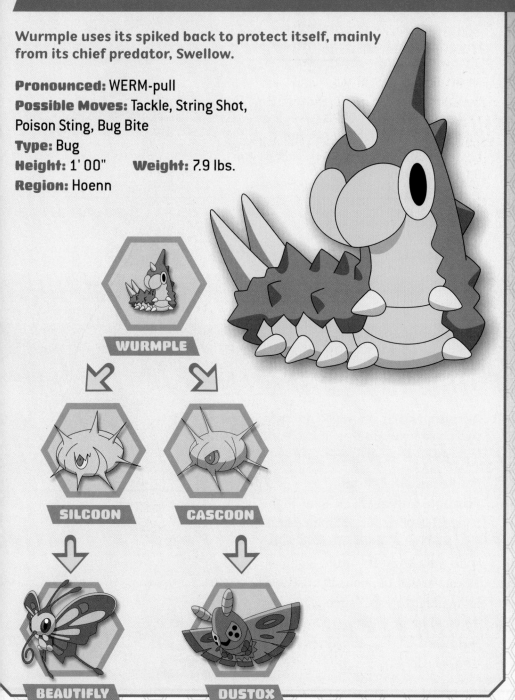

WURMPLE

SILCOON   CASCOON

BEAUTIFLY   DUSTOX

WYNAUT
BRIGHT POKÉMON

Wynaut loves to chomp on sweet fruit, and grows in strength by pushing up against others in swarms.

Pronounced: WHY-not
Possible Moves: Splash, Charm, Encore, Counter, Mirror Coat, Safeguard, Destiny Bond
Type: Psychic
Height: 2' 00"
Weight: 30.9 lbs.
Region: Hoenn

WYNAUT → WOBBUFFET

XATU
MYSTIC POKÉMON

Although Xatu seems to do nothing but watch the sun all day, it does have the ability to predict the future and see into the past.

Pronounced: ZAH-too
Possible Moves: Peck, Leer, Night Shade, Teleport, Lucky Chant, Miracle Eye, Me First, Confuse Ray, Tailwind, Wish, Psycho Shift, Future Sight, Stored Power, Ominous Wind, Power Swap, Guard Swap, Psychic
Type: Psychic-Flying
Height: 4' 11"   **Weight:** 33.1 lbs.
Region: Johto

NATU → XATU

YAMASK
SPIRIT POKÉMON

Yamask comes from the spirit of a person from the ancient past. It remembers some of its former life and holds a mask of the face it had when it was human. Sometimes, when it looks at this mask, it weeps.

Pronounced: YAH-mask
Possible Moves: Astonish, Protect, Disable, Haze, Night Shade, Hex, Will-O-Wisp, Ominous Wind, Curse, Power Split, Guard Split, Shadow Ball, Grudge, Mean Look, Destiny Bond
Type: Ghost   **Height:** 1' 08"
Weight: 3.3 lbs.   **Region:** Unova

YAMASK

COFAGRIGUS

YANMA
CLEAR WING POKÉMON

Prey will have a hard time hiding from this Pokémon, since its eyes can see 360 degrees without moving its head.

Pronounced: YAN-ma
Possible Moves: Tackle, Foresight, Quick Attack, Double Team, SonicBoom, Detect, Supersonic, Uproar, Pursuit, AncientPower, Hypnosis, Wing Attack, Screech, U-turn, Air Slash, Bug Buzz
Type: Bug-Flying
Height: 3' 11"
Weight: 83.8 lbs.
Region: Johto

YANMA

YANMEGA

YANMEGA
OGRE DARNER POKÉMON

Yanmega causes serious and critical injuries to its foes by creating shock waves with its wings.

Pronounced: YAN-meh-gah
Possible Moves: Night Slash, Bug Bite, Tackle, Foresight, Quick Attack, Double Team, SonicBoom, Detect, Supersonic, Uproar, Pursuit, AncientPower, Feint, Slash, Screech, U-turn, Air Slash, Bug Buzz
Type: Bug-Flying
Height: 6' 03"
Weight: 113.5 lbs.
Region: Sinnoh

YANMA → YANMEGA

ZANGOOSE
CAT FERRET POKÉMON

This Pokémon uses its sharp claws to defeat its prey. Zangoose's greatest rival is Seviper.

Pronounced: ZANG-goose
Possible Moves: Scratch, Leer, Quick Attack, Swords Dance, Fury Cutter, Slash, Pursuit, Embargo, Crush Claw, Taunt, Detect, False Swipe, X-Scissor, Close Combat
Type: Normal
Height: 4' 03"   **Weight:** 88.8 lbs.
Region: Hoenn

DOES NOT EVOLVE

ZAPDOS
ELECTRIC POKÉMON

Zapdos, a Legendary Pokémon, can control lightning bolts, which would explain why it likes to nest in thunderclouds.

Pronounced: ZAP-dose
Possible Moves: Peck, ThunderShock, Thunder Wave, Detect, Pluck, AncientPower, Charge, Agility, Discharge, Roost, Light Screen, Drill Peck, Thunder, Rain Dance
Type: Electric-Flying
Height: 5' 03"
Weight: 116.0 lbs.
Region: Kanto

DOES NOT EVOLVE

LEGENDARY POKÉMON

ZEBSTRIKA
THUNDERBOLT POKÉMON

Zebstrika moves like lightning and echoes like thunder when it runs at top speed. Whenever this short-tempered Pokémon gets angry, lightning shoots from its mane in all directions.

Pronounced: zehb-STRY-kuh

Possible Moves: Quick Attack, Tail Whip, Charge, Thunder Wave, Shock Wave, Flame Charge, Pursuit, Spark, Stomp, Discharge, Agility, Wild Charge, Thrash

Type: Electric

Height: 5' 03"

Weight: 175.3 lbs.

Region: Unova

BLITZLE

ZEBSTRIKA

ZEKROM
DEEP BLACK POKÉMON

Spoken of in ancient stories, Zekrom flies across Unova, hidden by thunderclouds. Its tail contains a massive generator that creates electricity.

Pronounced: ZECK-rahm
Possible Moves: Thunder Fang, Dragon Rage, Imprison, AncientPower, Thunderbolt, DragonBreath, Slash, Zen Headbutt, Fusion Bolt, Dragon Claw, Imprison, Crunch, Thunder, Outrage, Hyper Voice, Bolt Strike
Type: Dragon-Electric
Height: 9' 06"
Weight: 760.6 lbs.
Region: Unova

DOES
NOT
EVOLVE

LEGENDARY
POKÉMON

ZIGZAGOON
TINYRACCOON POKÉMON

Why do they call this Pokémon Zigzagoon? Because it walks in a zigzag fashion. It's also great at finding items in the grass, or even in the ground.

Pronounced: ZIG-zag-GOON
Possible Moves: Tackle, Growl, Tail Whip, Headbutt, Sand-Attack, Odor Sleuth, Mud Sport, Pin Missile, Covet, Bestow, Flail, Rest, Belly Drum, Fling
Type: Normal   **Height:** 1' 04"
Weight: 38.6 lbs.   **Region:** Hoenn

ZIGZAGOON

LINOONE

ZOROARK
ILLUSION FOX POKÉMON

It can fool many people at the same time, and it hides its lair with illusory scenery. Zoroark form strong bonds with one another and protect their pack by transforming into opponents.

Pronounced: ZORE-oh-ark
Possible Moves: U-turn, Scratch, Leer, Pursuit, Hone Claws, Fury Swipes, Faint Attack, Scary Face, Taunt, Foul Play, Night Slash, Torment, Agility, Embargo, Punishment, Nasty Plot, Imprison, Night Daze
Type: Dark   **Height:** 5' 03"
Weight: 178.8 lbs.   **Region:** Unova

ZORUA

ZOROARK

ZORUA
TRICKY FOX POKÉMON

Zorua protects itself by concealing its true identity, transforming into people or other Pokémon. Supposedly, Zorua often resembles a silent child, but it can assume an opponent's form to take foes by surprise.

Pronounced: ZORE-oo-uh
Possible Moves: Scratch, Leer, Pursuit, Fake Tears, Fury Swipes, Faint Attack, Scary Face, Taunt, Foul Play, Torment, Agility, Embargo, Punishment, Nasty Plot, Imprison, Night Daze
Type: Dark   **Height:** 2' 04"
Weight: 27.6 lbs.   **Region:** Unova

ZORUA

ZOROARK

ZUBAT
BAT POKÉMON

Using sonic waves that come from its mouth, Zubat can sense obstacles in its way.

Pronounced: ZOO-bat
Possible Moves: Leech Life, Supersonic, Astonish, Bite, Wing Attack, Confuse Ray, Air Cutter, Mean Look, Acrobatics, Poison Fang, Haze, Air Slash
Type: Poison-Flying
Height: 2' 07"   **Weight:** 16.5 lbs.
Region:
Kanto

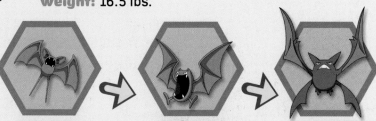

ZUBAT   GOLBAT   CROBAT

ZWEILOUS
HOSTILE POKÉMON

Zweilous always ends up overeating because its two heads don't get along and compete for food. Once it has eaten all the food in its territory, it moves on.

Pronounced: ZVY-lus

Possible Moves: Double Hit, Dragon Rage, Focus Energy, Bite, Headbutt, DragonBreath, Roar, Crunch, Slam, Dragon Pulse, Work Up, Dragon Rush, Body Slam, Scary Face, Hyper Voice, Outrage

Type: Dark-Dragon

Height: 4' 07"

Weight: 110.2 lbs.

Region: Unova

DEINO ⟶ ZWEILOUS ⟶ HYDREIGON